Tiger Lily

Part Three

AMÉLIE S. DUNCAN

Print Edition

Published by Amélie S. Duncan

Visit Amélie S. Duncan's official website at
www.ameliesduncan.com
for the latest news, book details, and other information

Cover Design by Damonza
Print Formatting Design by BB eBooks

DEDICATION

TO MY FAMILY

THANK YOU FOR THE LATE NIGHT

SINGING AND DANCING

CHAPTER ONE

JONAS CRANE. I sat on his lap, crushing yet another one of his designer suits. Normally, I would be worried about it, but not today. He had placed me here the second he sat down in the car. I was exactly where he wanted me to be.

He was dressed for work, which he missed yesterday and would probably miss this afternoon as well. Something unheard of for him, a renowned workaholic. I knew he thrived on structure and order. Nonetheless, I had somehow become the chink in his armor. He had chosen me.

I positioned myself to stare up at his face, and I couldn't help but gape. He was a gorgeous man, from his dark, wavy hair down to his polished leather shoes. High, sculpted cheekbones, a square jawline, and thick lashes that framed a set of sea blue eyes. If that wasn't enough, he had full sensual lips that I knew to be as soft as silk. And a muscular frame built for sin, which he wielded at every turn. Potent, masculine perfection.

He had beauty as well as brains, a savvy business mogul and a legend in his field.

Jonas was sought the world over to impart his wisdom or provide his golden touch to new ventures. That was how we had originally met. My company, Arch, wanted him. He wanted me. Still wanted me, after I had disappeared from his life, believing I could protect all I cared for, and myself, by being alone. But in the end, I fell apart, and Jonas came for me.

Just one of the many reasons that I love him.

A grin spread across my face, and Jonas's took on a suspicious glint. I didn't blame him. Mischief was on my mind. I leaned up and gave him a noisy kiss on the cheek, interrupting his phone call. He responded with a reproving shake of his head and mouthed, "Behave." A cute little pucker appeared on his brow.

I leaned up again and kissed his moving lips in apology.

"That won't save you," he whispered. A dark promise crossed his face and I shivered, such was his effect on me. Not because I thought he would hurt me physically. He had gained my trust there. And with that awareness, I decided to kiss him loudly once more, adding a giggle.

"I'll phone back," he said, ending his call.

He captured my chin and gazed at me intently. "What are you doing to me?" he asked.

My pulse sped up as I stared back at him.

His eyes glimmered and he used his free hand to caress the side of my face. He liked asserting his will, but also gave affection freely, which was one of the many reasons I loved him. He winked and tucked me back against him.

His warmth and the smooth ride through Manhattan traffic had me stifling a yawn. I closed my eyes and nuzzled his neck, inhaling his fresh scent. I loved the way he smelled. I loved everything about this man.

"You didn't get your nap. You'll take one after we eat lunch and talk." Jonas brushed his lips against my forehead.

The words "I'm not hungry…" were out of my mouth before my brain connected to them. Jonas gave me an empathetic, though critical, look. His body tensed underneath me. "I'll speak with Dr. Steinman. See what we can do."

My trip to the doctor's office yesterday had convinced me that I did have an issue with eating, as I was now underweight. A side effect of the extensive exercise routine I had cultivated in an attempt to exhaust my mind. Dr. Steinman ran some tests and I was waiting for the results. Or, we were. Jonas had included himself in the knowing.

He was taking me over and I wasn't certain how I felt about it. Though I was certain, no matter what happened, I wouldn't leave him again.

"I'm not sure how hungry I am." I corrected myself. He brushed his lips to my forehead again and slowly rubbed my back. "We'll eat lunch when we get there."

My brows rose as I looked past him out the window. We had long passed through Midtown and were halfway through Downtown Manhattan now.

"Where are we going?" I asked.

"We're staying temporarily in a furnished loft apartment in Tribeca," he replied. "I'd prefer to move closer to Central Park and the Upper West Side when we can. Dani is going to help search for a place."

I licked my lips. "I know you offered for me to stay with you, but you really don't have to do that. The locks have been changed at my apartment and I'll be finding a new place in a month."

"If he got in once, he could get in again. I'm furious no one told me," Jonas said, his tone sharp. He was talking about my ex, Declan, who had recently broken into my home and stolen photos and my prized possession—the *Peter Pan* book given to me by my father who, like my mother, was gone to me forever in a tragic car crash.

I curled my chin under in shame. If it had been my choice, Jonas would never have known what happened or seen me at my weakest.

He reached out and stroked underneath my chin, tickling the soft skin there, though I didn't feel like laughing. "You'll stay under my watch until we fix that piece of shit ex of yours," he said in a softer tone.

I swallowed hard. Generally, I would have told him that Declan getting inside again wasn't possible, but this time I just couldn't. He had assaulted and stolen from me. I had given him my word I wouldn't bother him if he didn't bother me, but he still harassed me. All he did was continue to find ways to hurt me. Most recently, he sent me nude photos I hadn't even known he had taken, the implicit threat being that he could easily post them on the Internet. He had the power to destroy my reputation and to hurt anyone else associated with me.

Even though I didn't want to further my embarrassment, I decided to remind Jonas of that much and added, "You can't. I told you what's at stake."

"You think I give a fuck about his threats to you?" he said, raising his voice. "I'll destroy him."

I flushed and closed my eyes. "I care. I'll be ruined. And your reputation, along with mine."

"Look at me," he said.

I raised my head slowly.

His eyes were steady and determined. "That isn't going to happen. I have people combing through his whole life right now. Trust me, he'll be shitting his pants when I'm done with him."

My pulse sped up. I was happy and terrified at the same time. Jonas's nature was to fight. He was a warrior in business. He crushed his opposition—and worse, based on what he had shared with me. And from where I sat, it was evident he had declared war on Declan. From the set of his jaw, there was little I would be able to say to make him change his mind now.

Truthfully, I no longer believed Declan would do the right thing. I knew I needed help dealing with this, but I worried for Jonas. "I don't want you, or anyone else, to get in trouble," I pleaded.

He grinned and kissed me lightly on the lips. "We won't," he said confidently.

I touched my lips and stared off, wishing his words were enough.

"What are you most scared of?" Jonas asked in a gentle tone.

I cast my eyes down. "I don't want anyone to see my body," I said, just above a whisper. The truth, without sensor or process.

"I don't either," he admitted.

I flicked my eyes up to him and my stomach lurched as my old, negative tapes chimed in. *He's embarrassed of me.*

"Whatever you're thinking, stop," Jonas said, breaking my thoughts as he assessed me. "Your body is beautiful, but I don't want anyone else to admire it. Only me." He paused for a moment, then asked, "You need confirmation of this again? You'll make me tell you."

A crease appeared on my cheek. Ever the general, Jonas. Commanding me to get him to remind me that I was beautiful.

My heart skipped a beat over just the thought, though I didn't see the beauty he referred to. Sure, my spa treatment had invigorated my skin. And Dee did wonders with my hair. I was pampered smooth all over. Some surface cosmetics to mask the darkness. But that wasn't enough. And the more I thought along those lines, the more worries arose. "But you haven't seen…"

"What haven't I seen?" Jonas asked. He stroked the side of my face, letting me know he wanted me to continue. But I didn't want to. "You need to tell me," he implored.

"He showed people at his job. He sent photos to my cell, with messages…" I stammered.

Jonas's facial expression turned lethal. "Show me."

I absently reached into my pocket and fumbled with my cellphone. Then I realized I didn't want him to see them either, and started to put my phone back. His hand closed on my wrist.

"No secrets. This, I will break you of. We won't work if you continue to hide things from me. Now, give me your phone," he said, releasing my wrist and holding out his hand.

My own hand shook as I placed the phone in his open palm. "That goes for both of us," I mumbled.

"I know this is hard for you, but you will learn to trust me," he said, kissing me on the cheek. A tear escaped the corner of my eye as I watched Jonas look through my cellphone history and the images Declan had sent of me. One, apparently new, had me naked in the shower. I could pinpoint the timeframe of most of the photos he had. They were taken right after I sank into a depression following my parents' death. I had gained weight, which he made fun of, and shortly after, he broke off our engagement. I covered my mouth to try to still the wave of nausea that went through me. The bile rose in my throat and I motioned to Jonas frantically.

"David. Pull over," Jonas called out. The car cut across traffic and double-parked. Jonas quickly opened the door and I climbed out just in time to expel what I hadn't digested from breakfast. Jonas took his handkerchief out and wiped my chin.

I took in a few quick breaths as I waited for the queasiness to pass. Once I was certain, I glanced at Jonas.

He handed me a bottle of water and I rinsed my mouth out, trying my best to pour the remainder over the piece of curb I had spoiled.

"I'm sorry," I said hoarsely.

"Shhh," Jonas said, as he helped me back inside the car. Another vehicle pulled up behind us and started blaring its horn, but David sat there for a few extra minutes before pulling out. That distraction broke the well of my thoughts. That, and Jonas placing me back on his lap, cuddling me close. After a few minutes passed without us speaking, I tilted my head up to look at him. His mouth was thin, but his eyes were kind as they connected with mine.

"I need my phone to call Mary. I have to tell her what's going on, but I don't want to over the phone...I don't want her to see me like this."

"I'll get you a phone to use and you can invite her down to visit when you're ready," he said.

I opened my mouth, poised in protest of him keeping my phone, but he held up his hand to stop me.

"You don't have to do everything at once. Your doctor said no stress. Let me handle it. I'll take care of things for you," he said.

"Like I'm a child," I stammered.

"No, like you're a woman I care for," he replied in a gentle tone. He kissed my parted lips and a flutter went through my stomach. Letting him take care of me was something I had tried my best to resist before, out of fear I'd come to rely on him too much and wouldn't know what to do with myself when it all inevitably ended. I worried he would only be caring for me out of pity, but we both agreed to put aside our fears and try to work on our relationship.

I had him and I was not leaving.

I gave him a small nod in agreement. The smile he returned didn't reach his eyes, but he kissed me lightly on the lips and tucked me back into the warmth of his arms before making another phone call.

CHAPTER TWO

THE CAR JOSTLED down a cobblestone street in the West Village, finally stopping before a five-story gray brick and granite warehouse. A stocky man with a dark brown crew cut and navy business suit stood poised outside the building with a notepad. Jonas opened the door and helped me to stand on the sidewalk. He walked over and greeted the man.

"Samuel," Jonas said.

"Mr. Crane," Samuel replied. He handed a key ring and a folder to him. "Everything is in order." I turned and thanked David, accepting my handbag. When I reached for my backpack, he smiled and stopped me, walking over and handing it to Jonas.

"Thanks, David. I'll see you later," Jonas said, ignoring my loud sigh and holding out his outstretched hand for me to take, which I did. "Samuel, this is Ms. Salomé."

"Lily," I said, awkwardly holding out my hand for him to shake. He smiled at me as he grasped my palm.

"Nice to meet you. We'll have some of your clothing

from your old apartment brought over later today. The rest will come tomorrow. I'll need you to make a list of things you would prefer to remain in storage..."

My mouth went dry. "You're done? I'll need to go over and organize. I need to clean and prepare it for my final walk through. I still have about six weeks and I have to find a new place—"

"Let's not overwhelm her," Jonas said with irritation in his voice. "We'll work it out later. She needs to eat lunch. Is Lin here?" He pressed his hand in the small of my back and guided me toward the building.

"Of course. Apologies, Mr. Crane," Samuel said and adjusted his tie. "Yes, Lin is here and she confirmed lunch is ready."

We walked as a group toward the backside of the building, stopping in front of a freight elevator. Samuel pulled the gate and then climbed inside. We rode to the top level. Once the doors opened, I was surprised to find we were already inside the apartment. It was a renovated penthouse loft with exposed brick walls, six floor-to-ceiling windows, and polished mahogany wood plank flooring.

The décor was contemporary, with mahogany and steel custom bookshelves, full of an array of leather and hardcover books. There was a closed, carved cabinet with a flat-screen TV and stereo that took up a third of the height of the fourteen-foot ceilings. A mix of brown leather and antique seating surrounded the centrally located fireplace.

"Your office is set up," Samuel said.

"Show me," Jonas said before turning to me. "I'll be right back."

I watched him walk away and couldn't help but admire the way his body fit his suit. Or the lean muscle perfection I knew was underneath. This temporarily distracted me, though I wanted to know more about his plans. I turned away and walked over to the black Steinway piano and lifted the case, pressing lightly over the keys and smiling. In tune. *Of course.*

I sat down and played "Alouette." When that didn't sound too bad, I played Brahms's "Lullaby."

"I was happy this place had one," Jonas said, walking up behind me. I stopped playing and smiled. "We used to have an upright piano in our house on Franklin Street. My dad would play and my mom would sing. I learned a few songs but, as you can see, I'm rusty."

"Paul plays, as you know. I was hoping to get him to play for us. Of course, that is if I can stop him from horsing around." His smile was wistful.

"Yeah, there's that," I said and laughed, but Jonas didn't join me. I reached out and took his hand. "I'm really sorry for what he overheard today."

Jonas's eyes glazed over. "Melissa was right, he's heard worse."

I pressed my lips together at the mention of her name. I wondered how he had left things with her.

Jonas cleared his throat. "Dani and I made some decisions in raising him that I now regret. I was under a strict regimen with my father. We kind of went overboard in trying to give him the opposite by exposing him to adult behaviors too early. Letting him have a lot of freedom. And, well, now I've got a lovable smartass."

I covered my mouth, stifling my laugh. "Well, he's a teen. We all push boundaries at that age. He's also kind and thinks very highly of his dad, I might add."

His brows rose and a ghost of a smile appeared on his lips. "Oh does he?"

"Yep. He told me as much," I said, and grinned when I saw the light in his face.

"Still. Melissa…I just don't understand her." He let go of my hand and ran his own through his hair.

"She said she loves you," I said evenly.

"Yes, there is that," he said it like it was a curse.

I blanched. "Yeah."

"She went too far. I don't know when I will forgive her," he said.

I swallowed hard and averted my eyes, reminding myself I didn't have Jonas's love either.

He ran his hand down my side and a tingle went through me, flaring our connection. He leaned close to my ear. "I don't feel the same way about her."

My heartbeat sped up. *As me?*

He turned me around to face him. "Maybe we can have Dani, Alan, and Paul over for dinner soon? We used to do that when I lived here."

I glanced at him. "We'll need to talk about how this will all be working first. I need to start searching for my new apartment. I'd like to know more about this storage Samuel was referring to. And I have to get back to work..."

"Slow down," Jonas reached out and took my hand, kissing the back of it. "We'll talk."

"But," I said, just as Samuel came back into the room, a folder tucked under his arm.

"It's all set. I'll call you later with updates, Mr. Crane. I'll just need your signatures," he said obliquely.

Jonas nodded and Samuel walked over and handed him a pen. He used the top of the piano to sign, before turning to me. "This is to give me permission to act on your behalf, to help you."

My lips parted as I eyed him questioningly. "In what capacity?"

"I need your permission to represent you through my legal division. Your authorization for me to proceed in the resolution of your apartment lease, and to pursue other issues. If possible, the theft of your property. Samuel will provide a copy for you to read over later," he said, holding out the pen.

I hesitated. This would not only be placing me further in his debt, but also under his control in the decisions affecting my life.

I trusted Jonas. He had shown his genuine interest in helping me, and had given me no reason to believe he didn't have my best interest at heart. Refusing would only leave me with the difficulty of trying to find and hire someone to do all of this on my own. But still, giving in felt too close to giving up, particularly after all I had tried to do to take care of myself.

I tried for a compromise. "I need a copy and for someone to explain this all to me, along with an added clause that states I can reject this agreement at any time, should I choose to do so."

Jonas's brow rose a fraction and he broke into a broad smile. "If that will make you feel better. Samuel here is your witness." The announcement of his involvement prompted Samuel to take a step forward and gesture with his hand in a semi-salute, acknowledging his willingness to do his part in the role assigned to him. Then again, the way Samuel was looking at Jonas had me thinking he would deny his own mother to stay in his favor.

Nevertheless, I reached out and took the pen, signing along the line where asked to do so. Jonas exhaled and handed the paper to Samuel, then walked with him to the door. My mind worried over the implications, but also reminded me that I didn't fare well on my own. In fact, things often got worse. I needed help, and he was willing to give that to me.

"Thank you for trusting me," Jonas said when he returned to my side, holding out his hand for me.

I walked over and clasped it. "I wish I could say I didn't need help, but I do. Thank you."

He led me out of the living room area and past the circular staircase to a modern, open-plan kitchen. Stainless-steel appliances, dark wood, and marble.

Modern lights. A long island bar with steel and leather barstools, custom cabinets and wine racks. A small breakfast nook completed the space.

A petite, elderly women with short, wispy gray hair and large, dark brown eyes stood before a five-burner stove. Her little bow mouth creased. "Jonas and…?"

"Lily. This is Lin, our amazing friend and housekeeper," Jonas said. "I had to bribe her away from Dani."

Lin laughed. "No, Jonas. I was more than happy to come over and help." She pushed up the sleeves of her pink shirt and came around the counter, surprising me with a kiss on my cheeks. "Lily, our little beauty. Or…what was that name you called her, Jonas?"

"Tiger Lily. Or did you hear me call her my lioness?" Jonas said, with a bit of huskiness to his voice that made me blush.

Lin beamed as her eyes shifted between the two of us. "Oh, yes. I see." Her eyes lingered on us for a moment, and then she added, "I've made my special homemade steak truffle pie with a delicious crème sauce and rosewater custard for dessert."

The smile froze on my face as my mind flashed. *Danger—bazillion calories alert.* Lin's face was prideful and my heart melted. I didn't want to hurt her feelings, but I wasn't sure about such a heavy lunch. "I had a big breakfast and my stomach has been upset."

Lin looked a question at me, her smile wilting a little.

"How about you try a bit, Lily. We can get you something light for dinner," Jonas said.

My brows rose. A compromise? Who was this Jonas Crane? "That sounds good. Thank you, Lin."

She beamed and squeezed my arm. "One more thing." She turned and held out a glass of water and a bottle. "Iron pills. This helped when my friend's daughter was anemic."

I took the pills and water without fuss. I wasn't sure yet that I *was* anemic, but I did want to get better. Jonas gave me an approving smile and motioned for me to take a seat at the built-in breakfast nook while he pulled out a bottle of wine.

"Take a seat," Lin commanded as she came up behind him and patted him on his back, taking the bottle from him.

I laughed as Jonas took the seat across from me, delighting in someone else ordering him around.

His stare warmed me all the way down to my toes. My heart skipped a beat as I returned his gaze with my own intensity.

"I love seeing you smile," he said softly.

Lin walked up and put our plates of food down in front of us. I shook my head to try to dispel the effect he had on me. I was utterly besotted with him. I needed to get ahold of myself or I might scare him off again.

"What are you thinking?" Jonas asked, no doubt picking up on the change in my demeanor. Nothing got past him.

I lifted the corner of my mouth. "Nothing," I muttered.

He frowned at me. "Why can't you just tell me?"

I shrugged. "I'm trying. You don't need to know every passing thought in my head."

"I do if it wipes the happiness off your face. I want to know," he replied.

I licked my lips. "My thoughts are…personal. Please give me time."

We ate in silence for a few minutes. The rich food was incredibly delicious and I nodded over to Lin when I noticed her smiling at us.

"I'd like to look over your spa treatment from this morning. You'll show me before your nap." His tone suggested he could have been discussing the weather, but his words made my breath hitch. His face remained straight as he continued to eat his food. I must have been staring off for a few minutes, because his next words were, "Your food is getting cold." Though he wasn't looking into my eyes, his mischievous grin told me he knew exactly what he had just done to me.

I shifted in my seat. "I'm enjoying it," I managed. "Thank you." I took a sip of my wine and went for my own change of subject. "So, how long before you have to go out of town?"

"I have a possible day trip to Miami Friday for work. Maybe in a few weeks we can go on a mini vacation," Jonas said.

I moved my food around my plate. My heart ached at the thought of him flying away on business so soon, but I understood. He enjoyed his work. I only wished we'd have more time together.

"If I decide to go, you'll come with me," he added.

I looked up and caught his eyes, a slight smile breaking across my face.

I ate more of my food and thought about the possibility. I loved that he wanted me to join him on his business trip, but I knew I wasn't financially in a position to pay to do so, let alone to go on a vacation. Finally, I spoke up, "I can't afford…I do appreciate your offer, but…"

"But nothing," Jonas interrupted. "I meant it when I said I want us to spend more time together. I think a compromise on both of our parts is in order. I'm making time, and you will too. You're on leave anyway."

"Yes. For a week, I suppose," I said and sipped my wine.

"I'll speak to Gregor and get him to agree to let me decide when you return," Jonas said, as if the thought had just formed in his mind.

My eyes widened. "He'd never do that.

Jonas sipped his wine and said, "Oh, he will. If I agree to publish my book with Arch, he'll do anything I ask."

I opened my mouth to tell him he was wrong, but thought better and closed it. Gregor would wrap a bow around me and hand me to him on a platter if Jonas agreed to give his business. Wasn't that how I had come to meet Jonas in the first place? Hell, he would be able to expand his office from the press release alone. "You can't…he needs me," I muttered.

But if that happened, would Gregor still need me?

My eyes darted as my mind raced onto what I would do with my life.

"Oh, please eat," Lin said, breaking my thoughts. She walked up to the table and added more pieces of steak. "I'll like to know your favorite meals, too. So I can cook them for you."

"Great idea, Lin," Jonas said and grinned. She beamed at him.

"Thank you, Lin," I said and plastered on a smile for her. When she walked away, I chewed my bottom lip and stared down at my plate.

"Calm down. I haven't done it," Jonas said. The word 'yet' hung in the air.

I exhaled. "So, you will be making the decisions for me? I know you found me the way I am right now, but I can fix these things on my own…"

"Not without me." He reached over and took my hand. "Not on your own."

I looked up at him through my long lashes. "Because you're my friend…"

A small smirk appeared at the edge of his lips. "You fishing, Lily?" he asked coyly.

I turned my head to hide my grin, thoroughly resolved to eat every last morsel of my lunch.

CHAPTER THREE

I WAS SURE I would burst after eating a small dish of the rosewater custard. I tried to help Lin clear the dishes, but she shooed Jonas and me out of the kitchen. He took my hand and led me to the stairs, where he started removing his shoes. The carpet was pale and soft underfoot as we climbed up to the second floor and down a short hallway, passing a few doors and a bathroom. At the end, we walked into a large and modern master suite with a small, floating fireplace and a sitting area that had modular couches and tables.

Four floor-to-ceiling factory windows dominated the space, draped by built-in blinds. A large, custom leather and steel bed with dark grey and white bedding and colorful pillow accents was against one wall.

Jonas let go of my hand and moved over to a walk-in closet that was divided by a short wall, while I admired the built-in shelves and groups of framed, abstract photos that decorated the space. I walked in the opposite direction toward the bathroom, which was also impressive—built-in cabinets, an extra-large garden tub with a large glass-enclosed shower with a stone bench, and a custom vanity area.

"Big enough for two," Jonas said. I turned to look at him and my pulse sped up. He had changed and was now wearing a shirt that showed off his sexy, muscular upper body. His pants hung low on his waist and looked oh-so right.

I forced my gaze back to the tub. "Or four. It's huge."

He kissed my lips, and I got a taste of mint. "I'd like to brush my teeth. Do you have spare toothbrushes?"

He walked me over to the cabinet, where I brushed my teeth and rinsed my mouth. When I finished, I asked, "Off for a workout? I could use one too." I rubbed my stomach.

His arms circled my waist. "Yes. My trainer will be coming soon. This place has a small gym, but," Jonas said, curbing my enthusiasm, "not for you right now." He kissed the side of my neck.

I sighed and he took my hand, leading me back into the bedroom and walking us over to the bed.

"Sleeping and eating," I smirked. "Just so you know, I gain weight pretty quickly."

"Good. I want you better," Jonas said. He sat down on the bed and put his hands on my hips, pulling me between his legs. "Now, I want you to take off your clothes and climb into bed. We'll talk until you fall asleep."

My body responded to his command. I enjoyed him

taking over when we were intimate. However, there was something besides my desire for him overtaking me now. Something different. I stared up into his eyes that were fixed on me, and my heart swelled. His need was reflecting back to me, but so was something else. I took in a shallow breath as my fingers trembled to work at unbuttoning my shirt.

Jonas's hands closed over my own as he leaned forward and planted a light kiss on my knuckles. "Want me to undress you?" he asked.

I nodded. I couldn't speak, but felt a tingle down to my core. He went at a slow pace and finished undoing my button-down shirt, then I helped him pull it off my arms and into his hands, where he paused to fold and place it on the side table. My breathing and pulse teemed with anticipation.

"Why do you always fold my clothes after undressing me?" I whispered.

He turned me away from him and unclasped my bra.

"How does it make you feel?" Jonas said, answering a question with a question. He eased the straps down my arms and kissed my shoulders. My breasts responded, swelling and hardening my nipples. He turned me around to face him. His eyes roved over my naked upper body.

My feelings were full of romanticism. I didn't trust he was ready to hear them, especially after his reaction to Melissa's love. So I answered, "I don't know."

"I think you do know," he said in a low tone.

I exhaled as he cupped and kneaded my breasts. He closed his lips around my nipple and traced it with his tongue as he continued to massage the other one. I moaned. I couldn't help but put my hands in his hair and hold his head there, arching my back to him. He gently bit down, then licked lightly, soothing the pain with his tongue. He suckled my other breast and my breathing became staggered. Heat coursed through my body. I thought he would take off my pants next, but he surprised me by capturing my lips and kissing me.

Deeply massaging his tongue against mine, he sucked my bottom lip, just to cover my lips again in a sensuous tangle that had me pressing in closer and squirming to get more from him.

"Don't be afraid to share your feelings," he said in a gentle tone as our lips parted. He placed his hands on my hips to still me. I looked over, taking in his half-lidded gaze and swollen, full mouth. I felt wetness gush between my thighs. He was so incredibly hot. I squirmed.

"I've got you," he said in a soft tone. He unbuttoned my jeans and hooked his thumbs in the sides of my panties, pulling them down together until I stood before him, naked and struggling not to cover myself. He wrapped his strong arms around me and pulled me into a hug. "I'm worried about you, Tiger Lily. I want you to gain weight and get healthy."

His term of endearment warmed me and the thickness in his voice constricted my heart. "I'm fine. I'm going to be fine."

"Yes," he rubbed over my hips. "You will be. I'll make sure of it."

His caress elicited a familiar spark, coursing across my skin. I shifted my legs. "Do you just want to talk right now?" I asked, my voice raspy.

He ran the back of his knuckle over the top of my mound in an unhurried manner. "So soft. I want to feel you on my lips, but if I start there we both know I won't stop." He was using his low tone. The one that turned me on to no end. He was also teasing me, making me desperate enough to do something I would likely find embarrassing under other circumstances. Like standing naked, parting my thighs in front of him and moving against where his knuckle stopped, making him press against my slit.

His gaze was dark as he watched me. "You're soaking my finger. Is that what you want?" he purred. He held his knuckle still as I slid it against my swollen clit. I moaned and moved faster, the sensation sending pulses of pleasure through me.

"Answer." He moved his hand back and rested it on his thigh.

My pulse pounded in my chest and I whined. "Why can't you just do instead of making me say…?" I hissed, frustration in my tone. He pulled me closer and kissed along my collarbone and neck. "Because I want you to tell me. Straddle my lap."

A blush crept up my cheeks. "I'll ruin your clothes," I whispered.

His eyes danced with amusement. “I know your pussy is wet. I don’t care. But since that bothers you, you can pull down my clothes. Just know, getting in my lap wasn’t a request.” His crass words and command worked as affectively as his hands and I heated up all the more.

Pulling down his pants and bringing his long, thick erection into view, I crawled on his lap. Before I could sit, he pressed the head of his cock against my clit. I whimpered, “Jonas.”

He inhaled sharply. “I’m not fucking you right now, though it’s tempting,” he gritted. “Mmm, but that whimper. So sexy.” He paused, seeming to think for a moment. “You don’t want my hand. You want my cock? Tell me.”

A smile formed on my lips despite his torture. This was a play on the dream he had woken me from last night. Oh, I had the answer alright. “Your cock, please, Jonas,” I rasped.

He laid back and dragged me up and down the outside of his shaft. He grabbed my ass and pressed in hard. “I want you to come on my cock.” Rocking my hips, I arched and slid against the base of his cock. Pleasure and need taking over me with every drag and press of my sex to him. *Oh, Jonas.*

His eyes were fixed on me as he groaned and panted below me. Even there he was in control. The last threads of my own broke, and I humped him unabashedly. He had reduced me to primal desire and all I could think about was that sweet release within my grasp. I grunted,

"I'm close. I'm, ohhh. Jonas!"

"Yes. Come, for me," he commanded, rubbing the head of his cock right up against my clit. I came, shuddering, collapsing against him. "God, Lily. So fucking sexy. I can't wait."

He let go of me and I eased to his side. He moved his hand down and gripped his cock in his hand, using my essence as a glide to stroke himself with.

"Lick me," he commanded.

I moved into action, licking him as he jerked on his cock until he exploded with force. Then I closed my mouth over him, sucking down his seed, tasting the heady mix of the both of us.

"Yes," he hissed. Jonas petted my hair as he came down, releasing himself from my mouth.

"My Tiger Lily. Come here." He pulled me into his arms.

Yes. Jonas had me. And as I held him close, I realized I had him, too.

"I do the things I do because I want you to feel closer to me," he replied, giving me an answer to the question I had asked earlier. How close, he didn't say. And I didn't push it. I was too bliss-filled.

After a while, he moved me on the bed and held open the covers. "Get in." I climbed in and he moved to lay on his side, facing me.

"Now, that's a look I'll enjoy while we are living together," he mused.

I glanced down at his mention of 'while.' It was best

to remember we had a time limit for our togetherness. "I'll start looking for a permanent place," I promised. "I'll pay rent here until then, though I suspect it's well out of my range."

He laughed. "I make your yearly salary quicker than you could turn over." I looked away, and he continued. "I'm not saying that to hurt you, but the idea of you paying rent here is ridiculous," he said.

My mouth went dry. "I don't think it's silly," I mumbled.

He stroked under my chin. "I do admire your willingness and pride. No one I have ever been with before has challenged me on this, and you have so much less than most of them."

My body went stiff. Jonas cleared his throat. "You're here because I want you here. What I want and do costs. And I want you with me. So we both benefit."

I didn't say anything, so he continued. "As I told you before, we ended the companionship. This is about us, together. I go to a lot of public functions and events. You will come with me. Right now, your clothing doesn't fit you properly. I want to fix that."

Now I wanted to respond. "So, what am I supposed to be? I wasn't raised to be a burden. I can't do that, not even if I only had a couple of dollars. Maybe I could clean and cook here? You can send Lin back to Dani," I said.

Jonas looked at me as if I had sprouted a new head. "Not a chance. I don't want you serving me. Well, not in that way," he joked, but leaned in and kissed my lips when he noticed how his words hurt me.

"So, I'm to take and take, until you're done and leave me? No way." I moved to turn over, but he took hold of my hips and pinned me down on my back.

"Where am I going? You already have me gone before we've even started. Stop telling me how I feel and listen to me, have a little faith in me. If you're worried about taking, how about you do something I want from you that doesn't cost money as payment?" he said.

"What's that?" I asked.

"You go to counseling for what happened to you. Dani has a friend, Isla, who could see you this week."

I furrowed my brows. "I appreciate Dani's offer, but I'm not a head case. I know I messed up with everything. I don't plan to do it again. I'm on board with fighting Declan, even though that scares me. But I took care of myself. I kept my apartment, went to work, and was trying to turn my life around."

He laid on his side, facing me, then placed an arm along my waist. "I know, and I admire that about you. I think you're resilient, trying to keep your life together after all that happened. But now you're not alone. I'll be here, and so will Dani, Alan, and Gregor. Even Paul would be willing to help you," he said, kissing behind my ear.

"Why? I don't understand. Gregor is my boss and friend, but your family barely knows me," I said.

"Because we trust each other and our instincts about

you. I went against them when you disappeared, but I trusted Dani to tell me what happened. Though we are both saddened that she kept your attack from me."

I took his hand. "Dani did that for me and I'm sorry. She wouldn't stop calling or texting, even though I didn't return any of her messages."

"That's how she's been since I met her. Once she declares you her friend, she won't let go. Even if you never spoke to me again, she would never have left you. Can you believe she still has friends from grade school? Even after we separated, she called me every day. She doesn't throw anyone away," he said.

My heart constricted. I kissed his chest. "I didn't throw you away," I whispered.

"I understand that now." He cleared his throat. "Anyway. Counseling may help you gain perspective on everything, and Isla can give you an introductory session before her scheduled sessions in a couple of days. You don't have to go forever, but trying would be an acceptable payment. I won't force you, but that's what I want," he said.

I huffed, feeling thoroughly ambushed. I wanted to whine that I should get a week to process, but there was no reasoning with the man that had taken me to my doctor's office immediately upon seeing me just a day before. This was the one thing he asked of me, and I had said I would try. "Fine, but I don't have to like it. I had a bad experience after my parents died. The counselor gave me a few brochures to read after…after I poured my whole heart out to her. It was useless. But I will try therapy again, for you. I still want to do something else, though."

"I'll think of something." He leaned over and kissed the back of my neck.

"Sex," I said, like it was a dirty word. He stopped.

"I wanted to find and explore what we have together without sex. We can't do that now," he said.

"Why not?" I asked coyly.

He reached over and placed his hand over my sex possessively. "Because I'm not going without sex. I don't go without," he said bluntly.

My mouth dropped open and I looked past him. "I don't want you to go without. I just didn't want to share you. But there is something that concerns me." I paused and he waited for me to continue. "Melissa mentioned there are things you enjoy that I don't…or we haven't…"

He pressed his lips together. "Melissa again." I could hear the exasperation in his voice, but he took a soothing breath and then returned to me. "We had a different relationship together. I was different, too. You already know some of my kinks, but the main thing right now is you staying here with me."

I put all my feelings into my gaze. "I meant what I said, Jonas. I'm staying, but I want you to tell me what's going on and for us to discuss it, and for you to compromise instead of taking over."

He grinned at me. "Feisty and full of negotiations.

Who are you?" He moved out of the bed and changed back into his clothes.

My cheeks warmed. I shrugged.

He kissed me. "I like it, but you'll find I'm not easily swayed. You won't get your way all the time, especially if I think my way is for your betterment."

I sighed. "Yes, I'm well aware that you're bossy and pushy."

"I'm not perfect, but you love me," Jonas said. His voice went up at the end, a rare hint of uncertainty.

Of course that hit me right in the chest and I answered without hesitation. "Yes, I do. That, I'm certain of."

Jonas cupped the side of my face and we stared at each other as electricity sparked between us. His thumb reached over and traced the outline of my lips.

The doorbell sounded. *Grrr!*

Leaning in to kiss me, he said, "That's the trainer. We'll talk more soon." He climbed off the bed and headed for the door.

"Jonas?" I called out.

He turned in the doorway. "Yes?"

My pulse sprinted as his eyes bore into mine. "The way you are with me makes me feel like…I'm special to you."

Jonas walked back over and kissed me tenderly on the lips. "That, I'm certain of," he whispered.

My heart swelled and I leaned forward, deepening our kiss.

The bell sounded again and we parted.

"Now, get some rest. I'll check on you later." That assurance was all I needed as I gave myself to sleep and dreams.

CHAPTER FOUR

I RUBBED MY eyes against the light coming from the table lamp. My body felt rested, though my jaw was sore from grinding my teeth. My heart sank as dread washed over me. Had I been having a nightmare?

I sifted through my thoughts as I took in my surroundings, narrowing in on a phone next to the lamp, along with a handwritten number scrawled across a piece of paper.

This is your new phone and number—Jonas

My stomach lurched at the thought of what might have appeared on my phone after giving it to Jonas.

Would Declan call to gloat? What would happen if Jonas answered?

The pain in my jaw flared again as I gritted my teeth. My mind raced ahead, worrying about what might be next. My heartbeat was even faster, and it had me seeking relief the way I had for some time now.

Pushing back the duvet, I climbed out of the bed and searched for my clothes, but I couldn't find them. I thought to run in place, to lunge, crunch or jump in my fight against the pain and exhaustion these thoughts plagued me with. But that choice had been taken away by my doctor and Jonas.

No. Truthfully, I knew it wasn't an ultimate solution. I wasn't running anymore. Not physically or mentally, since both had almost cost me everything.

Standing up, I walked back to the bed and sat down, covering my face with my hands. I took a few short breaths.

What was I to do now?

The sound of music drifted up from downstairs, interrupting my thoughts and bringing me back to the now. "Maybe I'm Amazed." I smiled. Jonas was here. We were together for a while, if I could help us. If I helped myself.

If I started letting people in to help me.

I dropped my hands and looked at the phone. I thought to call Mary, but she was another person I had shut out of my life in the midst of all this chaos. Would she forgive me?

I needed to find out. I picked up the phone and dialed her phone number. After a few rings, she answered.

"Hello. Who is this?" Her tone was cautious.

"Mary," I cleared my throat. "It's me, Lily."

"Oh. I didn't recognize the number. And I didn't realize you even remembered mine. Thanks for the message to say you would be back in touch," she said, her voice crisp.

I climbed back under the covers and curled on my side. "I deserve that. I was…I was trying to. I didn't want you to know about what happened. I didn't want you to worry…" I stammered.

"What happened? Are you hurt? Oh my god," her voice went shrill.

I sat up. "No." Then I took a breath. "Yes…I really don't want to do this over the phone. I just wanted you to know I'm staying with Jonas. And this will be the phone number to reach me at." My own voice wavered.

"I need to know more or I'm driving up to wherever you are this minute. I…I swore I would look after you after your parents died. And I've failed miserably." She was sobbing now.

I wiped my cheek. "No. I failed you again. I'm sorry."

"Tell me what's going on. I want to see you. Give me the address where you are and I'll leave right now." Her voice elevated.

I bit my lip. "Jonas said…we agreed…after a couple of weeks or so. When I'm better."

"I don't care what Jonas said. You're my best friend and I love you. If you're hurt, I want to be there to help you. Put him on the phone," she yelled.

"Calm down. Let me explain…everything. God I didn't want to do this over the phone." My voice broke.

"I'm grabbing my keys. I can't take not knowing what's going on anymore. You weren't doing well when I saw you after that asshole hurt you. I'm your best friend,

Lily. You're my sister. I love you. You have to tell me." My heart constricted at the sound of her crying into the phone.

My own eyes filling, I finally said, "After I returned from Boston…" I didn't stop talking until I had told her everything that happened after I left her apartment in Boston.

When I finished, she said solemnly, "I've failed you as a friend again. I had a feeling things weren't going right with you. I should have listened more during your visit or tried harder to come down to see you when I couldn't reach you."

I wiped my chin. "I didn't *let* you be a friend again, Mary. This is *me*. Not you."

"I want to be there for you. I'd like to take *your* Jonas up on his offer to visit soon. Please give him my number so I can speak to him," she said.

I groaned. "Jonas isn't exactly mine. He wants to help me. He has been helping me. But it's still complicated. I'd love for you to visit, but I just got here myself. I'll call you with a date soon. If you want to speak to Jonas, I'll have him call you, but I don't know what'll happen between us. If he decides I'm not…"

"Don't start down that path. He wouldn't have dropped everything and came for you, and he wouldn't have you living with him, if he was just going to drop you. The man is crazy in love with you. He's just too stubborn to admit it," she said.

I blew out a breath. "He likes me, I know that, but I

don't want to pressure..." My words were stolen at the sight of Jonas walking into the bedroom wearing just a towel around his neck.

He was unabashed in all his nudity. Was I drooling? Maybe, but who would blame me? Not with his incredible physique. He was flawless. From his smooth chest hair, trailing down his well-defined abs and trim waist, to his thickening cock.

I had to get off the phone.

His pace was slow. He didn't need to rush. He had already caught me.

"Um...can we talk later, Mare?" My voice was breathy.

"So, he's there? Okay. Be careful. I'll be calling more to check up on you. And you better answer or I'll just show up. I love you."

My eyes connected with Jonas's and electricity sparked between us. "I love you, too." I almost whispered. It was meant for Mary, but my gaze was locked on him.

I fumbled as I placed the phone back on the bedside table. "Mary," I said absently.

Jonas gave a nod and, with fluidity, removed the towel from his neck and pulled the duvet back, exposing the lower half of my body. "You ready for me? Show me," he said in a baritone.

All the air rushed out of my lungs as wetness gushed between my thighs. I only managed a grunt as desire overtook me. Closing my eyes, I stretched out on my back, gaping my thighs the way he liked. Oh, I was ready. And then some.

"Open your eyes," Jonas commanded.

I complied and watched him position himself between my thighs. "Don't hide from me ever again…know you're beautiful." Our gazes merged and we stayed suspended in that moment. Nothing Jonas ever said was without purpose. And with that thought, my eyes lit at the memory of when I had last heard those words from him. It was our first night together at the Waldorf hotel. Jonas battling my insecurities and assuring his desire for me.

Even though we had sex just 24 hours ago, he was starting over. And the depth of his understanding overwhelmed me. My eyes filled. "Oh, Jonas," I said. He called me a romantic, but I had nothing on him.

Jonas reached up and placed his hands on the sides of my face, using his thumbs to wipe my cheeks. His eyes shone as they roamed over me. "I missed you," he said softly.

My gaze didn't stray from his eyes. "I missed you, too."

He kissed my cheeks and down my neck, breathing me in. I kissed over the surface of his face, touching the soft waves of his dark hair. My breasts swelled and hardened before his sensual mouth reached them. And when he did, I arched, willing him as I watched him suckle and knead them in his large hands. Our breaths quickened, moaning on our exhalation. We were in sync in our desire for one another.

Groaning, Jonas let go of my breasts and captured my mouth again, kissing me deeply, delving his tongue between my parted lips and gliding it expertly against mine, kindling a scorching heat I felt all the way down to my core. His solid frame pressed against me, and mine answered by molding into him. Inhaling through my nose, I caught his intoxicating aroma, a collective blend that every fiber of my being recognized as *Jonas.*

My Jonas.

He reluctantly broke away and moved his lips down to my chest, forging a path to the flat plane of my stomach until he reached the top of my bare mound. He paused there, sought my eyes and bore into them. My heart stopped.

"You won't try to stop me this time," he said darkly. I sucked in my bottom lip and squirmed. *That I won't do, Mr. Crane.* The throbbing ache there surged, knowing he would soon soothe it and more. "Please," I whispered.

Placing my legs on his shoulders, he parted my slit with his tongue then closed his mouth around my clit and sucked. I called out an incoherent prayer, willing myself not to savor the sensation pulsating through my body as I clasped the sheets tightly in my fists.

"Mmm, you blessing me? I worship you," he mused, then kissed my pussy with a hunger as sure as he took my lips, lapping through the slick folds and swirling his tongue around my clit.

My heart pounding hard in my chest, I grasped his head and lifted my hips.

He groaned and managed to crook a finger inside as he relentlessly licked and sucked me. Knowing my body, he stroked his finger over my spot. I came, calling his name, my hands gripping and thighs crushing his head as pleasure flowed through me. When I came down, Jonas extracted his head and rolled his neck. “I'll need to tie you down,” he purred.

I shivered at his dark promise, imaging Jonas taking me over, and I heated all the more.

He journeyed up my body once more and lifted my head up. “Like that idea, my Tiger Lily?” He kissed my lips again and we ate my desire, still clinging to his tongue as he tangled it with mine.

Reaching his hand down between us, he guided his cock to my entrance. Lifting my hips, he pushed in one continual thrust until he was sealed deep inside of me. Every inch sending shocks of ecstasy coursing through my body.

“So perfect inside you,” Jonas growled as he rolled his hips.

Our gazes locked as he began short, hard thrusts.

My heart soared. I loved him. Did he see it?

The rhythmic strokes of his cock brought me close again. I felt my body stiffening and tightening once more. My eyes widened.

Jonas could feel it. “Oh. Yes. Come,” he hissed. He swiveled his hips as he ground his cock in deeper than he ever had before. My body wept in the feeling that arose within, and I climaxed, shaking underneath him.

"Lily," he moaned as my inner walls gripped and spasmed around his cock.

I wrapped my legs around him as he pushed in deep and erupted in his release. Putting my arms around his neck, I tried to pull him down, but he stopped me.

"I'll crush you," he whispered.

"I don't care. I love you." I said. I just wanted him close.

He pecked my lips and eased me over until I was lying on top of him, then he held me in his arms. My head resting on his chest.

This is perfect.

I pressed my head against his skin and listened to his heart, wishing he would give voice to what resonated between us in all that he had shown. But in mine, I knew. Jonas Crane loved me.

CHAPTER FIVE

"LILY," JONAS GENTLY shook my shoulder.

I stirred and lifted my head from his chest to look at him. "Sorry. I didn't mean to drift off."

He petted my hair. "I would have let you sleep, but I'd like you to eat dinner first. Were you uncomfortable?" The concern on his face brought a smile to mine.

I licked my lips. "I don't know why I'm still feeling tired. I felt like I'd woken from a bad dream earlier, but still felt rested."

He moved my body up so he could kiss my forehead. "I wish I would have been in here for you," he said.

A flutter went through my chest. "I'm fine. Or, I will be fine now. Thank you for the phone to use. I called Mary. She'd like to chat with you about a visit soon," I said.

He lifted the corner of his mouth. "She can come whenever you're ready. I'll tell her the same. And the phone is yours."

I half-lidded my eyes. "Thank you. You're too generous. The hotel spa, moving me in with you, not to mention all the other things. You shouldn't spoil me."

"That's hardly spoiling. Most of those are for my own pleasure. I plan to do better in spoiling." He kissed my lips lightly.

I lowered my head. "Why? You don't have to do anything else. I won't care. I'm just happy you're here. With me."

He cuddled me to him. "That's the reason I want to give you everything. You will be spoiled and adored, as you so rightly deserve."

His words were heartfelt, and I drank them in. But my mind grabbed hold of the last time I had heard similar words, and the change that had occurred in that relationship after those words were spoken.

Jonas cupped my face. His eyes fixed on me. "Did I make you sad?" The empathy in his expression had the truth I would normally hold onto flowing from my lips.

"Declan used to say things like that in the beginning, too. He was generous and kind. But then he wasn't. Towards the end, he called me a 'fat spoiled princess.' I guess the idea of being spoiled makes me think you'll think…"

"No. Never," Jonas said, cutting me off and cupping my chin. "I'll never do that to you." He squeezed me closer. "I know sharing those details doesn't come easily for you. So thank you for telling me. But please know, I'm not Declan."

I nodded, unable to speak. I tried to smile, but my lips trembled too much.

His gaze was pointed on mine as he continued. "He was leagues beneath you and never deserved you. He will pay for hurting you. That, I will make sure of." He kissed me tenderly.

"Have I received any more messages?" I asked in a small voice.

His jaw tightened. "If you did, I'd never tell you," he said bluntly. "That's a closed subject for you and your wellbeing. Promise me right now you will not try to retrieve messages or pursue any contact with him. This will be our resolution on the matter." From Jonas's stern expression, he wasn't open to compromise.

I gave him a nod and said, "I promise."

"It's late. Let's go have dinner and discuss what we will do with the rest of our week," Jonas said, changing the subject.

He moved us to a sitting position and my arms involuntarily moved around his shoulders. He then lifted and moved me off the bed, walking us into the bathroom where he sat me down next to the sink. Turning on the tap, he dampened a cloth.

I parted my legs a little and he moved between them, widening them more. He then thoroughly commenced with an embarrassingly intimate cleanse between my thighs. He had done as much before, so I didn't interrupt him, though it still puzzled me. Finally, I asked what this cleaning ritual was all about. But he responded with another question within a question, asking, "How does it make you feel?" for the second time today.

Though it irritated me, I decided to answer.

"It feels good, but it still embarrasses me. So why do you do it?" I asked.

He walked away and collected matching terry cloth robes for us to put on. Once his was in place, he held mine open. "Taking control, caring for you, even cleaning you; it turns me on. And I know, even though you blush pretty for me, that you're turned on too."

I put my arms through the sleeves of the robe and he closed and cinched the tie in place. "So you do it just to turn us on? You must have another reason. I'd like to know," I pressed.

He sighed and gazed at me, a hint of amusement at what I imagined to be a rapt expression on my face. "Because you're mine, and I want you to feel like you're a part of me," he said.

I beamed at him. "I want to be."

He rested his hands on my shoulders. "Then you are."

Jonas took my hands. "Lin left dinner for us. We need to eat and plan out the rest of our week."

"Can't we just wing it?" I whined. "I mean, I'm on stress vacation. Can't I just rest in front of the TV or read a book?"

He laughed as we walked together out of the bathroom. "I wish I could wing it, as you so eloquently put it, but to spend time with you and still meet all my business obligations, I have to plan."

We walked together down the stairs to the living

room, the sound of Paul McCartney and Wings still playing in the background. The song "My Love" started and a pang went through my heart. I lowered my head while Jonas eyed me inquisitively, as I realized too late that I had stopped walking.

"I love this CD. Thank you again for it." I recovered.

"It's one of my favorites, too," he said. I took steps and he continued his path back to the kitchen, where the table was already set and included our food, protected under metal place covers. I took the seat I'd taken earlier and removed the lid to find pasta salad with some sort of cream sauce and artichokes. Jonas poured me a glass of wine and himself a scotch before joining me at the table.

I ate a quick forkful of pasta. *Delicious.* We ate in silence, until I asked, "Have you seen my clothes? I didn't have much at the hotel and I wonder if David could drive me over…"

"They should be delivered tomorrow, and then Lin will put them away for you. You have a counseling session on Wednesday. Samuel has arranged for an appointment at Barney's on Thursday. While you were napping, it became clear I will have to go to Miami. So, we'll be flying to Miami for the day on Friday. I was to do a game on Saturday with Paul, but that depends on the weather. You can go to that, too. On Sunday…"

"Slow down." I said. We smiled at each other. "If I get new clothes now, I probably won't fit in them in a couple of weeks."

"Then you'll get more. But all that depends on how

you're feeling," he said.

I sipped my wine and glanced over at him. "So, where is this psychiatric session on Wednesday?" I asked.

"Upper West Side. You nervous?" he asked, then took another bite from his plate.

"Yes," I admitted.

"You can call me after the session, and I'll be here over lunch. I could get Dani to go with you," he offered.

I shook my head. "I'll be fine. I think I'm more worried about talking about everything."

"Isla is the best and comes highly recommended," he said.

"Have you ever been to a psychiatrist?" I asked.

He didn't answer immediately, and I thought he wasn't going to. But then he said, "Well, I was seeing Melissa at the end of our marriage. But that stopped once the situation changed."

I pursed my mouth. "She's not supposed to date her clients. That's completely unethical."

"Well, I wasn't her client for long. She was really more a friendly ear." He sipped his scotch.

"Yes, and then you became more than friends." I spit out the words.

"I was having problems adjusting to Alan with Dani and Paul. My brother Vincent was causing me grief when I decided to base myself in Texas. Melissa provided perspective, though now I know she wanted more from our arrangement." Seeing my face, he redirected. "And that's enough on her, Lily. I'm sorry about what occurred between you two, but don't be jealous."

I furrowed my brow. "Why not? You were jealous of Ian. I can be jealous of Melissa." I ate another bite of pasta.

"Yes, I was…am," he admitted.

I sighed. "You already know I don't want Ian, but you don't want me around him. I want the same for Melissa. I trust you, but…I don't trust her. And I would just feel better if you stayed away from her, like you want me to do with Ian."

"They are both friends that I know well. These situations are completely different. Melissa is going through a difficult time. I can't just disappear," he sighed in exasperation.

My face fell. "They're different because Ian doesn't love me, but Melissa loves you." He didn't respond, so I continued. "So, you plan to see her again?"

Jonas put his fork down. His eyes flashed at me. "Come over here, Lily."

I tilted my head down and stared at my plate. "I don't want to fight about your friends, but you still don't accept what we both witnessed today. She'll say and do whatever it takes to have you."

"Come over here, Lily," he repeated, this time enunciating every word.

I glared at him, though a thrill went through me. He appeared calm, but his eyes were stormy. He had moved his seat back and was waiting.

I inhaled and pushed back before standing. My pulse

increased with every step as I closed the distance between us and stood before him.

He took my hands. "I have few friends, Lily. My work and life are complex. I don't get to be as social and I was brought up to suspect everything and everyone. Alan, who's marrying Dani, like Ian, is one of those few who became my friend. I've known them both for over ten years. However, when it comes to you, I will let Ian's friendship go. I've learned that much. The only thing that saved him was finding out how he helped you in my absence."

He looked at me, examining my expression, then continued. "I don't want to play games. Ian wouldn't appreciate or deserve to be played, either."

I knew he was referring to my using Ian as a pawn to push Melissa out of our lives as well, and I immediately felt bad. Particularly because Ian *had* helped me. I nodded my head rapidly. I didn't want to be the reason their friendship ended. Just the thought made me ill. "I understand. And I'm sorry," I sighed.

He exhaled. "I accept. In regard to Melissa, she is an old friend I've known practically my whole life. Her life isn't perfect, and she's not perfect, but I won't throw her away because of her feelings. You didn't cast Gregor away, and he's in love with you."

My mouth dropped open. "He knows I don't feel the same way. And he accepts it. I don't believe Melissa holds the same sentiment."

"Gregor tried to warn you against me with Maggie.

Remember? I wanted you away from him, but you wanted to keep that friendship. That makes this similar. So you'll need to trust me."

My shoulders hunched and I looked down. My stomach dropped. "Gregor didn't do what she did. After what she did and said, you shouldn't be around her. I don't want you around her."

"I'm furious with her for her behavior this afternoon. That hasn't changed. But I shouldn't abandon her friendship because of her feelings. I chose you, Lily."

"For now," I said, interrupting him. I stared at my bare feet.

"Come here," I didn't fight when he tugged me forward and down onto his lap. "You know I didn't put a time limit on us. Have I given you reason to doubt me?"

I stared at my hands as they rolled up the ends of the tie on the robe. "I don't trust her. I don't feel secure with you being with her."

He took the ties from my hands and opened my robe. "I think it's more to do with you not having confidence in me. That will come in time, along with your belief that you're mine," he slipped the robe past my shoulders. "Take off your robe and fold it, then move your food over next to mine," he said.

I narrowed my gaze. "Why? You want to play a sex game in the middle of our argument."

"This is not a game, this is you being mine. I'm commanding and demanding. I'm all consuming. This is me, as I truly am. This is me giving you what I believe you need from me," he said and released me. I immediately felt empty, but I sat there and thought about what he had said. His demand was sexual in nature, and the heat that was working through me, along with the throb in my sex, had me ready to do what he asked. Still, my mind wondered if I needed to acquiesce to him to feel assured in his feelings for me and not Melissa. Wouldn't the same assurance be achieved by his saying he loved me?

My heart ached at how much I wanted those words from him right now. But he'd been given plenty of opportunities to say as much today, and he hadn't. He wasn't ready.

What he was ready for was to try to make me feel closer to him, and in that he was right. I needed that much from him right now.

Jonas exhaled long as I unclasped my robe, his stare fixed on me as I folded the robe, per his directions. Then I walked over to my seat and placed it down, lifting my plate and setting it next to his. I returned to stand before him and he sat me down in his lap, cuddling me close. My heart fluttered.

Jonas moved my hair and kissed the back of my neck and along my shoulders, resting his head against my back. "I need to be me and I need you to be mine," he said, as if answering a question. His words seized my heart. So much pain lingered in those words. He needed more than words as assurance. I understood that now, but I said them anyway. "I am yours."

He parted my thighs and cupped my sex possessively, then moved us close to the table. He lifted up a fork and fed me the remainder of my plate, before eating his own. He played with the wetness of my arousal there, and I moaned in the feeling of his fingers as they expertly stimulated me. I could feel his erection beneath me, and I shifted on his lap, willing him to action.

"Turn around and straddle my cock," he finally commanded. I felt the brush of his robe against my buttocks as I stood and faced him. His eyes were cloudy and the corners of his mouth were turned down.

My eyes bore into his. "Yes, Jonas." Reaching my hand down between his legs, I clasped his cock and moaned as I took his shaft inside me, my eyes never leaving his.

Jonas gripped my hips and pulled until I was flush against his thighs, then he covered my cry with his mouth in the joining of pain and pleasure as I took him all at once. But this was what he needed and wanted, for me to take all of him. I realized I needed the same. Our gazes fused as his hands held onto my hips and he controlled the rises and falls as I rode him. The way he wanted, and needed. As pleasure filled me up, I dug into his shoulders.

"Not yet," he gritted and stopped, until my orgasm passed then started once more. The anger at the interruption flared, but quickly transformed to pleasure as our bodies came together. The sounds of our slick connection filled my ears as his pace increased.

His face was taut as he came, then transformed to a beauty that stole my breath away. My legs trembled as I fought to hold on and he kissed me and whispered a message of mercy that I took, coming hard and shuddering in his arms as he engulfed me. I was his. We belonged to each other. We stayed linked together. My head resting in the crook of Jonas's shoulder, his hand sliding up and down my spine. "I forget you're unwell. I've taken advantage…"

I tried, but failed to suppress the yawn coming out of my mouth as I sought to protest. Unfortunately, he took that yawn as proof of his claim, deepening the frown on his face. I tried again to speak, and this time I was successful. "You can't take advantage of the willing. I want to have sex with you."

The words 'have sex' sounded weird in my head and voice, as I struggled to communicate what we shared together. We didn't just 'have sex,' making the description feel too clinical and cheap. *I touch him with love. He makes love to me.*

Pressing my lips against his neck, I willed him to understand. He exhaled long, though his muscles felt tense. I opened my mouth on his neck and sucked, trying to leave a love bite. This brought about light laughter from Jonas, and a clasp of my shoulders, disengaging my lips and stopping the beginnings of a mark on his skin. "No," he said.

I tried my best to blank my face. "Why not, Mr. Crane?"

"Because we're not teenagers and I have enough of a bad reputation that I don't want to add to," he said and smirked.

I grinned. "I don't think your reputation is bad. Everyone asks you for your advice and help with their businesses."

"Everyone has critics. Some of them rightly so," he interjected, his voice raised. He reached over for a napkin and wiped my thigh, then lifted me onto my feet.

I hugged him to my chest. "I can't ever think of you as anything but perfect."

He gave me a smile that didn't reach his eyes. "I'm not perfect," he said flatly.

"Then wonderful, brilliant, gorgeous," I said, then pressed a kiss on his chin, feeling the short spikes of stubbled hair growth.

"You keep that up and you'll forfeit your sleep. Then we'll see how perfect I am," he said in a low tone, kissing the space between my breasts.

I let go of him and rolled my eyes. As I turned to collect my robe, I felt a light swat across my buttocks. "See?" he said as I gave him a dirty look, one that blossomed into a mischievous grin on his face, so similar to the one I had seen on Paul's earlier in the day. Watching him, it took me almost a minute to stop laughing as I put on my robe and tied it in place. "Paul has that look down pat," I explained. "Did you teach him that?"

"Yes. He has picked up every bad habit I ever had. I guess it's genetic," he said, his eyes light. It caused a tingle in my chest. He was a gorgeous man, but beautiful when he smiled.

He started collecting the glasses on the table, breaking the spell, and I went about collecting the dishes and carrying them over to the sink.

"Were you a handful when you were younger?" I asked, rinsing the plates.

"I had my moments, but I didn't have the freedom Paul has. Or even what Vincent had. My father barely spoke to him," he said, adding the glasses to the water.

"Did your father suspect earlier…" I said gingerly. I knew the answer, as his mother in her fragile state had said as much. But Jonas didn't respond right away, instead loading the dishwasher.

I walked away and started cleaning the table area.

"Yes," he finally said. "Besides the fact that Vincent looks like a doppelganger of my father's best friend, Vincent was doted on by my mother." I walked over to him and placed my hand on his back. He continued, "My father cheated too, you know. But he prided himself on being careful when it came to having children. I was part of their pre-nup. A Crane son." He lowered his head.

I hugged him as tight as I could. "I love who you are and what you became. If I could, I would thank them."

He kissed the top of my head. "I'm alright, Lily. That's all in the past. So let's leave it there. It's late." And without another word, he lifted me off my feet and carried me off to bed, leaving me to continue to reflect alone on what he had willingly shared about his life.

CHAPTER SIX

THE SOUND OF my new phone buzzing like a banshee had my pulse sprinting as I desperately felt over the nightstand to answer it. *Note to self: Change the ringtone or destroy it.*

"Hello?" I drew out the words, letting my annoyance bleed in at the disruption from an otherwise perfect night of sleep.

"A grumpy morning, Lily. Or should I say, afternoon?" Jonas said.

My pulse sprinted in my chest at the rich sound of his voice. "Sorry. I didn't realize it was that late. I never sleep this long. Did you say afternoon?" I babbled as I forced myself to look around the room for the time and found a small clock on the ledge of the fireplace. *1:23!*

"Yes. Afternoon," he confirmed. "I didn't want to wake you, but I couldn't make it back to have lunch with you today. And now I know you didn't have breakfast."

I could hear the concern in his voice and sought immediately to lessen it. "I'll get up and eat right now," I promised. The sound of his breathing let me know he was still on the phone.

"I'll conference call the last of my meetings at the apartment office. Expect me in a couple of hours," he said.

I sat up and swung my legs over the side of the bed. "You don't need to alter your day to watch over me. I'm on my feet. I'm alright."

"I pushed you too hard yesterday," he said guiltily.

"You didn't do anything I didn't want to do. I could have said no," I offered.

"I'm awfully persuasive. Or what was that you said? 'Wonderful, brilliant, and gorgeous'?" he mused.

I giggled. "Perhaps I only said that as my own play at persuasion."

"You didn't. You're in love with me," he said brusquely.

My heart jumped into my throat, blocking the "Yes I am" from coming out of my mouth as I reeled from his casual acknowledgement of the depth of my feelings for him.

"I meant, you said you loved me," he recovered, as he sought to end the silence now on the line.

"Yes. I understood what you meant," I said and cleared my throat. "I should probably let you go so you can get on with work and come back soon."

"Yes. My next meeting started already. I'll see you soon," Jonas said.

Neither of us hung up.

He sighed. "I called because I miss you."

I ran my tongue over my lips. "I miss you too, Jonas," I responded warmly, before taking the phone from my ear and hitting 'end'.

I stared down at the screen for a few seconds before placing it on the bedside table. My shoulders hung as I walked over to the bathroom and into the glass walk-in shower, turning the nozzle and bracing myself for the shock of cold water on my skin before it settled to a warm temperature. Anything to block the lump in the center of my chest as I tried and failed not to reflect on my conversation with Jonas and our relationship.

He had my words of love and devotion to call on to quash any moment of doubt. Would I ever have the same from him?

Dampening the new sponge on the long shelf along the wall, I pumped what turned out to be a lavender body wash from the row of built-in dispensers, quickly washing over my body and draining the worries I had in the fragrant scent and the beauty of my new surroundings.

We were new, and Jonas needed time. A small smile lifted the corner of my mouth as I adjusted the warm spray to massage. *I have time.*

I turned off the water and took one of the sheet towels from the built-in glass cabinets and dried off, then cinched it in place as I went over to wash my face and teeth. Returning to the bedroom, I froze and felt my cheeks warm as I met Lin changing the bed linen.

"I could have helped change the sheets," I stuttered.

She paused and turned her head toward me and

grinned. "Don't be embarrassed. I love what I do. I've been with the Cranes a long time," she winked.

I blinked as the hint of what she must have encountered occurred to me and, with it, a wave of jealousy over the women who had shared his bed.

"You have some clothes in the closet," Lin said with a nod toward the walk-in closet. "I'll be leaving soon, but your lunch is in the warmer. Okay?"

"You didn't have to…thank you," I said with a lift to my voice. I padded over to the closet to find my clothes and quickly took out underwear, a tank top, socks, and sweatpants. I looked down at myself and laughed, imagining what Jonas would think if he saw me now. I touched my face. He was constantly on my mind now.

I collected my new phone and work bag from the room and, with another wave to Lin, I left.

I set up my laptop in the kitchen, planning to work while I ate, though my stomach wasn't giving any triggers to let me know it was empty. It was something I had ignored for a long time and now would have to retrain as I tried to get better.

Opening the fancy warmer, I found a shepherd's pie that had my mouth watering once I smelled the gravy. *Good.*

Internally, I patted myself on the back and carried the plate over to my laptop at the breakfast table. From the first bite, I was in love.

I skimmed over my personal email, then tried to log on to the company website and dropped my fork. *My email is blocked?*

I quickly took out my phone and called Gregor. On the third ring, I got him.

"Sorry, Lily. Can't talk now. I can call you later, unless this is an emergency?" he asked.

"Sort of. I can't get into my work email," I said.

"You're on leave. Your messages have been rerouted to Mark," he said.

"I have some things Mark won't know what to do with in my inbox. I'd like to at least clear them," I replied.

Gregor paused a beat, then replied. "Fine. You'll have access sometime today. Thanks, talk to you later."

"Thanks, Gregor," I said and smiled as I hung up the phone, then returned to eating the food on my plate. It was delicious and filling.

Standing, I searched through the cabinets and found wrap for what I couldn't finish, with a promise to myself that I would return to it later. When I opened the refrigerator door to store it, I found a note on a drink in front of me labeled, 'Lily', and a tingle went through my stomach at the thoughtfulness of everyone surrounding me, all so committed to my recovery.

Removing it from the shelf, I took a sip. Mango orange, with the additional aftertaste of something probably good for me. I carried it and my laptop into the living room and waved at Lin as she walked out of the apartment, leaving me to myself.

I sat down on the couch and turned on the television, numbly drifting between talk shows and news channels and nodding off in between. The sound of the door swinging open and voices told me that Jonas had returned and wasn't alone. My pulse sped up as our eyes found each other. He was gorgeous all the time, but especially stunning in his dark navy suit. He gave me a knowing smile as he crossed the room to me. My face flushed at my tank top and sweats. "Sorry I meant to change before you came back."

"Don't worry. You look beautiful." He kissed my lips.

"Lily Salomé."

I broke eye contact and looked over at the man by the door. Ian Unger. He was also in a dark designer suit like Jonas, but that was where the similarities ended. Ian was blonde and pale, with deep blue eyes and an angular face. The high cut of his cheekbones and perfectly shaped lips made him more pretty than handsome. His blue-eyed gaze was hard as he stared at me.

"Hello, Ian," I said hoarsely and tilted my head down. I had been shamefully rude the last time I spoke to him, amongst other sins I had committed when he took me to the gala fundraiser a month or so ago.

The seat dipped down beside me, and I felt Jonas's hand slide across the side of my face, lifting it up and capturing my lips. His tongue was hot and demanding as he explored every inch of my mouth. Branding his claim on me.

I knew my skin was bright red at his possessive performance for Ian. The corners of my mouth turned down as I met his brazen expression when we broke apart.

"Ian and I have a conference call. I've invited him to dinner," Jonas said as he tucked my hair behind my ears. It was a mess of tangles, as I hadn't bothered to do much with it today. I tried to finger comb it now, but Jonas took my hands and kissed the back of them. "You're fine," he said. I melted right on the spot and leaned in, pressing my lips to his mouth.

"I said I would join you for dinner later once you've settled in. Our call starts in five minutes," Ian said, bringing our attention back to him. I glanced over and watched his gaze shift between us.

"The office is down the hall. I'll be right there," Jonas said to him, motioning in the direction to aid his search.

"Good to see you again, Lily," Ian said and started walking away.

"You too," I called out.

Once Ian was out of sight, I shook my head at Jonas. "Why did you do that?"

"Ian needs to know you're mine," Jonas said bluntly.

"You could have just told him you're my…boyfriend," I said, playing over the title.

He scoffed. "Boyfriend? I'm not a boy. I'm a man. Your man," he teased, now playful. Nipping along my jaw and up to my ear, his fingers tracing the tips of my breasts that were poking out of my top.

I laughed and scooted back on the couch, out of his grasp, not ready to give in to Jonas's need to flaunt our togetherness in front of his friend, though I was pleased with his self-appointed title. "And I'm your woman."

He gazed intently at me. "You're mine," he said confidently.

"And that's how you'll introduce me?" I teased.

"Yes, I will," he said, all playfulness gone as his gaze remained steady on me. I wondered and decided to ask. "Did you introduce Dani that way?"

He smiled. "At one time. Our relationship was different. You and Dani are different."

I averted my eyes. "Yeah, she's strong, together, sweet, and confident."

He captured my chin and tilted my face upward. "I'm happy you admire her. She's very fond of you, too. But you are all those things as well, and will come into more once you heal." He kissed me lightly on the lips. "Ian recommended a new gourmet pizza place for dinner?"

I groaned. "Sounds good, but that's all I did today. Eat, sleep, and watch television."

He kissed the corner of my mouth. "You're on 'stress-free vacation,' as you put it. Your job is to eat and sleep. But we'll find you something to do. And when I'm here, I'll keep you busy." His face bore a wicked grin that sent a thrill through my body.

He took out his phone and ordered a pizza with cheese, olives, and sundried tomatoes. Then, at the last minute, he added an order for a chocolate truffle cheesecake.

"I'll eat it," he promised, hanging up the phone before adding, "I must go." He was rubbing the space between his eyebrows as he stood and walked back to his office.

It was then that I sighed. I was absolutely gone on him.

I stretched back on the couch and flipped through the channels, finding the selection process difficult once again. I finally paused when I found a show I had heard about but never seen before.

The entire episode was almost over, nearly an hour later, when the doorbell sounded with what had to be dinner.

"Just a second," I called, then placed my hand over my mouth, worrying I might have disrupted their work call.

I stood and dug through my workbag until I found my purse. But before I could walk to the door, Ian suddenly appeared, taking fast strides and opening it himself. I walked over and stood next to him.

"Eighty-three dollars," the delivery guy said, pushing his long hair out of his eyes as he smiled down at me. I squinted at the small box housing the pizza pie, my frugal brain calculating how many pies I could have gotten from other restaurants for the same price. As I was reaching in my purse to get the money and tip, I heard Jonas raise his voice from the office and turned toward the hallway in automatic response.

"I've got this," Ian said, handing money to the delivery man, who in turn handed me the pizza and dessert, as well as a smaller bag, before I could even argue. I carried it all over to the coffee table, opening the bag and taking out the fancy plastic plates and utensils.

The sound of the door to the office clicking shut had me turning my head. Ian gave me a small smile and walked over. "You don't have to be nervous, Lily. Jonas told me what happened. How are you feeling?" he asked. I didn't see or feel any animosity coming from him.

I shifted on my feet before him. "I'm better. Getting better."

I watched him lift his hand and drop it back at his sides. "I wish I had known you were in trouble. I would have helped. Seeing you now, I wish I had tried harder," he said.

I knew he was talking about more than just my avoidance of him, but I chose not to respond. "I doubt that would have changed anything. I was pretty determined to do things on my own," I said.

"Until Jonas came for you," Ian replied.

I met his steady gaze. "Yes…I love him."

"I'm happy for the both of you." A ghost of a smile appeared on his lips.

"Thank you," I said and glanced toward the office.

"I'm leaving now. But as your friend, if you ever need help and you can't reach Jonas, call me," he said.

I nodded. "Thank you. I will."

"Please make sure you do. This has nothing to do with me and you. It's about your safety," he said, then walked over to the front door and closed it behind him. A few seconds later, I walked over and locked it.

"Today was truly exhausting," Jonas's voice said behind me. "Maybe I'm getting too old for this." He walked up and put his arms around me.

I leaned back, savoring the feeling of being held by him. "You're only thirty-six, but you could retire?"

"I could, but that's not the Crane way. We die at, on our way, or right after work. Even Paul. He goofs, but when it comes to his piano, he's driven, passionate about it," he said.

I sighed heavily. "My father was passionate about his art and his ethics. My mother, her first graders and art program. But, well, unlike you, I ended up disappointing them over and over again. I didn't succeed at music. I didn't succeed as an anthropologist. I let Declan manipulate and hurt me many times."

He cuddled me. "You have plenty of time to get wherever you want to be, and from what you've shared about your parents, I think they would have been disappointed they couldn't protect you, but I believe they would be proud of you."

When I didn't respond, he added. "I'm here now and I'll protect you." He placed his arm around my shoulder and we walked over and sat down on the couch. He opened the pizza carton and steam rose up with the spicy aroma of the pie. "Ian claims this is the best pizza in New

York, and that's a tall order," he said as we each placed slices on our plates.

I took a bite and was an instant convert. "This is so delicious."

Jonas was halfway into his second slice before he gave his verdict. "It's close."

Snobby New Yorker. I mused as I reached for my own second slice.

"What are you watching?" Jonas said and made a face. He began flipping through channels without waiting for a response, finally giving up and leaving it on the news. We were both too engrossed in the food to care.

The pizza went quickly, and so did the cheesecake, with two bites from me. Once we were done, we cleared off the table.

"How about a bath and a read before bed?" Jonas asked as we left the kitchen.

"Milk and cookies and I'll agree," I teased.

"No cookies, but more rosewater custard if you want it," he offered.

I shook my head and groaned. "After all that? You're kidding!"

He shrugged, letting me know he wasn't. *Where does he put it?* I wondered, watching him turn off the lights. His body, muscular and toned, showed no signs of his voracious appetite.

I met him by the stairs and we walked up to the master bedroom and straight into the bathroom.

"This will be a soak. So keep your hands to yourself, Ms. Salomé," Jonas said in a light tone as he turned on the nozzle of the tub, dropping the contents of some of the jarred dispensers from along the back wall into the water.

I had already started brushing my teeth and almost choked on my toothbrush.

He walked over and joined me as he began to brush his own. I laughed at the ease of us together, despite all the chaos in my life. As soon as I finished, I told him how much I liked this…us living our lives together.

His eyes glimmered. "Yes. I like that too," he said. I gaped as I watched his skin cleaning and buffing routine, until he paused and opened a cabinet filled with all the things I had from the hotel spa, freeing me to go about my own ritual.

Jonas turned off the water and I noticed a bit of foam on the surface and the smell of lavender. "A bubble bath?"

He came up behind me and tugged up my shirt. I lifted my arms so he could continue to pull it over my head.

His phone beeped just then, so he paused touching me and took it out of his pocket.

"Get in. I'll be right back." He sighed and answered, "Hello?"

I slid my sweatpants down my legs and removed them. My ears perked in hopes of hearing the caller's voice, but he walked a few paces away before I could catch anything.

I looked at him inquisitively, but his eyes shifted away from me as he padded to the door. “I’ll be right back. Think about a book we can read,” he called out. I finished taking off my clothes and placed them away from the tub. Climbing into the tub, I marveled at its length, my feet unable to touch the end. This gave me a temporary distraction from the person my mind suspected was on the phone at…I looked around and found a small clock on the wall. *Ten? It’s not that late.*

I leaned back and tried to float, sitting up when Jonas walked back in a few minutes later, a puckering now appearing between his perfectly arched brows.

My eyes widened. “Everything okay?”

“Nothing for you to worry about. I’ll be holding an early meeting here tomorrow, so David will take you to your appointment in the morning,” he said, as if formulating a plan. He removed his clothing quickly, then climbed in behind me, splashing the water around as he settled his long legs on either side of me. My breath caught as his arm slipped around my waist and anchored me against his chest, feeling the soft hair brush against my back. I took a deep breath.

He lifted a sponge and dunked it into the water, then squeezed it over my hair repeatedly until it was damp. He next filled his hands with a lavender scented shampoo and started to gently massage my scalp.

“More spoils,” I murmured.

Jonas continued to massage and soap up my hair as I

drifted. "I take care of mine," he responded.

"I do the same," I said as I went to pick up a sponge to use on him.

"Another time," he said, stilling my hand. "You need to indulge me tonight."

I sighed, but let out a groan when he moved to massaging my shoulders. "Alright," I giggled.

He chuckled and kissed my shoulder. "I enjoy hearing you laugh. I want you happy."

My heart expanded. "I…I am with you. I want you happy, too."

He kissed my cheek, then began washing my shoulders. "I am," he said near my ear. "Have you thought of a book?"

I sighed and moaned when he reached around and massaged my breasts. "Byron, Burns, Yeats, Cummings?"

"Romantic poems we call out to each other in the night," he mused as he filled the sponge with body wash and massaged it lower over my stomach "I had something else in mind. Spread your legs wider."

I gasped, but complied as he washed my pussy. When he was done, he cupped me as he had yesterday at the table, making every nerve in my body rise in response to him and the significance of his claim.

I wiggled and he moved his arm around my waist to keep me still. When I was, he started rubbing the sides of my clit, his other hand journeying under me to the entrance of my anus. "I'll fuck you there soon."

The way he was teasing my clit, I wouldn't deny him

anything. I moaned and he took that as a yes to push his finger through the tight muscles there. I tensed as pain overcame the pleasure I was getting.

"Try to relax. Push back for me," Jonas eased his finger out and I tried again, but I was no longer focused on the pleasure. Jonas, ever tuned to me, removed his hands and cuddled me.

"I'll try with my tongue. Move up to your knees and lean over the edge and hold on," he commanded.

I shook my head and laughed nervously. "No way."

He paused, then released me. "I won't push you right now, but tell me why," he said, turning me around to face him. He quietly washed himself as I searched for a response, feeling my face burn. "Some things are just better left alone," I mumbled.

He chuckled. "For tonight. I'll do it when you become more comfortable with me and your body."

I bit the inside of my mouth. "I take it this is something you've done before?"

"Oh, you want to talk about this tonight?" he asked, his tone playful.

"Yes." I was quiet for a few minutes and he took the nozzle hose and rinsed my hair. "Has anyone done that to you?" I pressed on for more discussion.

"Yes, and I enjoyed it," he said.

I took in a short breath. "Oh."

This brought out a laugh from Jonas. "I forget how innocent you are. I've corrupted you."

I snorted though my skin flush. "I was in a sexual

relationship for three years. We didn't just do missionary." I didn't want to discuss my one and only past experience, but his cockiness still bothered me. He was right in a way though. Declan and I had occasional shower sex and sometimes tried doggie-style. For the most part though, he was focused primarily on his own pleasure. Our routine consisted of blowjobs, missionary, and me on top. The last one became my least favorite, because he would rest his hands behind his head and seemed content to let me do all the work.

Luckily, Jonas wasn't interested in the details. "I don't want to imagine that asshole touching you," he gritted, moving my hair back and squeezing out the excess water.

I looked down. "I only mentioned my past relationship because I didn't come to you a virgin. If I'm holding you back…"

He climbed out of the tub, pulling me up with him. Placing his hands on the side of my face, tilting it up, he said, "I don't want a virgin. You're not holding me back, and I'm happy with you as you are. I'm sorry if my teasing upset you."

I lifted the corner of my mouth. "It didn't upset me. I do like what we do together. I was just surprised." He kissed me deeply.

"I've only begun to explore that sexy body of yours, and fuck you all the ways I can and will. Including burying my tongue in that hot ass of yours," he said, adding in a swat on my bottom.

I swatted him back. This had him lifting me and wrapping my legs around him as he kissed me passionately.

"No sex tonight, my beautiful nymph," he said and put me down on my feet.

Who decided that? He kissed my pouting mouth as he dried me off. I began brushing through my long hair, but even that left me feeling frustrated.

Jonas seemed to sympathize and relented without a word, dropping to his knees and gently licking and nuzzling between my thighs until I opened for him. I moaned and almost lost my footing as all my senses went to the incredible sensation of Jonas, his tongue lashing over my slick folds and slipping over my distended clit. I didn't hold out as the orgasm came, just arched as his hand held me in place while he sucked. I shook and he held me, taking every tremble I had to give, until I floated down and was lifted in his arms. He carried me to bed and I crawled under the duvet. "Thank you," I spoke softly.

"Anything for you, my Tiger Lily," he whispered back and settled down next to me.

Reaching over to the bedside table, he pulled out a paperback book, his attention on me. "I also have a suggestion for a book. I found a new copy of Peter Pan on the shelves downstairs. How about we read from it?"

My jaw dropped open as pain took over my peace. "Absolutely not," I stuttered out as tears rose in my eyes and I stared back him in disbelief. He knew what that book meant to me. The memories it would unhinge, and the hurt I was still feeling over Declan stealing my copy from my deceased father. Reading it, I imagined, would be like a jagged knife cutting at my heart. "It hurts to even think about that book. I mean, why would you even suggest that? What are you thinking?"

I started to retreat, and he dropped the book and pulled me into his arms.

"I was thinking I wanted to be a part of the loving memory you shared with your parents. The first night we were together, you shared your story. I thought maybe we could create a new memory," he said in a gentle tone.

My vision blurred as tears dripped down my face. An indescribable mix of feelings ravaged through my heart and mind as I contemplated the depths of his understanding and care. I didn't think it was possible to love him more, but he continued to surprise and overwhelm me. Still, the pain of my loss was infused in the words of that book, which I could practically recite from memory. Memories of which I had both good and bad. But here was my lover, ready to create a new one with me.

My lip quivered. "I can't read it…yet."

He kissed me tenderly. "I'll read first. When you're ready, you will."

Jonas opened the drawer again and took out his glasses. Then he opened his arms for me to fill them. I did, resting my head on his chest.

"All children, except one, grow up…" he read.

CHAPTER SEVEN

I STOOD OUTSIDE on the sidewalk with Jonas the next morning, trying to convince him to return inside the loft. A light mist of rain fell down from the clouded sky above our heads, a less-than-veiled threat to open up and pour down on us at any given minute, something I had pointed out to Jonas before he sought to see me off for my therapy appointment this morning. Jonas, unruffled and with steady hands, busied himself instead with securing a scarf around my neck. Dressed in only a designer suit, crisp white shirt, and silk tie, he would fare worse from the rain than my simple button-down shirt and jeans would.

"The session is only forty minutes. Please go back inside," I said, renewing my argument after a loud clap of thunder.

He continued to fuss with my scarf. "If I get rained on, I'll change. My first meeting is… here soon. I wanted to see you off. I know therapy can be difficult."

My hands reached up and grasped his and we stared at each other. I was rendered speechless in this moment.

So overwhelmed by the feelings I had for this incredible man. His deep voice gliding over the passages of *Peter Pan* last night, pausing to wipe every tear that dropped from my eyes, easing the knot of pain I had attached to the work that brought me such joy and love growing up. With every page a memory came; good memories.

Jonas and the last few nights would forever be good memories. His concern and care had completely undone me, and I doubted I'd ever recover from the attachment he had orchestrated between us to instill in my mind and heart that I belonged to him. And now this morning, before his workday started, he was trying to ease my worries.

The thought of his work disruption had me trying to assure him once again that he didn't need to fuss over me. My mind worked to counter the thrill I had in basking in his care, fearful of indeed being the spoiled princess Declan had labeled me.

"I'll be fine. I'm going to try. And maybe it will help me," I said, giving him a wide smile I pushed all the way to my eyes.

"We'll need to leave to avoid morning rush hour," David said, opening an umbrella and holding it over us.

Jonas eyed me, then pressed his lips to my forehead. This action signaled David to open the door to his car, and I climbed in, with Jonas immediately seeking to belt me in place. "I will try for lunch, but if anything changes I'll text you. Perhaps we can go out to dinner this evening. And we should hear back from your doctor with your test results today."

I nodded and he pecked my lips before closing the door. David quickly moved to the driver's seat and started the car. My heart stuttered as I watched Jonas standing with the umbrella as David pulled away from the curb. He remained there until I couldn't see him any longer. I chewed my bottom lip, took my phone out, and sent a quick text.

You better go back inside!

After a few minutes he replied.

Better? You ordering me around?

I grinned and suspected he was doing the same.

If it keeps you from getting wet… I typed and pressed send.

Are you wet?

I licked my lips and moved my thighs against each other.

You should know. You checked before we left the loft :)

He responded.

Then your answer should have been yes.

I sent back.

Yes.

The car felt suddenly too warm. I eased my arms out of my jacket. Staring out of the window, I shook my head. A new text message arrived from Jonas.

Have you seen my glasses?

I wrote back.

You left your Clark Kent glasses on the bedside table.

He replied.

I'm Clark Kent?

I laughed to myself.

Yes. You're my superman too. After a minute, I got a text back.

I want to be for you, Tiger Lily.

My heart leapt.

You don't ever need to be. I'd take Jonas Crane any day.

Why?

I touched my lips. Then typed.

Because I love you. Do you love me? I quickly erased the message and wrote.

Because I love you. Now I don't want to be responsible for you missing your meeting so stop texting! Xox

He wrote back.

I'll have to remind you who gives the orders. My meeting is about to start. I'll talk to you soon.

I felt a pang in my chest as I stared down at the phone. I knew I needed to give him time. But still, I couldn't help the longing I felt to hear the words "I love you" back.

The car lurched forward on the brakes, and I wiped the condensation from the window to see what was happening. The traffic was bumper-to-bumper on the roadway. Would I be late and miss the appointment? *The appointment I don't want to go to anyway?* I grumped as I sat back on the seat. Sure, I told Jonas I thought it would help, but I couldn't help my skepticism. I looked out the window again. David had found a traffic break and zigged through the cars to take advantage. The car moved fast along the highway, leaving me with little time to prepare for my psychiatric session.

Before long, David was through the exit and up the

avenues, pulling up to park in front of a brick and stone building with an awning. I eyed the gold and marble lobby through the large glass windows as I opened the door and climbed out before David could make it around to open the door for me. He gave me an admonishing shake of his head and smiled at the sheepish grin I returned back to him. We walked inside and he handled the initial exchange with security, leaving his contact information as a further layer of Jonas's security. I didn't find this necessary, as Declan wouldn't even know about this place or location, but I didn't intrude in their conversation. Afterward, David offered an encouraging smile as we boarded the elevator to the eleventh floor.

My heartbeat sped up upon reaching the floor. We stepped out and headed to the wooden door with the gold placard that read, "Isla Bridgewater, M.D. Ph.D. Psy.D." *All bases covered*, I mused as I walked up to the door, already imagining a powdered elderly woman with a tight smile and polished leather office.

I pictured the space decorated with framed degrees and ultra-comforting music to lull clients into a relaxed state as they divulged the contents of their lives while Isla Bridgewater, M.D. Ph.D. Psy.D, would sit there and listen. She'd be politely taking notes and handing out brochures at the end of the appointment.

What I found when David opened the door to the office was not at all what I had imagined. Sure, the waiting area had the stuffiness I anticipated, complete with polished leather couches and tasteful pillow accents.

But Dr. Isla herself stood before a dark oak reception desk, wearing a white embroidered tunic. She was a short and curvy, with gray wavy hair that brushed her shoulders. Her dark-toned skin was smooth, with a few creases along the corners of her large brown eyes, and her wide mouth was turned up in a smile, which I surprisingly found myself returning.

"Thank you, David. Judy will call you when the session is over." We said goodbye and he left.

"Hello, Lily. The office is warm and has a nice, thick carpet. You won't need your shoes and may leave them on the stand." Isla motioned to a small wooden shelf and coat rack. I quickly removed my jacket and short boots, eyeing her white socks as I followed her into her office. The furnishings were similar to her receiving room but with more upscale eastern artifacts intermixed with framed honors on the wood-paneled walls.

She motioned for me to take a seat on a sofa with a short back and wide cushions. Crossing her legs, she sat down next to me.

"We will start with a breathing exercise. I want you to focus on your inhalation and exhalation," she said.

I raised a brow. "Seriously?"

She smiled. "Yes. When thoughts arise, bring it back to the inhalation and exhalation. Now, let's take two breaths together."

She flicked her finger against a metal bowl and a sound hung in the air.

Since she didn't leave the exercise open for discussion, I closed my eyes and tried to focus. *What is this?* Inhale. *How is this supposed to help me?* Exhale. *Is this how it's going to go?* Inhale. *How long is this going to last?* Exhale. Inhale. Exhale. Inhale. Exhale. Inhale. The bell sounded once again.

"I like to begin sessions with the practice of meditative mindfulness. An exercise in staying present and observing thoughts. Thoughts and feelings are separate. Sometimes our thoughts work against us. This will help you shift through the negative ones that may affect your overall health." She paused to let the words sink in, and had they ever. I could easily admit my thoughts, at times, were my worst enemy.

"So, let's take a step back. How did you feel after the short meditation?" she asked.

I ran my palms down my jeans and rested them on my knees as I thought on what she had asked. "I feel a little relaxed, I suppose."

She smiled warmly, and then continued, "I'd like to go over your goals for therapy and what brought you in today." She reached over and collected a pen and paper.

I grimaced. *And so it starts. I share and she writes, and after I'm miserable I'll be handed a few flyers and sent out the door. No thank you.* I knew she was waiting for a response, but I didn't have one. How would I know about goals when I'd just started? Hell, I didn't even want to be here.

"What went through your mind just now?" she asked, ending our silent standoff.

I crossed my arms. "I thought this isn't going to help me. I've done this before. The last therapist wrote a lot down, but not much became of it. Sorry."

"You don't have to apologize for your feelings. So seeing me pick up the pad triggered your memory of your past experience of therapy?" she asked, prodding me to engage with her.

I folded and unfolded my hands in my lap and took a deep breath. I was here, and I promised Jonas I would try. So I decided to share what I could or perhaps confirm what Dr. Steinman had possibly shared with her. "Yes. I went to a therapist and she did the same. She listened, but then…I don't know. I don't have many expectations or goals. I came here because my doctor and, well, my boyfriend, recommended I get help after I became ill and underweight from stress. I had been physically attacked and harassed by my ex-fiancé. He escalated after I reported him and, well, now you know everything," I closed my mouth and pressed my lips together.

"Seeing me with the pad and paper, ready to take notes, triggered a memory of past therapy and you thought and felt…what?" she asked.

I frowned. I just told her what was going on and she's talking about triggers? I sat there and tried to curb my annoyance enough to try to figure out what response she was after. "I felt like you wouldn't listen and I'd be left a mess of feelings with a bunch of pamphlets telling me information I could easily find on the Internet. I'm starting to feel happy again. I was sad for a long time. I don't want to start digging up stuff when good is coming into my life."

"So, would a goal for you be that I listen and you feel better from what we discuss together?" she offered.

I shrugged. "If that's possible."

"I believe so, but we have only started. So, my goal is to be mindful of your feelings about therapy and your goals. I'll check in often or ask how you are to make sure I help you meet that goal. How does that sound?" she asked.

I licked my lips. "Okay. I'd like that."

"You came in feeling good. Let's talk about that," she said.

I smiled and tucked my hair behind my ears. "Yes. Jonas," I covered my mouth as I realized she was a friend of Dani's and possibly knew Jonas too.

"Everything said here is confidential," she assured as if she read my mind.

I slid my teeth against my bottom lip. "Okay. I'm happy Jonas is back in my life. He's so good to me. He fusses, but truly he spoils me," I said. *Fat spoiled princess.* My face fell.

"What are you thinking right now? Did something you shared bother you?"

I looked at her blankly, not wanting to respond.

She continued talking. "You were smiling, talking about Jonas. How happy you were with him back in your life. He's good, fusses, spoils..." She paused between her words to gauge my response. I blinked when she got to the word 'spoil' and lowered my head. "What are you thinking now?" she asked.

I kept my eyes to the ground. "My ex used to call me a fat, spoiled princess. I tried not to be, but I don't know."

"What did you think of when you heard your doctor tell you that you're underweight?" she asked.

"I didn't believe it possible. My body doesn't look as thin as others, but Dr. Steinman said I'm unhealthy," I said.

"Do you believe Dr. Steinman?" she asked.

"Well, yes. He's a medical doctor. He has a thriving and well-respected practice," I said.

"Do you think he has anything to gain by telling you you're not fat?" she asked.

"No," I replied.

She nodded. "So, if Dr. Steinman doesn't believe you are fat and you trust in him…Are you fat?"

I crossed my arms. "It's not that easy. My becoming underweight wasn't intentional. I exercise to stop feeling. I didn't want to feel. I was miserable with Declan's harassment. You see, I gained weight after my parents died, and he taunted me. I…" I closed my eyes.

"Okay. Let's try another way. What does it mean to be a spoiled princess?"

I frowned at her. Couldn't she see how upset I was? I didn't want to keep talking about it. I sat there in silence, but she sat there with me and waited. I was the one to break. "A person that is treated like a princess. They are doted on, given things over and above what is necessary."

"Who judges what is necessary?" she asked.

I rubbed the space between my eyebrows. "I don't know. I guess I do. Declan did. I guess."

"So, let's say you both judge what is necessary. I want you to tell me how you came to believe it to be true. Tell me how you are a spoiled princess?" she asked.

I groaned. "My parents spoiled me. Declan was annoyed they called me numerous times throughout the day. They always wanted to spend time with me and even went as far as changing their plans to be with me. They helped pay my tuition for college, they met all my teachers, bought me clothes, took me on vacations. They always wanted me to be with them. They told me I was special. That I was a Tiger Lily Princess, beautiful, loyal…"

She passed over a box of tissues, and I realized I was crying now. My words didn't make much sense to me, but Dr. Isla wrote out notes and then responded.

"So, if I'm hearing correctly, you believe you are a 'spoiled princess' because your parents called you, their daughter, every day, spent time with you, helped you with college, took an interest in your education, bought their daughter clothes, and called you a special princess."

My face warmed. Hearing it back, I thought my explanation silly, so I tried to get her to understand another way. "Declan had a different life growing up. His foster parents were cruel. They didn't take good care of him.

He was beaten, left starving. It was horrible."

"So because Declan's life experience was different than yours, he told you that you are a spoiled princess, and that makes you spoiled?" she asked.

I shrugged. "No. I don't know. Well, my friend Mary's parents were the same. I thought we were normal until Declan pointed out we weren't."

"I want you to focus on you. You think of yourself as spoiled. You haven't proven it to be true, so let me ask another way. Say: 'I'm a spoiled princess because I' and fill in the blank."

"I'm a spoiled princess because I…enjoyed being treated that way," I said, my voice graveled.

"Did you do other things growing up besides enjoying the way you were treated?" she asked.

"Well, no. My father was strict. I studied and did extra homework at home. We volunteered. I helped with my mother's art program. I didn't believe I was spoiled, but their wanting to be with me and see me often, I loved that. I loved them. I wanted to please them. I wanted to be the princess they told me I was. I don't know," I sobbed.

"So a spoiled princess is perfect?" she asked.

I rubbed against the cramp in my stomach. "Yes. I'm not, but I can't shake the thoughts. I wanted to be. I wanted to be so he would see I wasn't so spoiled and he would love me."

"'If I'm not perfect…' fill in the rest?" she asked in a gentle tone.

I thought about what comes to mind when I hear I'm a spoiled princess, and the way things happened in my relationship with Declan when he sought to get me to change something about myself. He manipulated me. I wanted Declan to love me. I worked to get that love and acceptance from him. I tried to be the perfect girlfriend and perfect daughter. I exercised to lose weight. I tried to divide my time between him and my parents. But it didn't help. He didn't love me. He left me when I wasn't perfect. *If I'm not perfect...no one will love me.* "I'll need to think on that more. I feel awful, by the way," I said with irritation.

"Did your parents ever stop their care and concern? Did you ever do anything that changed their behavior toward you?" she asked.

I wiped my forehead. I felt turned inside out already, but still she was pushing me. I looked at her and saw her poised and attentive. I didn't see any maliciousness or disapproval on what seemed to be a glowing discussion of my stupidity. "You must think I'm silly after listening to all that I told you."

"No, I don't. And I'm not here to judge. I'm here to help," she said.

I exhaled. "In response to your question, yes and no. My father had a code Salomé's were to follow. We were to strive for perfection. We fought between us about Declan. They wanted me away from him. They thought he wasn't good enough. They fought against my changing, but they never stopped the way they treated me.

They loved me."

"Let's talk about what brought a smile on your face to conclude your first session and to keep my promise of not leaving you feeling sad. You said you're with Jonas and he treats you as good as your parents treated you, and you're enjoying it?"

I smiled. "Yes. Jonas is very good to me. I enjoy and love it. I love him. I feel he cares for me. Sometimes I think he loves me, but he doesn't say it." My smile wilted. I didn't have anything to support the thought that Jonas didn't love me, except that he hadn't said it. My understanding of love and his actions were the same. The only thing missing was the feeling I had at not hearing it, but even that was related to not hearing the words back from Declan for two years.

A beep went off, marking the end of the session. Dr. Isla cleared her throat and said, "I want you to write down what love means and how that relates to Jonas. Think about what proof you have to support your thoughts and feelings that he might not." Then looking through her notes, she added, "I want to give you some information about the type of therapy I practice. I prefer to send it by email, if you would like to continue?" she asked.

I sighed. "This has been really intense for a first session, but I'm feeling a bit lighter and emotional. You mentioned things I think I would like to discuss again. So, yes."

"Okay. I'd like to see you the rest of this week—

twice a week thereafter. I don't want to prescribe medication, but I do want you try yoga meditation and more relaxation exercises. We'll check in at the beginning of each session," she said.

"We may be going out of town on Friday," I replied.

She grinned and lifted a folder. "I'll send you some homework to make up for Friday."

I jokingly groaned as I gave her my email address. I didn't know if I would be able to grasp all her concepts or her pushing of things I didn't want to talk about, but having something else to use against my thoughts and past might be a good thing.

David was waiting for me when I exited Dr. Isla's office, along with a message on my phone from Jonas.

"How was the session? Dr. Steinman had the nurse call with the results of your test on your other phone. You're iron deficient and anemic, as he suspected. Lin will be adding iron-rich food to your diet. I won't be able to come back for lunch, but we'll be going out for dinner at 6:00."

I sent him a text.

I got your message. The session was intense, but helpful. I'll see her the rest of the week. Five days a week to start. Thank you for everything. Love you xox

I pressed send and closed my eyes, leaning against the window as we moved through the rain-drenched streets of the Upper West Side down to Tribeca. My mind navigated through my thoughts, and as I found myself questioning and checking my mood, I laughed. *It's already working.*

The ride went quickly, and once we were at the loft, I exited swiftly to avoid David getting out of the car and being soaked by the rain that was coming down. I managed to make it to the elevator without getting completely saturated myself. When I walked through the door, I heard Lin call out from the kitchen. "Is that you, Lily? Your lunch is almost ready."

I took off my shoes and coat, then padded over to the kitchen. Pausing in the opening, I watched Lin stirring a pot on the stove. She turned and gave me a bright smile. "I've made three bean soup and rice. You also have an iron-enriched smoothie from Dani. I would have been finished, but it was a busy morning here with people and deliveries. Jonas won't be able to make it back until dinner."

"Yes. He left me a message. Thank you for lunch. I'll be right back. I'm just going to go upstairs and change," I said and headed for the stairs.

I thought I heard Lin call out 'wait,' but I was already down the hall to the master bedroom. I stopped in the walk-in closet and went through my clothing that was placed there, picking out a wool skirt and turtleneck for dinner with Jonas later.

With or without underwear?

He didn't say and I wickedly planned to surprise him. As I was placing the clothing down on the bed, something shiny caught my eye. Scanning the area, I discovered a watch on the bedside table. From the shape, I knew it wasn't a man's watch. *Did Lin forget her watch?*

I crawled across the bed to pick it up. Before I reached the bedside table, my knee brushed against a lump under the duvet. I sat back on my heels. The bed linen had been changed, but something was there. I crawled the rest of the way off the bed and squinted. The bed was mussed. Leaning over, I could smell the faint fragrance of Chanel no. 5. I ran my hand over the pillow, shaking my head at my impromptu detective work.

Blonde hair?

My pulse picked up and I yanked the sheets back, uncovering the cause of the disorder. I found black lace panties that weren't mine. Freezing in place, I shuffled through the last twenty-four hours, trying to figure out how this had happened. My mind immediately confirmed that Jonas had cheated. Or at the very least, he had deceived and lied to me.

"Lily. Oh, Jonas is going to kill me," Lin said, appearing next to me. I realized I was still starring down at the panties, and that her gaze was now on them as well.

I hurried out of the bedroom and down the stairs. I grabbed my coat and shoes, closing the elevator before Lin could reach me with any lies I imagined she routinely told on Jonas's behalf. I ran down the street and around the corner, stopping beneath an awning in front of a gallery. I took in a few short breaths and pulled out my phone and called Jonas. After numerous rings, he answered. "Lily, I'm in a—"

"You had Melissa over at the loft," I barked, cutting him off.

"Yes. She came over before my work meetings. I didn't tell you because I didn't want to upset you—" he replied.

"Too late for that. I found her panties. Lin didn't cover up for you—"

"What panties? Lin doesn't need to cover up anything for me. I didn't have sex with her," he barked out.

"And I'm supposed to take you at your word when you purposely lied to and deceived me? You don't respect me. All that stuff about me being yours, no secrets," I spat out.

"Damn it, Lily, you *are* mine. Listen—"

"No. You listen! I've been a fool, but not anymore. I love you, but I deserve better. So do whatever you want, move her in next. I'm gone," I yelled and hung up. The finality of my words reverberated in my mind as the noise of the traffic and pedestrians on the sidewalk filtered past my ears. The buzz of the living city that didn't stop, even as my life was unraveling.

New York City was the place I chose to start over, and that was what I would have to do. Start over. With that thought, I walked on through Tribeca and over to Chinatown. I ignored the glances on Canal Street as I passed the buckets of frugally priced umbrellas. I actually could have afforded one, had I thought to bring my purse with me when I stormed out of the loft. I went with the impression that I was out of my mind, letting the rain soak my clothes to the bone. Fighting off my exhaustion and waves of nausea, I continued to roam the streets, creating a plan for what to do. Ignoring the vibration of my phone and my new reality.

In truth, I had nowhere to go. And I knew it.

Weighed down by this certainty, I turned around and started walking back to the place I had left. If nothing else, I needed to get my things.

As my steps grew heavier, I leaned against a clean spot on a derelict building, taking in the particular seedy area I had arrived at near a group of abandoned warehouses, some with scaffolding. A visual promise to improve, one I thought befitting of the promise I'd forged for myself just moments earlier. As I moved to stand under one of the scaffolds to block the rain, I fished out the phone from my pocket. Ten missed calls, all from Jonas Crane. The phone started vibrating once more in my hand, and this time I answered, my tone terse. "Yes. What do you want?"

"You. I want you. Where are you?" His voice was strained and elevated above the sound of traffic. *Is he out looking for me?* I pushed away the warm feeling that came with that train of thought, along with the wet strands of hair that were plastered to my face. "Why? You don't care. If you wanted me with you, her panties wouldn't be in your bed."

"I'm going to get an answer from her on how they got there, but I didn't touch her!" he yelled. Then, sighing audibly into the phone, he said, "I'm guilty here, but not of fucking around. I'm sorry I lost your trust, and you can stay mad, but I'm out of my mind with you out there alone. I need you with me. We need to have this discussion in person. Where are you?" He sounded despondent.

Tears were stinging my eyes, but I refused to let them escape. "I know I said I wouldn't run, but this is different. I deserve better than that. But then I left, and I didn't know where to go. You let me rely on you, and now I have nowhere to go…"

"Yes, you do. You have a place with me. You belong to me," My heart squeezed at the anguish in his voice. "Please, tell me where you are," he asked again in earnest.

Relenting, unsure of what else to do, I walked along the sidewalk, looking for the name of the building. "XR Industries building…" I read out what else marked my location and listened to Jonas repeat the information to David. Walking back under the scaffolding, I realized I was well beyond saving my clothing and wasn't fit for the expensive upholstery in his car. "I can't get in your car," I sighed. "I'm soaking wet. You go on to your meetings. I'll make my way back and we'll talk later."

"No, you won't. Listen to me, you're more important. You mean…everything to me. The world to me. I can't…I won't let you go, Lily. I won't be able to do anything until you're safe with me. Please don't hang up or leave. Let me come and get you." His desperation tugged at my heart, so much so the words tumbled out of my mouth as I cried into the phone. "I love you, Jonas. So much, it hurts sometimes. But when I saw Melissa had been in our bed…I realized you won't ever love me, and I can't…no, I won't, waste any more time trying to convince you to."

I searched for more words to say, but nothing else came, and the line went quiet. *Jonas has nothing to say back to me.* My mind raced with all the implications of his silence, none of which had me wanting to wait for his arrival and possible painful rejection. Nevertheless, I held the phone clutched to my ear, waiting and hoping for even the sound of his breath to let me know he had heard me. Every second that passed, a piece of my heart broke, fearing this would indeed be the end of everything between us.

As the dreaded silence grew longer, my hand slipped, easing the receiver away from my ear. I was about to simply press the 'end call' button, when I was distracted by a set of flashing lights on an approaching car. *Jonas?*

My heart jumped into my throat as the car slowed and halted in front of me. The back door swung wide, and out came Jonas Crane, wearing a stern but determined look on his face as he closed the distance between us. And there he stood, letting his suit grow damp, towering over me. Before I could say a word, he pulled me tightly into his arms, mouth right against my ear, and whispered, "I love you, Lily."

CHAPTER EIGHT

JONAS HALF CARRIED me to the car, but once we were under David's umbrella, I lifted my arm and said, "Please, let me go."

He hesitated and measured me for a moment, but then released me. "We have a bag for your coat and a blanket in the back seat."

I peeled off my coat and placed it in a bag, the whole time feeling the intensity of Jonas's presence surrounding me, his will pressing down upon me to surrender over to the love and care he had waiting in his arms. And all I wanted to do was bask in his declaration and let him take over. But I no longer felt as though I could, not with Melissa and his lie hanging over us both. Whether he was ready to admit it, there was something between them, and a true choice would have to be made if Jonas was actually mine. If he truly wanted *me.*

"Thank you," I said, my voice surprisingly even. I climbed inside the car and sat down on the blanket, crossing my arms to cover the shiver that had started up my spine once the adrenaline had waned. My awareness shifted to the cold air and chilly wind outside.

"David, turn up the heat for Lily, please," Jonas instructed as he took the seat next to me. His laser-like focus moved over me, though we sat in silence for a few minutes as the car turned and drove off down the street.

"Melissa called last night and pleaded to see me again," he finally said. "I was clear that you are with me. That we are together. Once she acknowledged that she understood, I agreed to see her, as a friend. I didn't tell you, not because I had something devious planned, but because I didn't want to cause you any more stress."

I pursed my lips together. "That's still a lie. Were you ever going to tell me?" I asked curtly.

A glance in his direction let me know he was working his fingers through his hair. "I planned to tell you tonight. I had hoped to resolve things today when she came over, but she was in a state I've never seen her before. Melissa was saying things like she couldn't live without me. She was threatening to harm herself. She took a sedative, and I asked Lin to help me get her to lay down. I didn't even think about anything beyond that, except calling her father."

I scoffed. "Melissa didn't display any signs of distress at the hotel when she tore into me, but if that's what you're ready to believe—"

"No, but I want Melissa to tell you the truth, and when you are ready, have her come over and tell you. So I can make things right with you, the woman I love and hurt." He lightly touched my hand, my heart lifting at once again hearing the word "love" from his lips. But still, I pulled back.

"I will make this right," he said. "But I won't force you. Just give me a chance to fix this. That's all I ask." His voice was just above a whisper.

Silence fell between us again as I sifted through his explanation. Finally, I turned my head toward him, my eyes on his chin. "I understand what you are saying, but I'm confused as to why you kept this from me. As the woman you love, I deserve more than to be shut out, even if it is something I would be upset about. I'm not ready for promises, but I'm here."

"Please look at me," Jonas said. I did as he asked and felt a knot in my chest at the sheen that I found in his.

"I'll take that much now, and I'll do whatever it takes to keep you here. I can't let you go. I can't lose you," his voice broke.

I rubbed the center of my chest and closed my eyes, letting the quiet return again as we rode the rest of the way back to the apartment.

On arrival, Jonas struggled to gain his composure next to the door as I climbed out once again on my own, moving next to him under a large umbrella. The loft door was blocked as a mattress was hauled out of the building, and we paused and waited as it was moved toward a truck double parked a few yards down the road. When we were alone in the elevator, Jonas offered, "They're removing and replacing our bed. Whenever you're ready to return to it."

I gave a little tilt to my head in acknowledgement but didn't say anything. If he was telling the truth and nothing actually happened between them, this wasn't necessary.

Jonas must have read me again. Reaching over and delicately moving the errant strands of hair the wind blew back into my face, he said, "I did it because this was supposed to be your place with me. I want you to have and hold good memories of us together here."

We rode to the top and climbed out. Inside, we found Lin directing the movers upstairs. Once she saw us, she quickly moved our way and we stopped in the living room area. Her eyes were red-rimmed as they set on me.

"I'm so sorry you left. She was sick, I didn't think she'd do that. I was distracted by setting up the other rooms. I didn't mean to get you upset…" she stuttered.

I reached out and clasped her hands, but then regretted it because mine were damp and cold. "I'm not upset with you, Lin. I'm upset with all that happened."

She nodded quickly and patted my hands.

"It's alright, Lin," Jonas said, placing his hand on her shoulder and guiding her a few feet away to talk. I hesitated, not sure if I should wait for the movers. Before I decided, Samuel and Ian walked into the living room, followed by a thin woman with short, slicked-back salt-and-pepper hair. She reminded me of the executives at work, dressed in a black power pants suit and pointy-toed heels.

They all took in the state of the two of us, particularly me being soaked down to my now bare feet and dripping on the hardwood floors. Maybe that was why the woman's mouth was gaping and Ian had a deep frown creasing his smooth forehead. Glancing at Jonas, the woman recovered. Putting on a tight smile, she spoke first. "Jonas, I'm going to have to get going, but I'll send an update to you on the status later," she said.

"Sounds good, Diane." He turned to me. "This is Diane Langston."

My eyes widened and shifted away from her once I recalled how I knew her. She was the lawyer I had avoided speaking with about Declan. Was she here about that?

"We've met only on the phone," Diane confirmed, turning back to me. "And I'm sorry I'm out the door now. I know you want to get out of those wet clothes, so I won't keep you," she said, waving her hand as she hastened her steps to the front door.

"I'll see her out, Mr. Crane, and will be back soon, Ms. Salomé," Samuel said and followed after her.

I looked questioningly at Jonas, but his gaze was fixed on Ian, whose narrow stare I found on me. "Jonas, I see you've got everything under control and are handling things as perfectly as you said," Ian said icily, his mouth set in a firm line.

I lifted my chin. "I'd like to know if Diane coming by has something to do with my case," I said to Jonas, ignoring Ian.

"She was here as a consultant," Ian answered, as they both glared at each other. "I'll be in your office."

"Or you can leave. In fact, I insist," Jonas replied abruptly.

I held up my hands. "I'm tired and am going up to change."

"And eat, you haven't had anything since breakfast hours ago," Lin interjected.

I blinked rapidly. "Eat, and I'm…" I swayed a bit on my feet.

Jonas immediately rushed over and swooped me up and over his shoulder.

"Put me down, please," I protested as he walked toward the stairs.

"Bring the drinks and food up, Lin, thank you. Ian, go home. We'll talk later," he called out.

Jonas walked toward the master bedroom, but I tugged on his shirt. "I'd like some time alone to think over everything that happened. I'll…sleep in the spare room, just for tonight."

"You don't have to sleep in there with me," he said, his voice coarse. "But the bathroom is big, and set up. You can change and dry off. I'll have someone stock the spare bath, but…" he walked us inside the master suite, and I looked at the large four-poster bed in the process of being built. "There is plenty of room for you in the new bed if you don't want to sleep in my arms." He stopped inside the bathroom, closing the door behind us.

I turned my back and shivered, my heart aching at

the sadness so evident on his face. "I'd like to be alone right now, too," I said, my teeth chattering. I could feel him before he touched me. "Lily, not taking care of you is going against my instincts, but I don't want to pressure you," he said.

I tilted my head down, and started nervously unbuttoning my shirt to try to keep my hands busy as he watched over me. The moment I faltered, he took over, his hands rushing through the buttons faster than my mind could keep up, pulling the fabric off. "You are justified in your anger with me, but don't deny both of us what we want and need right now," he said as he unhooked my bra.

My mind screamed, *I shouldn't,* as I pulled of my bra and Jonas unbuttoned the front of my jeans, easing the soaked fabric down my legs. "You're cold. You need to warm up," he said.

"I need a drink of water," I murmured. Walking over to the sink, I picked up a glass, filling it with cold water, which I quickly drank down and then refilled. Once I drained my second glass, I replaced the cup on the sink.

"A shower would heat you up," he said as he reluctantly took my wrist. I let him lead me over to the shower and turn the nozzle to warm. I stood under the spray with my eyes closed, holding my arms. "I should be alone," I said in a small voice.

"No, you shouldn't. It's okay. I'm here and I'm sorry," Jonas said. He removed his clothes and stepped inside the shower. His arms circling my waist and his head resting on top of mine. My emotions swelled to bursting at the feel of his warm, firm body encompassing me, and I split apart and started crying. He held onto me, as if I was his last lifeline, his mouth kissing over me as he repeated, "Shhh…Don't cry. You're mine. Please don't cry."

He took me over to the bench and laid me back along the cool surface. He then kissed and touched over every inch of my body until I calmed. It was everything I wanted and needed without even asking. Jonas almost had me believing that he understood and that he may love me more than I ever imagined possible.

Yes. He loves and cares for me, but does he respect and trust me enough to stop keeping things from me?

As I calmed, I broke from his embrace. He hesitantly let me, as I asked one of the questions that was nagging me. "Why was Diane Langston here?" He folded his arms and didn't answer.

With a huff, I went back under the spray. Reaching for the vanilla-scented wash, I started washing over my body. Jonas walked over and started doing the same to himself.

After a few minutes, he finally offered, "She came to look over what happened with Declan, and to offer advice to those I have looking into the situation, mostly in regards to the theft and photos, but that's not all we are looking at."

I pursed my mouth as I lathered my hair. "Were you going to tell me?"

"If I found it necessary," he said.

I turned and met the jut of his chin with my squint. "You can't keep this from me. I'd like to be involved in whatever you have planned, or you stop now."

"I may be guilty of not fully disclosing Melissa's visit, but I'll be damned if I'm called to the carpet for protecting you. This is one of those situations where you won't get your way, and that's my final word on the subject," he said.

I gaped at him and his brazen domineering display. "You can't do that." I whipped around, not caring if my long hair hit him as I rinsed it off and walked out of the shower, knowing my juvenile actions didn't support my cause. Still, I seethed over his cool control over my life. It was also clear he would continue to keep secrets from me. *And I'm the one with the habit to break!*

Taking one of the bath towels, I dried off and tied another in my hair. He stepped out of the shower and I had to force myself to look away as he walked over and took a towel to dry himself with.

"I don't know if the workers are finished," he said. "I'll go get you something to wear."

I crossed my arms. "I'm sorry for my behavior in the shower, but I can't believe you think it's acceptable to exclude me from what affects my life. My being with you doesn't give you permission to control and run my life."

He narrowed his gaze. "So caring about and protecting you comes with limits? If you think for one minute that I'm going to let you go up against that fucker that abused you, then you don't know me. Now *that*, you can stay mad about. But I promise you, Lily, it won't change a damn thing." And with that, he snatched his robe and shut the door with force.

Now we are both being juvenile, I thought as I continued to dry off.

A few minutes later, my pulse increased when I saw him come back into the room in a pair of low-hanging sweatpants, carrying my favorite blank tank top and sweats. I accepted the clothing from him, neither of us speaking. This time he closed the door softly when he left.

By the time I was finished getting dressed and drying my hair, the movers were gone and I was alone in the bedroom. The smell of food crossed my senses, and I eyed the large platter left for me on a small table. My stomach growled. I was hungry.

I sat down and ate the three-bean soup, salad, and bread in front of me. I was half finished with the smoothie when Dani walked through the door. My expression must not have been a good one, for she said, "I'm not going to stay. I just stopped by to make sure you were okay and to bring more food for you to eat. And also, to pick up Lin so we can go to yoga tonight."

I shrugged. "I'm taking this down, then going to sleep," I announced.

"I'll take it down for you," she said, waving for me to stay seated. "I heard what happened, and I don't blame you for being mad," she said. "Paul was quite animated when he described how Melissa behaved the other day, and it sounded like she was certainly being awful. I told Jonas as much." When I didn't say anything, she continued, "She is manipulative, but is she worth stilling your happiness?"

"What kind of happiness is built on lies and deception?" I asked and covered my mouth as the irony washed over me. I realized I was just as guilty of doing that and then some. I drooped my shoulders. "I'm sorry. I didn't mean for that to come out so harsh. Today, with Melissa, just really surprised me."

"That was one part of your whole day. One part of your experience together. Jonas isn't perfect, and he was blindsided by her. He will work to fix this. But all he wants is for you to be happy. His way of getting there wasn't right this one time, and he knows that now. But please don't shut him out," she said.

I nodded. "I don't want to. It's hard for the both of us. I'll try, and I hope Jonas will do the same."

She smiled and exhaled long. "I have been where you are for years. There will always be women after him, but you must remember how he feels about you."

She gave me a hug, and picked up the tray, ignoring my attempt to do it myself. I followed her out of the bedroom, stopping at the spare room one door over.

"Thank you, Dani. You're a good friend. To both of us." She gave me a kiss on the cheek before walking back towards the stairs, and I entered the bedroom and closed the door behind me. Climbing on the queen-size bed, I slipped under the duvet cover and eventually fell asleep.

"Stop, Dec. Let go of me," I yell, but no sound comes out.

His hands grip my head tight as he slams it down against the dashboard

His hands come across my face.

His hands grip my arms and shove me on the floor.

I scream.

"Lily!"

I continue to scream as strong hands hold me down. He has me.

"It's Jonas, Lily. Please wake up."

My eyes opened and darted around, finally settling on a set above me. *They're not green. No, they're blue.*

Jonas.

He loosened his hold on me and sprawled beside me, bringing me into his arms. "I'm here. Nothing will ever happen like that again." I flushed as awareness returned to me. And then I found myself trapped between my anger at Jonas and my need for the comfort he was giving me.

"I know you're still upset, but you're still mine. Just let me hold you, even if you're not ready to forgive me," he said and kissed over my damp forehead.

I yielded to his arms. "Please."

Without hesitation, he wrapped me close and rubbed

over my back, repeating soothing words, lulling me into the security of his embrace from the nightmare that had robbed me of my sleep.

As my awareness returned to me, I noticed his hard erection through his sweatpants.

My body awakened with need, and Jonas, catching my shift, froze next to me. So unlike the man I knew and loved.

Taking a breath, I said, "Are you. I mean, do you want to make…have sex with me?"

He turned me around and gave me a look that I felt down to my toes. "Love. You can say 'make love.' I meant what I said earlier. I love you. But I'm not going to make love to you until you're ready to give yourself back to me."

My heart skipped a beat at his use of 'make love' to describe our intimacy. But I didn't like being given ultimatums. I furrowed my brows. "So now you're withholding yourself?"

"No, because in that we both know I would lose," he said and smirked. "No. I mean you can have me, but you'll initiate."

My frown deepened. "You know that's not what I want."

"But you're still upset with me," he said.

"No. I'm confused. You are upset with me," I replied.

"No, I'm not. But after that dream, there is no way in hell I'm leaving that piece of shit ex of yours alone. I am going to make sure you never have to worry about him again. I'd do it even if you chose to leave me." His eyes shifted.

I rubbed the stubble on his face. "I don't want to leave you. I'll leave the Declan situation alone for now." I almost left it at that, but then thought to continue while I had the guts to do so, "I love you, but you need to make a choice. I don't trust her, and I can't have trust in us if she continues to be around. I need you to choose. Her or me." I held up my hand. "And before you say you have chosen, I need more than a promise."

His face lit up and he smiled. "You're my charging Tiger tonight."

I lifted the corner of my mouth. "And?"

"I love you," he said and kissed me tenderly on the lips. "Would you like to get up and eat? Or go back to sleep? I'll leave…"

"No. I want to fall back to sleep in your arms. I'll eat a large breakfast before therapy in the morning," I said. Without hesitation, he laid on his back and I positioned myself on top of him and closed my eyes and sighed.

"As Rubin says, 'morning will come, it has no choice.'" He turned off the bedside lamp. Life would go on, and whatever was to come, I did not know. Nevertheless, I wasn't alone or left with nowhere to go.

Jonas was here and in love with me.

CHAPTER NINE

"BEFORE WE END our session today, on a scale of one to ten, one being miserable and ten being perfect, how are you feeling?" Isla asked at the end of my session the next day.

I paused and thought on all that happened and said. "Six."

She nodded. "What keeps you from being a five or a seven?"

I tucked my hair behind my ears. "Jonas telling me he loves me back. Melissa coming around trying to get him back, and Jonas keeping things from me. I know he does it to protect me, but after my walk through the city yesterday, I realized I can't allow myself be completely dependent on anyone."

"Was it dependence or receiving help? You mentioned you were having difficulty managing your ex on your own?"

I rubbed the sleeves of my soft turtleneck. "Yes. I have. And I will admit I need help there. But, like today—I'm going shopping later for clothes at a place I can't afford. I'm on leave from work, and I don't have my own place."

"What do you want to do with your life?" she asked.

I lifted my shoulders. "Ultimately, I want to be able to work and expand the Salomé Love Legacy Art program and make it a cultural exchange, but with work and everything…" I let the words die in my throat. "I suppose I could look into that now. And, well, everything else."

"Then that's one of your assignments. But I also want you to think on your relationship with Jonas. I know you experienced this before, but imagine your life away from him now. We'll discuss both next week. Are you still going out of town tomorrow?" she asked.

I smoothed the front of my wool pencil skirt. "Yes. At least, I hope so. He hasn't said anything."

"Talk to him. If he's shutting you out, show him what sharing can do for the both of you. This is a little leading, but something to contemplate over the weekend," she said. I sighed and took the hug she gave before I made my way out of her office and the building.

I was lost in my thoughts for part of the drive, until we were stopped at a traffic light in Midtown. And not just anywhere in Midtown, but a couple of blocks from Arch. A sinking feeling took hold of me, and I climbed out of the car the second it stopped in front of the building. I pulled out my phone and called Gregor. On the second ring, he answered.

"Do I still have a job?" I blurted.

"Lily?" I couldn't tell if he was glad to hear from me or just shocked by the sound of my voice. "Of course you have a job. Jonas just left our meeting. How are you feeling?"

I sighed in relief. "Good. Over-rested."

"It's only been a few days. No rush," he said.

I frowned. "Oh."

"Lily Salomé?"

I looked up and made contact with the large brown eyes of a tall waif of a female with mushroom bobbed hair standing a few feet from me. Her business attire had me thinking she was from Arch, but I couldn't place her, even when she took steps toward me. The closer she came, the more details of her face came into view. Her skin was pale and scaly, despite the humid air following the on-and-off rain of the day. Her eyes were puffy and dark circled, and I thought for a minute how similar I must have looked just short of a week ago, had I not gotten to Dee and the spa treatment, as well as food and sleep. Her lips thinned, then formed a small smile.

"Hi. I don't think we formally met…" she stuttered, interrupting my call.

I held up a finger to her in a gesture to wait as I spoke into the phone. "Someone is here, Gregor. Would you mind sending me one manuscript to work on? I need something or I'll go crazy."

He chuckled. "Fine. Check your work email. But don't tell your boyfriend, as I think he's warming to using Arch to publish his book."

The woman thrust her hand out in introduction, bending her wrist in an odd manner that had me thinking something was wrong with her hand. But then my eyes zeroed in on the boulder-size diamond on it.

I ended the call and put the phone away, then awkwardly shook the tips of her fingers. "Are you okay?" I paused, waiting for her to tell me her name.

"Heather, I'm Heather. And yes. I just need to talk…" She lifted her face and stepped past me and grimaced. "I must go. I work a few blocks from here. I'll be in touch soon." She turned and ran down the sidewalk.

That was odd.

"Wait." I called after her. I was about to take a step in her direction, when I felt a familiar presence and decided against it.

Turning around, I found Jonas. He was causing a stir around us in his dark navy suit and white shirt opened at the collar, low enough to show off a peek of his smooth chest hair. His dark hair was coiffed back in waves, showing off his gorgeous profile. I felt like one of the many admirers on the sidewalk, pausing to gawk at this scorching hot man. His eyes were all for me though, and the intensity in them had me shrinking in his striking presence.

"Come here, beautiful," he said in a baritone. I unconsciously moved closer and he gripped my hips, pulling me into a kiss that went from innocent to adult pretty quickly. This got us a few 'Get a room' catcalls from the onlookers and had my perpetual blush creeping up my skin, but it wasn't enough embarrassment to let go of him. So when he broke it off, I was delighted at the surprised look that passed across his face before it settled into his all-too-familiar amused glint. "You alright?"

I sunk my teeth into my bottom lip. "There was a woman who came up and talked to me then ran away."

Jonas frowned. "She ran away?" he repeated incredulously.

I lifted my shoulders. I had nothing to offer as an explanation. He looked around and I did also, but she was long gone.

"Did she say anything?" he asked.

"She just introduced herself then left," I replied.

"Hmmm…odd," he said. Then he brushed a strand of hair away from my face and said, "I've got time between my next meetings to set you up at Barney's. We're going out tonight before we leave for Miami," he said, smiling down at me.

I raised my brows. "I'm still going?"

He gave me a chaste kiss. "Yes you are, but this trip isn't something I would have chosen to have you on. I'm just too selfish to leave you here."

I gave him a small smile. "I love that you want me with you. I'm here in any way you need me."

Jonas cupped my face and ran his thumb over my bottom lip. "I need you, but for tomorrow it's all business, and I plan to make this trip as short as possible. There is something I could use your help with, though. I need someone to take notes. Just a brief on attendance, topic…"

I rolled my eyes. "I know how to take notes."

He grinned. "Yes, but I'm…I've been called persnickety. I don't want everything, just particular pieces so we can leave immediately afterward."

I reached into my purse and pulled out a note pad and pen. "Well, go on then, Mr. Crane, sir?"

His eyes darkened. "Mmm say that again," he said and kissed me. "We'll talk about it on the flight." The rain started again and we quickly settled inside the car.

I licked my lips. "So, how was your meeting at Arch? I didn't know you were going there today," I asked cautiously.

"I had the business meeting I rescheduled after I left with you. Remember?" His stare was bold and seductive, and I shrunk beneath its weight.

I dipped my head. "Yes. Right. I forgot," I answered in a soft tone.

He reached over and twirled his fingers in my ponytail. "Why are you being shy now? Not that I don't enjoy it. I'm just curious," he asked as a smile spread across his face.

I glanced at him through a fan of lashes as a ripple of excitement went through me. I didn't know how to explain, but I tried. "I don't know. The way you're looking at me, like you want to do…something."

"Like I want to fuck you? Yes, I want to." He tugged slowly on my hair, exposing more of my neck. "Do you want me to?"

I licked my lips. "Yes, but we have an appointment soon, right? I mean, you don't have time, right?" The words came out like a sigh.

Jonas moved closer and nipped along my neck. The beginnings of stubble brushed against my skin to my ear, where he closed his lips on my earlobe. "Oh, I always have time to fuck you. I don't care. We'll be late." His breath was hot, tone seductive. I moaned and leaned my head, taking in his scent. His expensive cologne and what I knew to be his natural smell had my body blooming, heating and tightening for him.

He moved a hand across my full breasts and took in a sharp breath. "You need me to fuck you. Tell me," he purred.

My breathing staggered and I gapped my thighs. "I need you, please," I said, breathless.

"Fuck, my sweet Lily," he gritted as he tightened his grip on my hair and slowly moved his hand down from my swollen breasts to my knee. He licked and lightly sucked my neck at a painstakingly slow pace before moving his hand up my skirt until he reached the apex of my thighs and stopped. "Tights?" he hissed.

My face heated. "It's cold outside," I mumbled as he tugged the nylon fabric aggressively down my legs, taking my panties with them. "You're going to rip…" The words died in my throat as he trapped my clit between his fingers, and I let out a staggered breath.

"Unbutton my pants and take my cock out," he said,

assuming command. I felt a gush of liquid from my pussy, dripping down on his fingers.

He let out what sounded like a groan and a laugh. "Mmm. That for me?" He grinned, slicking his fingers around my sensitive flesh. "I should eat your sweet gift, but you need to get fucked? Decide."

I mewled. I didn't want to think. I wanted him to do! Do me. Fuck!

He was right. I wanted him to fuck me. He imprisoned my clit again, as I moved my hands blindly behind me, pulling down his pants and freeing his cock. He took it in hand and slid the tip against the liquid heat at my entrance. "Take me," he commanded.

I bore down on his dick, shifting to accommodate his thickness. Jonas took my hips in hand, and pulled me the rest of the way down to take his incredible length.

"Jonas, please," I cried out as pain and pleasure intermixed.

"So tight. You're killing me," he hissed out, and my sex clenched. He groaned and dug his fingers into my hips, as he started gliding me up and down his shaft. I titled my head back and closed my eyes as I arched with him, matching his tempo, taking every inch of him. "My Jonas," I must have said as I felt his head against my back.

"Yes. Yours, Lily, and you're mine." He punctuated with every relentless surge of his cock. I was gasping, my heart pounding against my rib cage as I lost myself in the pleasure of the strokes of his throbbing flesh inside me.

I cried out incoherently as I came, and he picked up the pace, working my walls as I clamped on to his dick, bringing on his climax, his cum spilling into me. He held me there for a few seconds longer, then I lifted up and he went about cleaning up both of us.

I went to collect my clothes and put them on, even though now they were mussed. Angry runs decorated my tights. "I can't go in there like this," I whined.

"Oh, yes you will. Kate will get you a pair of thigh highs. She can take those flat shoes too," he said and mockingly wrinkled his nose, then caught my hand before it connected with his arm.

"Why do you look so together?" I said. He had a few creases here and there, but was otherwise ever the striking businessman. Years of practice, I suspected.

He lifted my hand to his mouth and kissed my wrist. "I always prepare. I have a spare suit in the trunk too. I'll get you another outfit inside. Kiss me."

I leaned forward and he claimed my lips. In fact, he had demonstrated complete possession of me, though he told me that I was in charge. "I thought you were going to hold yourself back and let me lead?"

Jonas laughed. "You're complaining now? Let's go in so David won't have to drive around for us anymore."

I looked out and noticed we were a block away from the front entrance of Barneys, on West Seventy-Fifth and Broadway.

My lips parted. "How did he? Never mind. Have you heard from Melissa?" I asked as we got out and made our way inside. Jonas took my hand and we passed through the fragrant aisles and busy patrons.

"No. Arthur said she is resting, though he did mention she's working to bring her practice back to New York."

I snorted and tugged on my hand, wanting away. But he held on firmly.

"I told you because you wanted to know. Her coming here won't change how I feel about you, my Tiger Lily." He rubbed the back of my hand with his thumb. A simple gesture of assurance.

I calmed as we made our way to the women's section and up to a counter where a woman made a call to his personal shopper, Kate. She came a few seconds later, a walking *New York Style* magazine finest, in what had to be designer dress and four-inch stilettos. Greeting both of us with a handshake, she said, "This way, please."

We followed after her into what appeared to be a private fitting suite, complete with plush couches, chairs, and racks at every angled mirror. Jonas settled in a chair, and Kate took me around to a closed room. "I'll just take your measurements, and you can tell me what you feel comfortable in. Then I'll add that to your work and formal wear."

I shifted on my feet. "I just want a couple of shirts, skirts, and jeans. And maybe a pair of heels."

She smiled and leaned by my ear. "Mr. Crane said you would say that. Just try on some of what I've picked for you. I promise, I'll make this fun as I can manage."

I plastered on a smile and we returned to the room. Jonas was busy on a call, but paused to give me a wink. And then it started. Kate and another associate brought back dresses, skirts, shirts, and heels for me to try on. All under the attentive gaze of Jonas, whose eyes lit up every time I came out wearing a new outfit. The more pleasure he had on his face, the more comfortable I felt, until I was happily trying on more clothing. When I came out in one of the final pieces, a swing-embroidered dress, Jonas stood and came over and kissed my lips. "I'm taking you out for dinner tonight." He leaned over my ear. "Thigh highs, heels, and this dress."

I gave him a small smile and he kissed my lips. "I have to go now, Tiger Lily. David will come up in half an hour to get you," he said.

My bottom lip quivered. "I enjoyed this, but I don't need all of these clothes. I'm gaining weight, and I won't fit half of them in a month. This would be a waste."

"Well donate them if that will make you happy. Seeing you happy works for me," he said with a wink. "Get a purse, too. But don't throw this one across a room to hit me with like you did at Sir Harry's."

I giggled. "I most certainly did no such thing!"

His eyes danced and my heart flipped over. "It worked. You got me," he said in a soft tone.

My eyes misted and I lowered my head to hide the overwhelming feelings I had in the moment.

He lifted my chin. "No crying. Happy thoughts. We'll have a read later." That, of course, had my tears flowing down more, He clicked his tongue in mock admonishment and took his handkerchief out to dab my eyes. "See you soon."

I nodded and touched my lips, staring after him as he strolled out.

"That was beautiful," Kate said softly, calling my attention back to her. I smiled and followed her back to finish up as memories of the serendipitous encounter with Jonas at Sir Harry's played through my mind. That night had been perfect until Declan interrupted our conversation. After six months of silence, he arrived with a surprise fiancé that couldn't wait to show off her ring. Her boulder-size ring, like the woman on the street.

My pulse increased as recognition surfaced. Heather, Declan's fiancé. The one he claimed he had broken up with. She was the woman who had been outside Arch looking for me.

Did Declan send her to me? Was he angry about not being able to reach me by phone?

I absently changed back into my old clothes as Kate chatted about a delivery later today. My mind was too preoccupied with worries and the implications of what could arise from more contact with Declan.

Jonas wasn't willing to tell me about what was going on. Perhaps I could find out from Heather? But would finding out cause Declan to do something even more desperate with the photos?

Even as I stood waiting for David, a plan hadn't formulated. It took me a few minutes before I realized someone was tapping me on the shoulder. I looked up at the stunning blonde trying to get my attention. *Melissa.* She was dressed to the nines, as she had been a few days before, in a fitted dress and heels. Her face narrowed as her eyes shifted over me.

"Well played. I have to hand it to you. Bravo. You not only duped Jonas into buying the whole collection, but he left with a ridiculous smile on his face. He keeps missing work for you, but you obviously don't give a shit about his career or him because you don't have one."

I lifted my chin. "I didn't mean to…" I took a breath and stopped myself to rethink what I was saying. While I had problems, she wasn't my therapist, nor did she in any way have any objectivity, being that we were both in love with the same man. "It's none of your business what we do together. He's heading off to work right now and his smile wasn't ridiculous, it was genuine, because he's happy. Something I doubt he ever experienced with you."

She flinched a little, but seemed to regain her composure quickly. "Oh now you have claws? I was out-trumped yesterday. You running out into the rain after you found out we had sex." Her eyes darted and returned to me.

I glared at her. "He didn't have sex with you. You left your filthy underwear in our bed." Then another thought occurred to me. "How do you even know about what happened? You spied on us? I understand now that you're a pathetic liar, but a stalker too?"

She narrowed her eyes. "Now I see why your boyfriend hit you. But don't worry, I'm above such primitive means."

I lowered my head. "That was low, even for you," I said, my voice hollow.

She lowered her eyelids. "That was terrible. I didn't mean it, but Jonas and I did share the morning in bed and that must hurt. You can chose to believe it or not. I just thought you should know. We did things you can't even imagine together," she said.

I shook my head. "I know he didn't, but let's just say he did. He's still with me. He chose, relocated, and moved in with me. Jonas loves me, and that must hurt."

Her lips curled. "Jonas doesn't love you," she snapped. "Jonas doesn't know what love is after Dani. He loved her. You may, in your inexperience, believe he loves you. But he doesn't."

I folded my arms. "He said he loved me. I'm surprised you missed that in your stalking."

She blanched. "Even if he said the words, he's impulsive," she said, speaking over me. "He gets bored easily too and is virile. Why else do you think Dani agreed to an open relationship? She knew the score. Don't believe me? Ask Kate how many women have come here. How many he's done the same routine for."

I bit the inside of my cheek and glanced toward Kate, who was boxing up the clothing. Had Jonas done the same with other women?

"He has his slip-ups, like he did with you at the gala

when he was starting again with me. He'll do it again. I'll leave you to think on that."

"Lily," David came up and I went to follow him, but turned back and said, "Even if Jonas becomes bored and leaves me, he won't return to you. He's had plenty of chances to and keeps choosing otherwise. How about you think on that."

CHAPTER TEN

I BREATHED IN and tried to relax, letting my thoughts drift back to all that had happened during the day. I watched the dark sky overhead through the glass of the car, guessing there would be another downpour coming along at any minute.

I pulled out my phone and typed, *Guess who I ran into at Barney's.* My finger hovered over the send button, poised to tell Jonas all that had occurred in the shop between Melissa and me. But I stopped and thought for a second.

What would I gain by running back to Jonas, equipped with her words?

Melissa was aware that my insecurities were my weaknesses and played on them. I had little doubt her words had been carefully crafted in a way to cause a rift between us. I had to be smarter. After all, Dani had been married to him for sixteen years, and she had warned me that there would always be women like Melissa after Jonas. I shuddered at the thought. But it was up to me to try to rise above them.

Then again, that didn't leave Jonas without some

responsibility. He would need to do something.

I erased the message. No. Her words were not going to come from me.

Miraculously, there was a momentary break in the clouds as we reached Tribeca. The sun shone, warming up the cold industrial area surrounding the loft apartment and brightening my view of the day. As I played it over again in my mind, Melissa was a small bump in what had otherwise been a joyous day.

There was something else my mind tried to conjure to dampen my mood, but I pressed it down and gave David a grin as I practically skipped up to the loft. I went about my new ritual of changing into comfortable clothes (a tank top and sweatpants), collecting my lunch (tuna on rye) and setting up my laptop to check over my messages. As I settled down at the table, I was pleased to find a new one from Ms. Parker, head of the Salomé Love Legacy Art program. I immediately opened it up to read.

Dear Lily,

The program is coming along great so far this year. We had a surplus in donations, as well as the large contribution from the Finch Foundation. I wanted to know if you would be interested in assessing a few new schools to include in the program for next year. This is getting bigger than me, and with the class and summer coming up, I won't be able to take on more. We may be able to hire someone from the colleges as an intern for the summer? Let me know.

Ms. Betty Parker
Marymount Elementary School

I beamed as I wrote out a quick reply.

Dear Betty,

I'll take over the responsibility of the assessments, and possibly more.

I'll be in touch soon.
Lily

I tapped my finger against my lips, then sent a text message to Jonas, though I knew he wouldn't get it until later.

Do you know anyone that I can speak with regarding learning how to manage the Love Legacy Art program?

I ate the rest of my lunch and cleaned up, then carried my laptop to the living room and turned on the TV. Flipping through the channels, I discovered there was a rental option and chose an old movie. I watched it between researching evening courses and programs at the local universities that would work around my job. As I finished sending my last inquiry email, my phone buzzed with a reply message from Jonas.

I'll get someone to help you. Glad you asked.

I grinned and placed my phone down on the table, then stretched out on the couch and drifted off to sleep.

I don't know how much time went by before I heard, "Oh don't wake her. She looks adorable curled up."

My eyes blinked open and I found a pair of eyes hovering above mine. I startled.

Paul laughed. "Hi, kid. Ready for our date?"

I rubbed my eyes. Was I dreaming? Nope. Jonas's son, Paul, was leaning over me, dressed smartly in a button-down shirt and dark slacks. His longish dark wavy hair was even neatly tied back. A doppelganger of what I imagined a teen Jonas had looked like, though his smile was all Dani. Even his eyes were assessing me in a manner so similar to Jonas, it was unnerving.

I broke his laser-eye gaze. "What's going on?"

He gave me a lopsided smile. "Game's postponed for Saturday and Dad didn't know if he would get back in time after Miami tomorrow to hang out, so he invited me to come tonight. Right now, he's working up to dinner. So as his wingman, I'll be your escort."

"Yes. Jonas called," Lin said, entering the room and confirming their arrangement. "He'll meet you there. Your shopping is upstairs."

I lifted the corners of my mouth. "Thank you very much, Lin." I looked at Paul and smiled. "Great. Where are we going? I should get dressed." I sat up with an enthusiastic bounce.

He chuckled. "Oh, this is going to be fun."

"No, it won't be. You'll behave," Lin said to him in a stern tone. He gave her the cutest sad look, which had her giggling. "Why don't you play the piano and let Lily get ready," she suggested.

"It's my day off, too," he said, his full lips poking out as Lin half-dragged him over to the bench before the piano.

"Oh, I'd love to hear you play," I said, clasping my hands together.

He flashed a bright smile at me. "Do that a few more

times and I'll play all night," he said.

"Stop flirting with your Dad's girlfriend," Lin scolded. "Lily, it's close to five. You really need to get dressed."

Paul titled his head. "I'll play you out. Your own theme song."

I stood up and headed for the stairs as Paul began to play. The musical arrangement was nothing I recognized, but his playing was nothing short of brilliant. I slowed down at the stares and glanced back to watch him. The playful teen was replaced by a skilled master, completely absorbed in the music. I wanted to stay and listen but forced myself up the stairs to change.

I took a quick shower and used my daily skin moisturizers before leaving the bathroom. Standing at the closet, I found the new lingerie was already there and quickly changed into it and thigh highs. I applied a little makeup and decided to wear my long black hair down. I ended with a little fragrance and the embroidered dress Jonas had selected. Collecting my heels, I went downstairs and was delighted to see Paul was still playing. When he saw me, he started banging out Fountain of Wayne's "Stacey's Mom."

"Knock it off Paul," Lin said.

He gave her a sheepish grin. "How do you know that song?"

Laughing, she said, "Your face told me."

"I'll have to work on my poker face then," he said and kissed her cheek.

He turned to me. "You ready, doll? David's downstairs ready to take us to Per Se." He held out his arm.

I put on my heels and hooked my arm to his. "I haven't broken these in, so I'll need your help on the cobblestones."

"You look beautiful, Lily," Lin said, kissing my cheek. "See you Monday."

"Thank you so much, Lin," I gushed before the door closed and we left for the restaurant.

We walked arm and arm through the glass doors housing Per Se in Columbus Circle, and a new Paul took over. He helped me out of my coat and spoke quietly to the hostess, who immediately had the staff collect our coats and gave us a personal escort to our table in the main dining room. The formal cloth tables had elegant chairs, along with soft lights and floral arrangements decorating them.

Our table was situated before one of the large windows, and I was in awe of the view. We were looking out at Central Park, which was spectacular, even at night. Paul held out my seat and I sat down, "Thank you."

His phone buzzed as he took the seat across from me. He held up his hand to answer it. "It's Dad. He said he tried to phone you, but got voicemail."

I searched my purse, realizing that I didn't have my phone. "Sorry," I said sheepishly.

Paul gave me a wink. "She's fine." He held the phone away from his ear. "He stopped by Mom's for a quick change. He should be here in ten minutes. Oh, and he said to order a glass of wine for me."

I squinted at him. "He didn't say to order you wine." He gave me an innocent look, and was ready to hand me the phone. But before I took it, he put it down and laughed.

"I thought you were fun. Mom lets me have a glass with dinner," he said and simpered.

I lifted my shoulder and offered the only compromise I had available. "If Jonas says it's okay when he arrives."

"Then the answer is no," he said and laughed.

The waiter brought waters and a basket of bread and left.

"Dad already set us up for the tasting menu and champagne for you. I get some sparkling kiddie drink, but I don't care. The food here will blow your mind," Paul said.

"Paul, what was that music you were playing earlier?" I asked.

"That was something I've written recently. It's not finished," he said.

"It's brilliant," I enthused, and he actually blushed for me.

"Thank you," he said in a soft tone.

"How long have you been playing?" I asked.

"For as long as I can remember. Mom says two. I sat down at one of her hippie chants and pressed down on the harmonium, and someone said I was an old soul, but dad didn't buy it. He gave in once he was convinced that

I was a natural. He gave me the 'as long as it makes you happy, son,' speech. Ba da Bing, I'm at Julliard."

I laughed then grinned. "Yes. Jonas mentioned you were there. My Dad was a principal viola for the Boston Symphony before he passed away."

Paul took a hold of my hand and gave it a squeeze. "Mom and Dad told me. That must be hard. Sorry."

I couldn't help but smile at the teen. *Old soul, indeed.* "Thank you. It is…was…I think it gets…it becomes little less painful every day. They'll always be a part of me."

He patted my hand. "Good. I'd love to hear his performances. I'll give you my email and, well, now you'll have to come to my performances."

My heart expanded. I could have hugged him at that moment. "I'd like that very much."

He laughed. "You look like I gave you a Christmas present. Sweet. I've got to toughen you up. Throw a tantrum while Dad's here." We laughed.

"Time to put you in the hot seat." His tone became serious. "What are your intentions with my dad?"

My mouth dropped open. "Uhm…we…"

"We plan to keep your nose out of our business," said a deep, rich voice behind me, and Paul laughed.

I looked up and my heart stopped. Jonas looked devastatingly handsome in an impeccable dark grey suit. His dark waves were slightly curlier, due to the humidity and rain I suspected, but that only added to his beauty. He leaned in and met my eyes and I forgot to breathe. I could feel the heat of his skin, even before he kissed the side of my face.

"You look stunning," he said in a low tone.

My eyes flicked to his lips and back to his eyes that were glimmering. "So do you."

"Okay, we all look hot. Am I going to have to watch you two ogle all night?" Paul said, exasperation in his tone.

Jonas kissed my lips lightly and took the seat next to me. "One day you'll understand."

"Ha. I already do, Dad. Mom didn't tell you?" Paul said mischievously.

Jonas's eyes widened and then narrowed as realization crossed his face. "Please no, way too soon," he grumbled. He took a generous sip of the Scotch that the waiter placed before him.

I suppressed a giggle by holding up my glass of champagne and drinking it too quickly, though I could see Jonas had shifted his reproving glare to me.

Paul pushed out his chest. "What? I'm almost sixteen. I'm a man. Well, soon will be if all goes to plan."

"Is this what you want to talk about over dinner?" Jonas said in a tone that made it clear he didn't. "Lily will never want to go out with us again."

Paul shrugged his shoulders. "The tables are private here, so no one besides the three of us can hear what we're talking about. And anyway, we have to squeeze in these talks when you're around."

Jonas looked like he had been stung, and tapped his

finger on his glass.

"I didn't mean that like it came out. I added to your calendar everything that's coming up," Paul said with a lift of the side of his mouth.

"It's alright. I'm changing, son. I'll be around more. And taking off more time, too, now that I'm back in New York. We'll be seeing each other outside of the dates," Jonas said.

The waiter came over and announced our first course, "Sabayon of Pearl Tapioca with Island Creek Oysters and Sterling White Sturgeon Caviar."

The presentation was so pretty, I didn't want to ruin it. But then I bit into it and moaned, flushing as both sets of sea blue eyes swung over to me.

Paul batted his long lashes. "You'll need to control yourself, Ms. Salomé. I'm an impressionable child and this is an upscale establishment."

Jonas snorted. "Who was just talking about a losing-his-virginity plan?"

Paul laughed, then said, "How about you, Lily? For a minute act like Dad's not here. Did you have a plan to lose your virginity before it happened?"

"That's enough, Paul," Jonas interrupted, but I answered truthfully anyway.

"My plan was to wait until I was married. I got engaged in college and convinced myself that was enough. We were together for three years before it was called off. So my plan didn't exactly work out. But, yeah…that was the original goal," I said and drank more of my champagne.

"You're serious," Paul said, looking at me as if I was an oddity from another planet and time.

Jonas winked at me and mused as he watched Paul quiet for the first time since he sat down. Then he looked to Paul and said, "I didn't have a plan. I had an opportunity and should have waited. I want better than that for you."

Paul let out what sounded like a groan and sigh. "No freaking way I'm waiting for marriage. Sorry, Lily. I'd be old and grey by then. I'm taking the first opportunity that comes my way. And it's coming soon."

My head felt light as I grinned between the two of them. Jonas looked at me inquisitively.

"What's your rush?" I said, a little too loudly, giggling as the words came out.

"No more champagne for you," Jonas said and moved my glass out of reach. We all laughed.

Jonas met my eyes and we gazed at each other for a few moments before he kissed me. He leaned over my ear. "I can't resist your happiness, even if it's enhanced by champagne." I kissed him.

"Influential child here you're trying to talk out of having a good time," Paul bemused with a wave of his fork. He stared at Jonas.

Jonas sighed. "I see you're determined to do this. I'd like to discuss this alone with you later tonight. Can you wait as long as that?" he asked and smirked.

A pleased grin spread across Paul's face. "I can do

that."

We ate duck foie gras and lamb, both with a beautiful presentation that matched the taste. Then we spent the remainder of dinner singing praises to every living thing that went into the divine meal. When the tray of assorted desserts came, I held up my napkin as a white flag. "I can't eat anymore."

"Just one bite of the…" Jonas and Paul said together and stopped.

I laughed and ate two bites of the chocolate torte and crème brûlée as I admired both of them. Once we were done, Jonas settled the bill and we rose and left the restaurant.

The Dakota apartments, where Paul lived with Dani and Alan, weren't too far from the restaurant, but I still fell asleep with my head on Jonas's lap on the ride back to Tribeca. The rain continued to pour down and Jonas swooped me up in his arms to run to the elevator and up to the apartment. "Bed," he commanded. "You need your sleep before our early flight tomorrow."

I slipped off my shoes and headed up to the bedroom, where Jonas took the time to unzip and remove my dress.

I took a deep breath. "I enjoyed dinner with Paul tonight."

His face fell. "With all my work and travel, trying to give Paul a different life, he's turning out just like me," he said in a disgusted tone.

I furrowed my brow as I undid his shirt. "I happen to

love you, Jonas. So I do hope he turns out just like you."

"You love what you know about me," he said wryly, taking the shirt from my hands and pulling it off, then walking into the bath.

I took my clothes off and found my robe, then joined him in cleaning up for bed. "I'd love to know more about you, if you'd give me the chance."

He turned his head, his gaze as soft as a caress. "You'll know enough living with me to learn my faults instead of having me point them out," he said, looking around for his phone and returning with it in his hand.

"Is work okay? Have you been missing too much because of me? Melissa said…" I covered my mouth.

He sighed. "David told me about your run-in with her at Barney's. She's avoiding me."

I shook my head. "Sorry. I didn't want to bring it up, or to waste time on her tonight. I'm trying to trust you to deal with this, when the time is right."

Jonas paused and touched my chin. His eyes brimmed with tenderness and passion as they searched mine, "If only you knew how much you have me. You'd never worry about anyone else."

"You have me too, Jonas. I'm yours." I leaned forward and he crushed his lips to mine, almost hurting me in his possession. Then he let out a sigh of relief.

"Work is fine. It's just me using time I haven't used and actually leaving things to those I hired, like I should do tomorrow. But I think we both need to go to this one." He pulled me up against his side and walked us back to the new bed.

I climbed inside and rolled over as the mattress formed to my body. "Mmm…a mattress from the Gods. You may never get me out of it."

He laughed and tugged me back to his side. "I'd keep you right here next to me."

I snuggled back. "I'd love that."

He kissed my neck. "You ready to read?" he said softly.

I shook my head, unable to speak. He reached over and pulled the book out and I crawled into my space, resting my head on his chest with my arm around his waist. I listened as he read from *Peter Pan* until I got lost in the perfect world between awake and dreams.

CHAPTER ELEVEN

THE RAIN HADN'T let up overnight or when we arrived at the airport at six in the morning the next day.

Six!

"You can sleep on the flight," Jonas said, with a small tap on my backside as he urged me to climb up the short flight of stairs and into the cabin of his private plane.

The plane itself took me back a bit. While I knew Jonas was wealthy, he usually kept his shows of wealth subtle enough that I, for the most part, felt comfortable. His plane was another story though. It was a level of luxury that surpassed anything else I had been exposed to in his life.

The interior reminded me of images I'd seen of the President relaxing on Air Force One. Plush grey leather seats with built-in desks. A television already playing stock and news updates. A few modern colorful accents here and there to brighten up the space.

I headed toward the back before Jonas took my elbow and steered me to take an aisle seat. Placing down his briefcase, he removed his iPad, phone, and a stack of papers, then handed the rest to the flight attendant.

His mouth twitched. “Take a seat, Lily,” he said, motioning again to the aisle seat next to him.

I dutifully sat down in a couch-like leather seat with a recliner that I immediately tested, though I noticed David was settled into the one behind us. I worried for a minute that I might be encroaching upon his space, but then looked around and noticed that even fully reclined, I was nowhere near him. There was plenty of room.

“Comfy?” Jonas asked. “You can do that after you eat.”

I rolled my eyes, but smiled at him. “You’re always in command, Mr. Crane.”

“That you can be sure of, Ms. Salomé,” he responded.

The pilot walked out of the cockpit and began speaking. “We need to stay ahead of the weather and will be taking off shortly,” he announced.

As I glanced over at Jonas nervously, he took my hand and gave it a squeeze.

This wasn’t my first flight. I had flown to see my father perform in other countries and had vacationed abroad. But as I listened to the lashes of rain beating against the plane, accompanied by a flash of lightening, I shivered.

Even the flight attendant seemed anxious. She played the safety video and quickly secured herself in a seat. The crack of thunder had my pulse sprinting.

Jonas pressed something that made the shutter close

over the window. "Relax. We'll be fine," he assured. He was completely Zen.

Before I could respond, the plane lurched forward as we taxied down the runway and wobbled in the air. I had a white-knuckle grip on the seat rest and poor Jonas's hand. He leaned over and stroked my face and kissed my lips, distracting me as the plane hit every air pocket in the sky as we flew.

My shoulders lowered once I saw the sun coming through the windows. After a few more minutes, the emergency lights turned off. I released my grip and leaned over close to Jonas's ear and said, "I love you so much." He gazed at me longingly, then kissed my lips.

The flight attendant came back with coffee and orange juice. She then brought us an assortment of cream muffins and slices of fruit, granola, and yogurt. I mixed up a small bowl and watched as Jonas put on his glasses and multitasked through his papers, electronics, and eating.

Between spoonfuls of granola and plain yogurt I asked, "Is this for today? If you need help, let me know."

He took off his glasses and rubbed his eyes. "No. Today has been set. I'm working on something that will be presented in a couple of weeks."

I lifted my brows at him as he continued to move around his work. "Have you always worked so far ahead?"

"Yes. Well, it's the way my father worked, so it became the way I work. He used to say 'only losers wait for others to define the path for them. Cranes set the path and standard.' I check and set," he said.

His screen went blank as he sipped his coffee. A picture appeared. It was a charcoal sketch of a woman's back and the curve of her hips.

I felt a flash of jealousy, until I realized the sketch was one he had done of me during our first week together at the hotel in New York City. My hand shook as I delicately touched the screen.

"You never forgot about me," I said in a hushed tone.

"No. I carried you with me," he responded just as quietly. I leaned over and kissed his neck. "You were always with me too, though mostly in my dreams."

A crease appeared on his cheek. "Oh, I enjoyed the dream I got to wake you up from at the hotel."

I covered my face. "That was embarrassing."

"You got past your embarrassment pretty quickly, as I recall. One of my favorite Lily traits." He reached down and adjusted the front of his pants. "You'll be on your knees sucking my cock if we don't change topics."

I looked around to see if David had heard, but was relieved he had on earphones. I next located the flight attendant, who was busying herself in front. "With everyone around?"

He chuckled. "David listens to folk music on plane rides, so don't worry. There's a bedroom in back. But before your eyes get smoky and you lick those sexy lips of yours, I'm not fucking you right now."

My jaw unhinged. "What? I didn't…you turning down sex." I made it a statement, but truly, Jonas seemed to always be in the mood.

"Because you, my beautiful Tiger Lily, don't have a poker face. And I don't want my friend, or anyone in the office, to know what's going on between us," he said candidly.

My face fell and I stared dully at the food on my tray, stirring the yogurt and granola as the pain of his words ripped through my chest.

Jonas cursed. "That came out harsh, and nothing at all like I meant," he said, picking up on my shift in mood. "It has nothing to do with how I feel about you. More about what this day will bring. I need to keep this meeting professional, no matter what Phil Keane tries to do today."

I looked at my hands. "Okay."

He studied me for a moment, then pushed his work away and tugged on my hand. "Come here."

I didn't budge. "I'm not to be played with when it's convenient, or brushed under a rug when you don't want others to know. If I'm really yours, as you claim, I'm yours all the time," I said nasally.

"You are mine all the time. Fine. I'll take you back there and fuck that into the torturous landmine that is your mind. I'll introduce you as my 'girlfriend,' if that will please you. But that doesn't even touch the depth of what I feel for you, Lily," he said.

My chin trembled and I took his hand.

"I'll tell Phil I'll use his assistant, and you can spend the day at a spa or something in Miami. But you can't be with me there. My feelings for you make it too hard for me to be professional when you are around, and the way you look at me after we make love would make it impossible." He was formulating a plan before me, and at the same time slaying the demons in my mind and soothing the pain in my heart.

I blinked back the tears that were standing in my eyes as my heart tumbled over. "I love you so much Jonas."

"Come here," he commanded, making room in his lap.

"But your suit," I protested.

He smiled at me. "I've got another. I don't have another you."

I moved everything out of the way to climb in his lap and inhaled his incredible scent, pressing my lips to his neck. "I want to go with you. I'll go along with your plan."

He kissed my cheek. "Alright. Pay attention. Here is a briefing and schedule of today's presentations at KeanexTech. It's Phil Keane's company. Phil and I…have known each other a long time." He cleared his throat. "Anyway, we should conclude close to 2:00 p.m. You will sit in on everything but the partners' meeting at the beginning. I don't want to involve you in the ins and outs of that, since you'll have to spend time with staff. I'll see that Phil gives me an office you can use before the presentations. You understand?"

I smiled. "Yes, Mr. Crane."

"Good, Ms. Salomé. Now kiss me and eat the rest of your breakfast, then get the rest of your sleep."

I leaned up and kissed him.

He looked a little sad, and I rubbed his cheek. "What's wrong?"

"I wish I could keep you this innocent and protected, but I can't. This is part of my life too, and…" he said, his voice hoarse.

"And nothing. I love you, nothing will take that away." I kissed him. He didn't respond, but slowly released me to return to my seat, where I ate the rest of my breakfast and he went back to multitasking for the remainder of our flight to Miami.

Jonas lifted the window and let the sunshine pour in as we landed. Once we exited, David split off to collect the car and we walked through the breezeway of the arrivals terminal to get out of what quickly became more heat than my dark crepe navy dress and blazer could handle. I cursed the nylons, though even I had to say the designer ensemble, along with the chignon hairstyle, looked great.

And then there was Jonas, wearing a dark designer suit of a similar shade and a crisp white dress shirt open at the collar. He didn't appear affected at all by the heat. With a pair of sunglasses pushed up in his hair, he looked more like a movie star. With the lingering and questioning glances that were coming from the people around us, I had no doubt there were those wondering if he was.

"Jonas Mathias Crane." A voice somewhere in the crowd said.

I stifled the giggle that rose in my throat as Jonas stiffened next to me. The sound of his full, given name being broadcasted across the terminal set him on edge.

The man attached to the pleasant, booming voice finally came into view, and quite the view he was. The phrase 'beach babe' came to mind. A handsome man, I guessed similar in age to Jonas, with a thick head of light brown hair and ice blue eyes that stood out against his copper-tone skin. He was dressed similar to Jonas, though his suit was light grey. His hand extended on approach, "You stubborn old bastard. I offered for you to stay over at my place, but you chose to fly in the middle of the night?"

Jonas gave the man a smile that didn't quite reach his eyes. "Phil. You didn't tell me you were moonlighting as a chauffeur? It wasn't necessary, since I'm flying back to New York after the meeting."

"You still could have taken me up on my offer to stay last night at the house. Dottie and I would have loved to catch up with you. I don't think we've had a full day together since back when you and Dani would escape to my parent's beach house every summer in college."

"You know there were other times," Jonas said, and they stared at each other for a heartbeat. He exhaled and motioned for me to step forward, "This is Lily Salomé, my assistant." Phil's eyes glimmered as they slowly roved over me.

I glanced at Jonas. *Poker face.* I knitted my brow and pressed my lips together. "Hello, Mr. Keane. Nice to meet you," I said politely, offering my hand to shake.

Jonas hid a laugh with a cough. *Did I blow it?*

Phil gave me a wide smile and closed both of his hands over mine, letting me know I must have done okay. "The pleasure is all mine. I'm here to convince your boss to stay for dinner. You are welcome to join him."

Jonas blanked his face. "We won't have time, and we should all head over to KeanexTech now."

"Not so fast, Jonas." A beautiful brunette in bohemian wear approached, holding the hand of a pretty toddler with blonde curls and ice blue eyes. "You must say hello to Holly."

Jonas smirked. "Dottie, please tell me Phil didn't drag you to the airport with Holly." She walked up and planted a kiss on Jonas's lips. "How could we miss out on the celebrity business mogul dropping in on us mere mortals," she said, and they laughed.

Jonas turned to me with glances between Dottie, Phil, and Holly. "We all went to boarding school and college together. They were New Yorkers for a long time, until they decided to give it up for Miami. And don't let Phil fool you, he's successful and has numerous businesses."

"Yes. But KeanexTech is my primary business," Phil said and stared at Jonas.

I nodded. "Nice to meet you." Dottie shook my hand, though her focus was on Jonas. I leaned down to Holly and said, "Hello."

She gave me a smile that showed off the cutest dimples I'd ever seen, then clutched the leg of her mother.

"She's shy. You like kids, Lily?" Dottie grinned as Holly took steps toward me and took my hand.

"I love them," I blurted. I could feel Jonas's gaze on me, but I kept my eyes on Holly, who was now getting me to help her twirl in a circle.

"You'll get dizzy, Princess," Dottie laughed and picked her up. "Your boss here was quite the reluctant dad, to put it mildly."

"She is lovely, but we must go," Jonas leaned down and kissed Holly's cheek.

"You know we were invited to your brother Vincent's birthday next Friday. He still thinks of us. Are you going?" Dottie asked.

I shot a questioning glance at Jonas, and then looked away.

"I didn't realize...No. I'll be working," Jonas responded quietly.

"Well, then I bet a lot of people will be disappointed," Phil said.

David stepped forward on cue. "The car is ready, Mr. Crane."

"Please agree to come for dinner tonight. I'm making paella." Dottie tried again.

"You mean you'll have a chef deliver paella," Jonas

said, correcting her, and they laughed. "We'll see you soon? Or do you need a lift to your office?"

Phil grinned. "Splendid idea."

Jonas shook his head a little. "I should make you take a taxi. Good to see you, Dottie." He gave her a light kiss on the cheek, and we all moved out to the sidewalk. A gust of air hit me, immediately heating my skin, and I gratefully climbed in the open door of the estate car David held ajar for us.

Once Phil said a quick goodbye to his family, he climbed in the car and settled in next to Jonas. I sat on the seat close to the window as they launched into a discussion about the business. I nodded and listened while staring out at the beautiful pastel stucco structures intermixed with the new buildings. We arrived at a white glass building with a row of miniature palm trees lining the front and a white and chrome stylized sign that read 'KeaNEXTech.'

"I'd like a quick word with my assistant. I'll see you inside," Jonas said to Phil, who grinned at me and climbed out.

"Vincent's party?" I asked.

He blew out a breath. "I wasn't aware or invited to the party."

I curled my lips. "He didn't invite you? We'll *we* wouldn't go to his party anyway."

Jonas suppressed a grin. "No more of that. Please, focus on what we have to do today. Keep yourself together, and follow my lead. Understood?"

I stared up at him and, wow, was he good-looking. "Yes, Mr. Crane."

He kissed the end of my nose. "Stop that look too."

"And what am I saying right now?" I asked and blanked my face.

"You're saying 'trust me.' I do, but this is one of those times I expect you to follow," he said.

I almost choked. "When are the times I'm not expected to follow?" Jonas pointed his chin as his answer.

We exited the car and I fell into step next to him as we entered the building. Once inside, I couldn't help but wonder if I was in an office or an upscale playroom. There was an oversized sign for 'KeanexTech,' and the 'Orion App' prominently on display, along with a few colorful custom couches that stood out against the white polished lobby. But what got me salivating, besides the smoothie machine, were the circa 1980–2000 game machines in the lobby, where a few people were dressed in pajamas.

Oh, Phil. Can Mary and I work here?

Jonas sighed and leaned over my ear. "Poker face, Lily. Or I'll have David pick you up now."

I pursed my lips, but sucked in my cheeks and lifted my chin.

Jonas suppressed a laugh and shook his head, then put on a real poker face. It was all stiff and business and practically chilled the air around us. I even noticed the pajama clad workers leaving the games, as the only one in a shirt and tie approached us. "Mr. Crane. I'm Dex, and

I'll be your personal escort for the day. I'll be right with you for your entire visit. I just want to send out a quick text letting everyone know I won't be down in reception."

Jonas motioned to me. "I brought my assistant. I don't need an escort."

Dex looked perplexed. "I was told to be your escort. If you…and?"

"Ms. Salomé," Jonas responded, and I nodded.

"I must insist," Dex replied.

Jonas looked as if Dex was see-through and walked off toward a glass elevator while I fell into his pace. Poor Dex continued to mosquito buzz by the elevator. When we climbed in, the energy around Jonas killed his advance and we watched him stare at us as the door closed.

"What was that about?" I asked.

"I made it clear the last time I didn't need an escort, but Phil insisted. Having you here I had hoped would stop the unnecessary use of his staff to take me around what I can find easily on my own. I detest the fuss," Jonas explained.

The elevator doors opened and I marveled at the floating stations around us. We walked over to the large glass room along the center. I could see Phil already seated, along with a few other men and women in suits.

Jonas turned to me. "They're waiting for me. This won't take long, and you'll be in for the next presentations."

Dex appeared, a bit out of breath, having clearly taken the stairs. "I'll set her up, Mr. Crane, sir."

Jonas clenched his jaw and walked past him into the room. We both stared as everyone stood and walked over to Jonas, who held up his hand and took the seat at the head.

The king has arrived.

"Sorry, I didn't catch your name?" Dex was saying.

I glanced at the room and was surprised when the glass frosted over. "Lily," I blushed. "Uhm…sorry?"

He laughed and put his hands on his hips. "You're good." Then his eyes wandered back to the room Jonas had just entered. "The legend continues. I should be honored. I got a bite from Jonas Crane, and I survived. He must be in a good mood," he said, then looked at me and clamped his mouth shut.

"Oh I don't know. I just started," I said, my stomach churning.

He grinned at me. "Well, take a load off, lady. At least take the breaks you can. In fact…" he paused dramatically and pressed his finger to his lips. "You look like a smoothie lady. What would you have?"

Enthusiasm crept in my mind and my face, and then I remembered I was supposed to be professional. I shook my head. "I'm to wait here."

"You'll be waiting for an hour and a half. Blame it on me. I'll be the martyr. Come on, a drink before being trapped in boredom for the rest of the morning and early afternoon? That's the motto around here at KeanexTech:

we get the job done and we have fun. So come on."

I glanced at the door, hesitant at first, but then I followed Dex, though I knew I would blame myself if it turned out I was needed and absent. I wouldn't want to get Dex in trouble.

We went down a floor and over to one of the rows of floating stations, where a woman was working on her computer next to a corgi sleeping on a dog bed.

Dex introduced me with a theatrical wave of his hands. "This is Lily, Mr. Crane's assistant. She's my cool new friend," he said, loud enough for others around to hear. And suddenly, everything became like a scene out of the *Wizard of Oz,* as I was surrounded by people I'd never otherwise met. "Wow, with Jonas Crane? What is he like?"

I shrugged. "I'm new."

"You know Lily signed a billion confidentiality agreements," Dex said.

"Lily, would you come over and look at what I'm doing?" a woman named Fran said. I was tugged over to see a game. "Pretty cool, right? This is what we're working on."

Even the corgi pushed his head into my hands, seeming anxious to be around me. I found myself petting him.

"Oh, can we keep you?" Dex said.

The place was easy and relaxed, even more so than Arch, and everything seemed to run smooth. No matter where I stopped with Dex, there were workers testing, designing, or discussing the ongoing projects at the company. I couldn't understand why Jonas was dreading coming here.

"I promised a smoothie, and you will be in heaven after one of these," Dex said as we walked into a café that would rival some of the fancy coffee houses in the West Village. Dex pointed to a small group gathered at one of the longer center tables.

"I'll bring the drinks. Go join them. They're good people."

I nodded and walked slowly but confidently over to the 'cool' table.

"Got my resume ready. The shark is in and Jonas Crane doesn't nibble, he devours," I overheard.

"He could devour me anytime," someone said. They all laughed.

"I'm serious. He guts and disposes, he doesn't build. He demolishes. That's what's made him rich, the motherfucker. He couldn't give a damn about how well we did last quarter."

"He flew in on a private jet for an afternoon meeting? Tell us who's wasteful."

"He's a billionaire and we cost his shoe budget, but he's too selfish to see what we have to offer. I mean, come on, he put his own mother in a home. Think he'd blink about closing us down?"

My stomach dropped and my blood ran cold as I listened to them continue to badmouth Jonas. Was he here to close this place?

"Hey. Where you going?" Dex said from behind me. "I was serious, they're good." I hadn't realized I had walked over toward the door. I followed him back to the group, sitting silently as he gave the same spiel from earlier. "This is Lily. She's Mr. Crane's assistant. She's also my new friend. So give her a KeanexTech welcome."

Some of them went red, and some averted their eyes. No warm KeanexTech welcome this time, and I didn't have one to give back.

I turned to Dex. "I probably should go over my notes and see if Mr. Crane needs me." Dex looked questioningly at his colleagues, but handed me the smoothie. "I'll escort you..."

I shook my head. "Not necessary."

"Well, at least let me show you to Phil's office. Mr. Crane can use that one, as it has everything. It's also a great place to hide out." He laughed and the rest of the table made a sound that seemed close enough to a laugh for him. As it was, I made the faux laughter sound too, before following Dex out of the café. He led us back up to the third floor and down a corridor, where he pressed a button and the glass slid back and opened to what looked like a large suite with the same modern furnishings and game-centric décor as the rest of the place.

"I'll come get you in about twenty minutes. Sorry for whatever happened back there." He had an urgent energy about him, as if he wanted to leave but thought he might need to stay.

I plastered on a smile. "I'm fine." I took out my

phone and held it up. "I'll just check my messages."

His shoulders relaxed a little. "Cool, see you soon."

I let go of the breath I was holding when the door closed, then looked through my phone for a distraction from the negative thoughts that were starting to plague my mind. I was happy to find one from Mary.

BIpIv'a' Tigress Lily!

I covered my mouth and laughed. Klingon for 'Are you healthy?'

I smiled wistfully as I read the rest of her message.

Can't wait to see you. Tell Jonas thanks again for the ticket.

I touched my lips. Jonas hadn't mentioned anything about a ticket to me, which explained her next text:

Ooops! It was a surprise. Uhm. Errr. Sorry lmao!

I giggled and quickly wrote a message back.

jIpIv. bIpIv'a! I am doing well. So happy you slipped up and told me! When are you coming? I can't wait to see you. Love you MB

She wrote back.

We're lining up to board my flight now.

My eyes widened and I quickly dialed her number.

"Mary. We're in Miami," I blurted out when she picked up the phone.

"Oh really? I thought you weren't going with Jonas to Miami? He mentioned you staying back when I talked to him." I could hear her hesitate for a minute, and didn't know what to say. "Shoot," she continued. "I changed my ticket to an earlier flight, but I couldn't reach him. And I couldn't call you, because it was supposed to be a surprise."

"It's alright. Jonas is in a meeting right now, so if you could text your flight information I'll see if I can get someone to pick you up," I said.

"Uhm okay. I'll text it now, but I can just hang out until you return."

Mary chattered on and I laughed internally. I really missed her, and was happy she was coming, though I needed to make sure she was able to get into the apartment. "I've got to go."

"So do I and thank you both. I can't wait to see you tonight!" Mary said excitedly and hung up.

I chewed my lip. What was I to do now? David was here. *Ian?* I quickly found him on my contact list and dialed his number. He answered on the first ring.

"You alright?" Ian asked.

I paced. "I am. Well, my friend Mary mixed up her dates for her visit and is on her way to New York, but we are still in Miami…"

"And she needs someone to pick her up and get her to your place," Ian said filling in the rest. He sighed. "Text me her phone number and flight information. I'll take care of it from here."

"Thank you very much," I replied.

"I'm glad you called. We'll see you both when you return," Ian said and hung up. I stared at my phone and waited for Mary to send the text message through so I could forward the information to Ian.

I went back to sipping the smoothie and walked over to the window. Staring out the large windows, I took in the amazing view of the beach and ocean. I imagined Arch could fit Gregor's office and part of our floor inside of this one office. Phil had quite the setup here in Miami. I settled on a leather desk chair before one of the largest desks I had ever seen. The desk was covered with high-tech computers and office equipment and a digital frame displaying Phil's family. I sat and watched the images change. Most of them were of Holly at various stages in her young life. A few were of Dottie, and one featured Phil with Jonas. They were in flight suits, in the air.

Jonas and Phil jumped out of a plane together? Another photo was of the Keanes with Dani, Jonas, and a younger Paul on a beach. They were closer than Jonas let on, and I was puzzled as to why he hadn't mentioned them before today.

Looking around the whole room again, I had to agree with Dex. The office was incredible. In fact, this whole place was incredible. That was until the staff spoke negatively about Jonas. My Jonas. They were cruel.

"Lily," I looked up to see Phil and Jonas standing there. I met Jonas's eye and all I wanted to do was put my arms around him.

He smiled at me. "Phil. I'd like to talk to Lily alone for a second."

"We'll start the next meeting when you return," Phil said, lifting his brows and smiling at me before walking out. When the door closed, Jonas held his arms open, and I rushed over and crushed myself against his chest.

"What's wrong, Tiger Lily?" he murmured against my head.

"Please tell me you didn't come to close this place? Oh, I don't have a poker face. Phil is so nice and you jumped out of a plane together, and he has a family." I realized I was rambling, but I couldn't stop. "I overheard the staff saying things, and I hope it's not true. Even though they were gossiping. But we all gossip, you know? And Mary is on her way, but Ian is going to pick her up," I babbled.

Jonas rubbed my back. "Mary is on her way? She's early, but that's fine. Good that you called Ian. He'll take care of it." He looked at me for a moment, and then sighed. "Taking you to KeanexTech was a bad idea, but it's too late now. I need you to pull yourself together for me. No sad face. Put back on the funny, stern expression you came up with for me earlier. Can you do that?"

I took a deep breath and nodded, though my stomach twisted.

He pulled back and held me at arm's length so he could study me. Once I put on my best stern face, he chuckled and kissed my temple. "You're a delight. Come on, they're waiting for us."

I STRAIGHTENED MY shoulders and took out my notepad and the folder he gave me and we walked out of the office and over to the boardroom. Once inside, Phil motioned for me to take a seat in what appeared to be Assistant Row, a row of seats with women and men holding iPads. My heart swelled in admiration as Jonas made a point of connecting with all staff that came in the room. Some I hadn't seen from other floors came shaking his hands and gushing over him. Jonas even came over to Assistant's Row and greeted us. I couldn't hide my smile.

When he was done, he sat down at the head of the large conference table with Phil on his right. They then went around the table introducing themselves, and I wrote down all attendees.

A man with microphone headgear took the front stage of the room and everyone quieted down as he started the presentation.

"KeanexTech was started in 2010. A brain child of Phil Keane, with the backing of Crane Holdings, it took form in 2013…" A large screen lowered and lit, thus beginning the presentation.

It went on for almost two hours, ending with the projected profits for the next quarter and plans for 2016 and beyond. At the conclusion, there was a round of applause. Jonas stood and more chatter erupted, until finally the room emptied.

"Lily, come take a seat," Jonas said.

I glanced at Jonas and Phil, then sat down at the large conference table with my notebook poised.

Phil sat down at the table across from us. "Okay. Now that you've seen everything…"

"My decision stands. This is our plan," Jonas said, handing a leather-bound folder over to him.

"And as I told you, our contract has a clause that allows a four-month extension. I'm asking you to extend it for an old friend," Phil said.

"No," Jonas replied.

Phil dropped the folder on the table and gave Jonas a tight-lipped smile. "So you came down here to bring me this? I seem to recall KeanexTech bringing in twice the projected revenue for Crane four years ago."

"Four years ago. Nothing you showed me today proved this company is worth further investment by Crane Holdings," Jonas said.

"Your father would have—" Phil interjected.

"My father would have stayed at your house, ate your food, tried to have sex with Dottie, and given you the same answer," Jonas replied crisply. He stood and held out his hand.

"You're just as miserable as Mathias. Why did I think you would be different? After all the years of friendship, you can just brush off me and my family like that? Good luck," he said, shaking Jonas's hand, despite the sour look on his face.

"You keep trying to make this personal," Jonas admonished. "Fine. You knew the stakes. I went against my instincts investing in you in the first place. Good luck to you."

Phil pulled out a card and looked at me. "I'd offer you triple whatever he's paying."

I looked at his hands on the table. "No. Thank you, Mr. Keane," I said quietly.

"Tell Dottie and Holly it was good to see them," Jonas said.

"Fuck you, Jonas. And I mean that sincerely," Phil said.

My skin was burning as I followed Jonas out of the room and kept his leisurely pace, though I would have left faster if I was on my own. A crowd gathered through the building and Jonas stopped to shake hands and chat all the way out.

Once we got into the car, I turned to him. "That was brutal."

"That was business," Jonas said and folded his arms.

My stomach sank. "You flew us down and listened to everything, but still planned to close the company. Will they all lose their jobs immediately?"

"Sixty-five percent in the first wave but, ultimately, yes. That is unless Phil finds new backers. But honestly, once I pull, no one will touched KeanexTech," he said bluntly.

"What about your friendship?" I asked.

Jonas lidded his gaze. "Phil and I are friends, but if we are no longer, I accept that. He knows my coming down was an act of friendship. He's upset. He's good, but he's not one to run the helm, and a good last quarter and projections are meaningless at this point."

I tried my best to mask my disappointment. "How could you be so kind and do that to them? It seems so cruel."

He set his jaw. "Because that's how things work. It's

what's best. I don't have anything against the people there, Lily. This is business. I have a reputation for excellence. I can't keep afloat a sunken ship, even if that partnership came from friendship. Many companies show what they can do, but most, like this company, had their chance to prove it, and failed at every turn. I don't continue to invest in what doesn't profit. Phil's far from destitute, and he knows I don't play fools games."

I didn't know how to answer him, so I stared out the window at the cheery, brightly colored buildings. I was searching for the words that would help ease my troubled lover, as well as my conscience, as we drove onto the road to the terminal entrance that housed his private plane.

But I could come up with none.

CHAPTER TWELVE

THE SMELL OF tiger lilies filled my nostrils the second we returned to the plane. Looking around, I didn't see any. Our flight attendant stepped forward. "Your room is ready for later."

I eyed Jonas questioningly.

"We won't be needing it after all," he said and handed her his briefcase. "Scotch neat, please. What would you like to drink?"

I stared at him, but he still wouldn't look at me.

I crossed my arms. "Vodka with ice, please."

Out of the corner of my eye, I saw Jonas's lip twitch, though his eyes were dull. "She's joking. A glass of wine for her." He removed his blazer and David took it to place on a hook. He then sat down in his previous window seat.

Frowning, I sat next to him. "What's in back?"

He took out his phone and started going through his messages. "A mistake."

My pulse increased as I stared and waited for him to talk to me. A few minutes passed and the flight attendant returned with our drinks. Jonas took a sip, while I drained my glass. That got me a pause, but still nothing from him.

"Can we go back there and talk?" I asked, my voice loud over the hum of the jets heating up for takeoff.

He rubbed his brows. "I'm tired. Let's wait until we land." I clipped myself in and stared down at my hands as the plane started to taxi and lift. Jonas reached over and took my hand, though this time I didn't get the kisses and cuddles I'd received on our earlier flight.

What had changed?

My reaction to what happened at KeanexTech. I didn't understand or agree with all that occurred there. Truthfully, I didn't think I had to. But as I stared at him and willed him to look at me, I realized he had shut down, and thus shut me out. What I wanted was for us to be right again. I needed to find a way back in.

My heart pounded as I formulated a plan and waited impatiently for the emergency light to go off. The second it did, I unbuckled my seatbelt and took off at a quick, though jagged, pace for the back of the plane.

I could hear Jonas curse behind me, but still I went, finding the door marked 'suite' and opening it.

The bedroom had the same modern décor of grey and wood as the rest of the plane, with a large bed complete with a matching decorative bedspread and sheets turned down. But what had my heart singing were the bouquets of tiger lilies on every surface. My eyes watered at his thoughtfulness and their beauty.

Slipping off my shoes, I fell back on the bed and sighed as its contours encompassed me. The sound of the door clicking closed behind me had me up on my elbows, and my heart skipped a beat as Jonas walked up, his face raw with emotion, his gaze intent.

"I had misjudged…I'm sorry that I took you with me today. I never let Dani come to one. Oh, she knew everything, but I knew it would break something in her to see the truth. And you, so innocent and loving. But I couldn't spare you. I wanted to be the philosopher, lover, artist, man of your dreams, but this is me. And I needed you to know me as I truly am. I don't expect you to understand everything, and I understand if what happened today makes you love me less. Or perhaps not love me at all. I understand." His eyes clouded over, as pain closed around his body.

Pain that I was a part of and desperately didn't want to be.

My heart constricted and tears welled in my eyes. He was so unlike the confident leader that I, and others, knew him to be. His self-loathing was there. I knew it well, because I suffered from it myself. But I loved him. All of him. He bared a piece of his soul, and as the woman that he loved, I gave back my own.

"No. This isn't all of you. As I said before, you employ thousands of people around the world, and do a lot of good outside of business. I'm shocked and saddened by what happened today, and would like to understand more about your work. But I do know I couldn't make those decisions, and I respect the fact that you have to. My therapist asked me to imagine a life without you, but even a second is too much for me to take. Love isn't something waiting for perfection. My love isn't dependent on you being perfect, Jonas. I love you. Nothing will ever make me not love you," I said. My speech didn't have the finesse or eloquence of his, but my passion for him was there. I moved to the end of the bed and took his hands and stared into his eyes. "You don't have to quote Shakespeare or poems. You don't have to be anything. I want you as you are," I said.

He gave me a smile that didn't reach his eyes. "Even though I'm a greedy, selfish businessman who's taken over your life?" Jonas said, half-joking. Words weren't going to be enough right now. He needed me to show him.

I kissed his lips and unbuttoned his shirt, pulling the end out of his trousers and down his strong arms, finally easing it off while Jonas sat there and watched me. I scanned the room and decided to drape it across one of the built-in seats. I then unzipped the back of my dress and stepped out of it, removing my bra and panties until I was naked. I quickly moved over to the cabin door and locked it.

A low chuckle filled the space and I turned back to find Jonas laughing at me. I lowered my brow as I walked back over to him. A dip in the plane had me losing my footing and he reached out and pulled me on him and the bed.

He cupped my face as his eyes roved over it and said, "You have worked your way in and I don't know how to defend myself against you. The love I have for you is chaotic, I can't control it."

My bottom lip quivered as the center of my chest ached. He captured the lip between his and sucked, then kissed me more, his hands caressing me down my back to my buttocks, where he lingered. My body heated and tightened at his touch, knowing the ecstasy he could give me. But this wasn't all about me. This was about my Jonas. He was mine as much as I was his, and I needed to show him that.

I turned my head to the side, breaking the kiss and catching my breath. "Let me." I wanted to take over. He stilled his hands, his eyes glimmering as they met mine. A bit of uncertainty was there, as well as curiosity, but he let me know without a word he was handing himself over to me.

I pressed a kiss to his mouth and tugged off his t-shirt, tossing it toward the chair as I moved my body down between his thighs and unbelted his trousers and tugged. He lifted for me as I worked them off his body and put them aside.

Climbing back up his body and pressing mine against him, I took his lips again, then kissed down his neck and to his chest, brushing against his smooth chest hair and to his nipples. And like he often did to me, I licked around one and lightly pinched the other one. He tensed under me, letting out a short breath as he touched my head. I could feel his cock twitch as I moved between his thighs, then kissed and caressed my hands down the cut plains of his chest and abs. He truly was a beauty. I moved my body between his thighs as he widened them for me without my asking, and I looked up at him.

His look back was dark and carnal. "This is how I want you, open and ready for me," he said, sending a tremor through me. Stroking over his toned thighs, I kissed and licked along the soft trimmed hair just above his cock as my hands closed around his shaft. Running my tongue over the weeping head, I closed my lips over the top and sucked the tip, then slid my tongue down the underside as I placed my hand on his balls and fondled them in my hand. Jonas let out the sexiest moan, which went straight to my clit. His hands gripped the sheets and I moved my head down and licked over the seam and around the sack as I worked his swollen cock that had grown fuller in my hand.

"Suck my cock, Lily," Jonas commanded, his voice rough and his patience gone. I gave him a wicked smiled as I licked and kissed around his shaft on my way back up, then drew his length between my lips. His hands were on my head, willing me to take more, and I swallowed around him as I sought to take him to the back of my throat.

"Oh. Fuck. Yes," he growled, tightening his grip on my hair and lifting up his hips a little, seeking more. Easing up, I sucked him down to the back of my throat again and again. Jonas held my head in place and I knew he was there. He let out what sounded like a grunt and a hiss as he came. His cock rippled and I gagged as his cum filled my mouth. I swallowed over again, knowing he loved when I drained him to the last drop. He released my head and I slipped him out of my mouth, pressing my face against his stomach that was covered in sweat. Hell, I was covered in sweat, and breathing just as heavy as Jonas, who smoothed my hair. I didn't care. Jonas was my heart and I wanted him happy.

He pulled me up his body and kissed my swollen mouth. "That's my Tiger. I like you taking over," he said.

I let out a snort. "You still took over in the end," I said, but I really didn't care. We laid together for a while, listening to his heartbeat in his chest. His hand started moving down and turned me over on my side. "I want this time to be about you," I said.

"It can be about the both of us," he said, pushing my hip down flat on the bed and trying to get a hand between my thighs, which I had now locked together.

"No. I'm fine. You always take care of me. I want this to be about you. It would please me if this was about you," I explained and kissed over the sulk that was forming on his face.

"But what if I want you?" he said.

"Then take me. However you want to, but later. I'm hungry," I replied, knowing that was the magic word that would stop a determined Jonas.

"Fine, but this ends when we get back," he partially

relented. I let out a breath.

He sat up and pressed a call button. "Please bring lunch and refill our drinks. Thank you." I slipped under the sheets as Jonas got up and moved toward a door on the opposite end. He came back a few minutes later with a towel around his waist and went to the door and waited there. I got up and went to where he had come out of, only to find a full bathroom. I washed my hands and opened a cabinet, discovering toiletries and creams as well as extra towels. I tucked a towel around me. The sound of the cart and Jonas talking had me pause, waiting for the flight attendant to leave before I re-entered the room.

Once it was quiet, I slipped out and found Jonas was seated before a table with our lunch of steak and new potatoes and mixed vegetables. I took the seat across from him and we both started eating the food. The steak was tender and the potatoes melted in my mouth. "Oh, thanks for inviting Mary. I know I said I wanted to wait until later, but I'm really happy she's coming," I said between bites.

"I wanted it to be a surprise," Jonas said.

I giggled. "Mary sucks at keeping secrets," I replied.

"I like her already," he said with a wink. "She's worried about you. I thought this would ease her fears and help you too," Jonas said and sipped his scotch and returned to his plate.

"Jonas," I said, a question on my tongue.

"Lily," Jonas teased back.

"Does what happened today at KeanexTech happen often?" I asked.

"No, but it does happen," he said. "I broke a rule with Phil by investing in his company. My friendships dwindle with each one. Exactly what happened to my father, but he didn't care. He bought and disposed of people often." He went silent and focused on his plate.

"You're nothing like him. Phil was upset about his company," I said in his defense, before eating the rest of my vegetables.

"I know, but there is some truth about losing friendships over business. As far as business friends, I have plenty of them. Some went the way of Phil after choosing to cut ties with their companies. Some friends I have through the yoga center, but those were mostly Dani's scene," he said looking out the window.

I reached over and took his hand. "Are you…we…are we going?"

"Not now." He must have seen the concern flash across my face, because he added, "I'm alright, Lily. I've accepted my life. I love my work and family. I love you. I knew long ago I would have to make decisions I didn't want to for the betterment of the company and those I care about. Vincent never had those restraints, though if you saw him with my father, you would know he wished for them."

"I guess we all want something that we can't have, or wish things were different from time to time. I wanted to get my advanced degree and expand the cultural program with the Love Legacy Art program. I wanted my father to walk me down the aisle, or my mother to fuss over my children…" I said.

Jonas went quiet, and so did I, as we finished the rest of our meal.

Once every bite was gone, we cleared up and Jonas rolled the cart back into the hall under my request, as I didn't want the flight attendant back in the room since we were barely wearing anything. I went back to the bed and slipped the towel off under the sheets.

"My choice," he said as he walked up to the edge of mattress, as if he had to remind me. He wasted no time letting me know he was back in command. "On your knees, arms at your side and your head down. I'll be right there," Jonas said, leaving me to maneuver into the position he chose for me. A warmth filled me as I waited in anticipation of what Jonas would do to me.

I didn't have to wait too long, and when he returned, the bed dipped with the feel of his strong legs on either side of me as the rest of his frame molded against me. I was vulnerable beneath his powerful body that was covering and sheltering me. I closed my eyes as Jonas remained there cocooning me, letting me soak up the mindset he had given to me. I was his completely.

He ground his growing erection against my buttocks and my breath caught. "All of you." He lifted up and moved my hair off my neck and planted a kiss there, using his lips to create a trail along my spine, ending at my tailbone. His hands were on my hips, lifting me higher and moving himself between my legs. My skin felt hot and my body went rigid at being so exposed. He rubbed my hips and moved his hands to my cheeks, spreading them apart. My pulse sprinted and my breath came out harsh. Before I could say no, his tongue slid along the seam, rimming me.

"Jonas," I puffed out.

He paused enough to say. "Try to relax and feel."

He stopped and kissed both cheeks. "You'll come first." He flipped me over and grabbed my thighs, tugging me down on my back, his broad shoulders settling between my legs. He moaned as he sealed his mouth on my pussy and plunged his tongue in and stirred it inside my walls, slipping and sucking my folds.

"I'm close," I hissed as I bit my lip. Jonas knew my body well, so I didn't stand a chance of prolonging my pleasure. And just as I thought that, when my thighs shook, he swiped his tongue hard around my clit and I came on a jolt of bliss. But I didn't have time to revel.

"Back into position," he commanded. I flipped back over on my knees and this time he spread me apart, his tongue traced the puckered flesh there. I felt light slips of his tongue as his breath heated the tight flesh at its barrier. He moved his tongue out and kissed and licked my ass as his fingers thrust inside my pussy. I panted as I heard the sound of something being squeezed out of a tube. Then I felt his finger replace his tongue, pushing against the ring of muscles and out. He added another finger and I whimpered as he twisted and stretched the opening. A deep guttural sound came from me as I rode between relaxing and tightening. Jonas moaned with me.

"You're so sexy, every piece of you. Oh, Lily. I can't get enough." I closed my eyes and braced myself, waiting for his cock, which he slid between my slick folds, coating himself with my juices. "Fuck."

He lifted my hips up and pressed the head of his cock inside my rear. I tensed and he rubbed my back.

"Relax, Lily." He moved slowly, easing more of his shaft inside of me, reaching around to tease my clit as he pressed further still.

"Push back for me and breathe," he commanded, his voice rough.

I took in a deep breath and did as he said, stretching the tight ring and whimpering as my muscles clenched. He pumped slowly until he slid deep inside my buttocks. "Yes. Lily. All of you. Mine."

I reached back and touched his thigh. "Wait," I muttered.

He slid his fingers around my clit and I jolted as pleasure again mixed with the pain, then he started to rock his hips. Jonas grunted as he thrust in and out. Pleasure arose and I push back and moaned. He took my hips and pressed his head against my back as he came. His thick fingers pumped inside me as his thumb teased my clit.

"Give it to me," he gritted, and that made me come apart for him. I quivered and he held me to him. He removed his cock and turned me around and hugged me.

"I love you. Thank you for trusting me." I closed my eyes and tightened my arms around him. I wasn't ready for him to let me go after he had touched and marked every part of my body.

"Love you," I said back to him. He lifted me and carried me to a bathroom, where he placed me in the shower and turned it on. The shock of the cold spray woke me some and I balanced back on my feet as the scent of vanilla filled the small space and his hands moved over to wash me.

"Did I hurt you?" he asked as he washed over my buttocks.

"I feel tender," I muttered. When we finished our shower, he took me out and stood me before the sink.

"Bend over," he instructed.

I complied and for the first time, I didn't blush as he bent down and examined me. It was as if I believed he had a right to do so.

"I've got cream that should make you feel better." He went into a bag on the sink and pulled out a tube and rubbed it against the sore, sensitive rim at my back entrance, then kissed both cheeks. We both washed our faces and brushed our teeth, even then pausing to touch each other.

When we were done, he guided us back to the bedroom, where we worked to fix the sheets before settling back down in them. Jonas pulled me in his arms and I wrapped every part of my body I could around his. There were no boundaries remaining between us. I belonged to him. After a while, Jonas woke me. "We're back in New York. We need to get ready for landing soon." He was already dressed in a shirt and slacks and was trying to work my dress over my hips, which I took over.

He kissed my naked shoulder, then took back over zipping me up. I stood and picked up my shoes and handbag that had made it back there. Pulling out my phone, I made my way over to the bouquets.

"What are you doing?" Jonas asked.

I smiled. "Memories." I took a photo.

He took out his own phone and snapped one of me.

"Mr. Crane?" The flight attendant knocked on the door.

"Come in," he said and chuckled as I rushed over to the bed and tried to straighten the sheets. He pulled my waist and that spark that we shared flared from his touch.

"We're preparing to land," she said.

"Would you mind taking a photo of us?" he said to her as she walked further into the room. She smiled and took his phone and poised it up to take a picture. "Ready?"

Jonas placed his hands low on my stomach and she snapped the photo. I couldn't imagine my expression, but when I looked up at Jonas I noticed he had that faraway expression I'd seen on his face earlier. "Jonas?" I asked. He came back from wherever he was and gave me a wink.

"Would you please take one more? I wasn't ready for that one," I pleaded.

Moving Jonas's hands up to right under my breasts, I covered my hands with his and she took another photo. I turned to face him and wrap my arms around him, and she took another two. "I want a copy of that one," I said as she returned Jonas's phone and we walked out of the room to our seats.

"Yes," I said as I stared down at the photos of us both together, letting my heart fill with the image of the love and care I felt being in his arms. He took my hand and the plane started its descent into New York City.

CHAPTER THIRTEEN

THE RAIN HITTING the surface of the cabin sounded like thousands of spikes hitting a metal plate as the plane dropped, shook, and jittered in what was turning out to be an infinite journey to landing. This time, no amount of kisses from Jonas could ease my grip on the arms of my seat. The pilot continued to loop over the area, causing the queasiness in my stomach to return. I took deep breaths and a sip from the bottle of water Jonas handed me.

Once we leveled, Jonas opened the shutter on the window and pointed at the lights and buildings coming into view, soothing my fear. We flew closer to the ground, until the wheels hit the tarmac and his lips brushed against mine again. His attentiveness and care truly had my heart.

"I love you," I said.

"I know," he replied and held my hand as we taxied to the designated arrival area. We had made it, together.

Once we came to a stop and the emergency lights went off, Jonas pulled out his phone and turned it on, immediately greeting us both with millions of beeps as all his incoming messages poured through. This brought a curse to his lips and a sigh to mine.

David rose the minute the flight attendant opened and secured the cabin doors, taking Jonas's briefcase along with him as he went to get the car. Before I put on my jacket, he was back, making me think I had lost time. Or that something was wrong.

Based on his expression and the hurried manner in which he approached Jonas, my gut told me the latter was true.

"We have press," David announced.

I lifted my brows and moved to peer out the window, but Jonas blocked me and closed the shutter. "Lily, I need you to leave with the flight attendant now," he said and frowned as he quickly put on his suit jacket.

"The uniform, please." He motioned to our flight attendant, who went to the front of the cabin and opened her trolley, retrieving a flight uniform shirt and skirt, which she then handed to me.

I turned to Jonas. *Was this necessary?*

"Put the uniform on as quickly as possible," he ordered.

As I reached for my handbag, Jonas passed it to David, who exchanged it for his briefcase.

"I'll return your bag soon," David assured as he placed it in a paper bag that the flight attendant was now holding open in front of him. He then rushed with the bag up the aisle and out the exit.

Jonas was back on the phone and motioning me off to change again. So I headed back to the suite and quickly removed my dress and suit jacket, awkwardly putting on the uniform, which was snug on me. I then took my clothing and made my way back up to them.

The flight attendant handed me a flight bag to put my clothes in, then beckoned me to follow her.

I turned to Jonas. "What about you? And why are they here?"

Jonas paused mid-conversation. "I need you safe. Go with her. She will get you to David. I'll explain later." He called out to the flight attendant, who was now at the cabin door, "Thank you."

My pulse raced as I hurried up the aisle after her, down the steps and onto the tarmac. She met me there with a small umbrella and we huddled under it together in a dash toward the small terminal building. On our approach, I could see a row of glass windows where a few passengers milled around in arrivals. I spotted one man with a camera. This had me thinking Jonas and David were being overzealous in their security measures. *Did he really need all of this?* Still, I followed the hurried pace of the flight attendant as she moved with purpose across the square room toward the main exit.

It was there that I finally noticed the press, swarming with cameras around a couple of uniformed airport security guards. This wasn't just one man. It was a mob. And we were heading right toward them.

The flight attendant motioned for me to keep up,

but the second we breached the door that was to be our exit, flashes of lights blanked my vision. I felt a hand grab onto mine, pulling me forward, but I stumbled. Once I recovered, I blinked rapidly and swiped the rainwater from my face before walking forward. The cacophony of voices speaking all at once made it hard to understand what the throng of press may have even been saying. All I could manage was to stare down at my feet as I rushed along, with airport security moving in to unblock the jammed path that only the flight attendant knew would lead to David and the car. My chin was skimmed as microphones were pushed into my face.

"Flight attendants. How long was the flight from Miami?"

I would have rolled my eyes at the question, but my head was still down, looking for places to step as the crowd surrounded us.

"Will Jonas Crane be coming out to give us a statement?"

"Will there be a joint statement tonight?"

The questions were flying faster than I could keep up. *A statement about what?*

"Move back," a security guard hissed, stepping in front of me and blocking the arms stretched out in front of us as we took more steps forward.

The voices of the press started to blend even further together.

"...coming here?"

"Combined fortune estimated..."

What are they talking about?

The security guard became even more determined to clear a path. "Stop taking pictures. You are going against our safety policy. Police are on their way," he yelled out repeatedly as we inched further along.

"I'll sue!" I heard someone call out as a new security guard joined us, moving with a bit more aggression. I was now hustled forward as the crowd was being forced to conform to their restrictions. I panted and glanced around the massive bicep of the security guard directly in front of me, with a blessing on my lips for the beefy warrior, as we continued down the pedestrian area.

"Jonas Crane!"

A surge in the opposite direction left enough of a gap for us to manage a quick retreat. *Is Jonas behind us?* My heart ached, thinking he might be left alone to face the crowd.

"Lily," I heard David call out, not realizing he was close enough to touch my arm. David took my hand and we ran to the car. I could now see the parking building ahead. Our flight attendant ran off to short-term parking. *I didn't even get a chance to thank her.*

"Get in, please," David said as the door opened.

Without a pause, I climbed inside the driver's door and crawled over to the passenger side as David scrambled into the driver's seat. He slammed the door to more flashes of cameras, quickly driving off and aggressively maneuvering the car away from the parking area.

"Why didn't anyone warn us?" David grumbled.

"Will Jonas be okay?" I asked.

"Mr. Crane will be fine," David answered with a curve of his lips.

I wiped the condensation off the window and noticed we had joined other cars on the road leading out of the airport. "Do you know what's going on?"

"I didn't get a full briefing," David said cryptically.

"Please, David. Tell me what happened," I tried again, but to no avail. David was now focusing hard on the road or hard on avoiding me. Just when I was about to give up, he gave me a half-answer. "Mr. Crane said he would prefer to discuss it with you later. I'm sorry."

I nodded. I liked David, and I knew he was only following orders. But he left me with the even more futile task of calling Jonas, which I ultimately decided against, only because I didn't wish to distract him from getting away from the airport.

Once belted in, I pulled the shopping bag with my handbag in it from underneath me, reaching inside to retrieve my possessions that had scattered along the bottom. David pressed the horn, increasing his speed to get us the rest of the way out. I closed my eyes and took a deep breath, using the sound of the windshield wipers flicking across the glass to settle my nerves. We were in the clear and off to Tribeca.

My shoulders relaxed into the leather seats as we crossed the RFK Bridge over to FDR Drive down to Tribeca, my mind moving just as fast imagining all kinds of scenarios to account for the scene we had landed in.

Jonas was well known, but not enough for the frenzy we had encountered at the airport. New York City had plenty of celebrities walking around, and in the years I had been here, I had never seen such a display unless something big and newsworthy had happened.

Was the closing of KeanexTech big news? I doubted it, for Jonas would have planned for that. Something else must have happened. And what did they mean about joint statements? I glanced back over at the tight-lipped David and folded my arms, sulking all the way back to Tribeca and dashing inside once he stopped in front of the building.

Walking in, the faint smell of patchouli oil crossed my senses and I remembered Mary was here, but had maybe just left. I turned on the lights and then took off my shoes and headed up the stairs to the master bedroom. Pausing for a look in the spare room, I spied Mary's fabric trolley next to the closet. *Why didn't she call?* I wondered.

I remembered then that I had turned my phone off for the flight. Turning it on, I watched it flash to life and looked at the time: 8:49. Placing the phone on the bed, I padded over to the walk-in closet and changed into a pair of jeans and a v-neck t-shirt, opting for a more presentable look rather than my usual choice of a tank top and sweatpants.

I cleaned up in the bathroom then returned to the bed and collected my beeping phone to retrieve my messages. There were three in total, from Mary, Dani and Gregor.

I sighed. Still nothing from Jonas. I decided to send him a text.

Are you okay? What's going on? Please tell me so I won't worry.

I immediately received his reply.

I'll be home to explain everything soon. Please trust me. I love you.

I exhaled and smiled as I went on to listen to the rest of my messages. The first was from Mary.

"I'm here! Ian picked me up, thanks. He's now taking me to Mars. See you both later."

Saucer Burger. I smiled and played the next message from Dani.

"Lily. I'm sorry about what happened. But I know Jonas is doing his best to make sure the damages are minimal. He loves you. We all do."

Damages? The ease I had experienced from Jonas and Mary's texts quickly evaporated. My stomach sunk. But I pressed on to listen to Gregor's message.

"Hi, I have some news. And, well, the damage is minimal compared to what else is going on. If you want to talk about it, or want me to pick you up, give me a call."

My pulse increased as my fingers swiftly navigated to Gregor's name and pressed connect. I knew Gregor would be more forthcoming with answers. He answered on the first ring.

"What happened?" I blurted out.

"I spoke to Jonas and he said he wanted to tell you,"

he said apprehensively.

My heartbeat picked up. "Tell me what?"

"You can call me after, no matter what time, and we can talk about it then," he responded.

"You're my friend and I'm really worried now. I have no idea what's going on, and Jonas isn't saying anything. Please just tell me. I'll think the worst if you don't," I pleaded.

He was quiet for a few seconds, but then said, "Okay, but keep in mind that it's been handled. A…photo was sent as a group message to everyone at work from your work satellite email address. But since we have a flag on adult material, it was blocked by our firewalls, quarantined, and flagged by IT pending review. The manager contacted me and, well, I contacted Jonas and the list of contacts he gave me. I also reported the breach to the police. I just wanted you to know that I took care of it and stopped it from spreading. So you have nothing to worry about."

My mind raced as I tried to understand what Gregor was telling me. "Wait. What do you mean?" Then awareness washed over me. "You saw me? My body? Declan sent photos."

"One photo," he muttered, and we both went quiet.

My pressure rose as my pulse leapt into my throat. Was it the same one Declan had sent me? Gregor would tell me the truth. "Are you sure it was me? My hands in my hair twisted up…"

"Yes," he finally responded in a hushed tone. "But it

didn't go any further. I'm sure Jonas's team is working to seal it. It was in the shower, that's all I know. I barely saw it. The second it came it was flagged, quarantined. It wasn't copied and the entire IT team knows that sharing it will result in a loss of their jobs. Not to mention prosecution. Nothing will come from Arch. I will never mention it again. I promise." He jabbered on, but I had tuned out as the implications of what he was saying heightened my nerves and scorched my skin.

"You, and people at work, and a legal team, and the police…have all seen the photo?" My voice was thick.

"Yes. I don't know. Not many. It wasn't widespread. We took steps to make sure it didn't go any further." He sighed, clearly uncomfortable. "I'm not saying this right," he replied and cursed.

All those people saw me? The phone slipped out of my fingers and onto the floor. My stomach muscles cramped and I ran to the bathroom, where I dropped to my knees before the toilet and vomited.

It didn't matter. His words had confirmed my fear. Sure, I knew he was trying to ease my worries, but the thought of that photo etched into his memory or the memories of all those who had seen it caused just the opposite. *How can I ever look at Gregor again? Or anyone else at Arch?*

Walking out of the bathroom, I dropped to the carpeted floor in the bedroom and started doing crunches and running in place as thoughts swarmed my head and tears blocked my vision. I felt like I needed to move, if only to clear my head.

The damage had been done. There was no going back. I stopped and wiped my now damp brow, yelling out a curse.

How could this have happened?

I sought to catch my breath as the adrenaline rushed through me. Picking up my phone once again, I paced as I called my old phone to check my voicemails remotely by password, only to find it had been changed. *Jonas changed it.*

He was determined to shut me out. But being in the dark didn't protect me, and now I needed to find another way to fix this. I was too far gone to sit down and idly wait or to listen patiently while my life went to hell.

I dumped the phone on the bed.

Knowing Declan, he would have called and warned of his plan. My mind crowed. *If only I had kept my phone and dealt with this myself.* I would have been okay.

I was lying to myself again.

I knew how angry Declan must have been when he couldn't reach me. I should have seen this coming. Once again, I had underestimated him. He truly was a boy, one who petulantly lashed out when he didn't get his way. And even after I did all he asked, he still hurt me more. Truly, he reveled in my pain.

I clenched my fist as I snatched my phone from the bed and pressed hard enough on the keys to hurt the tips of my fingers as I typed in Declan's phone number. It went to voicemail.

"You fucking asshole..." I yelled out venomously as I started to tell him once again what he had done and how he had hurt me. *No.* I reminded myself. *Don't give him your pain.* He would only delight in it. "Not a chance," I said, gritting my teeth.

The phone line beeped. Was that before or after I spoke? *Never mind.* I hung up and threw my phone down on the bed again. *Fuck Declan. He will pay for this somehow.*

"Lily, where are you?"

I heard Jonas's voice coming from downstairs and I sprang to my feet and rushed to talk to him. I found him in the living room, standing by the couch with his hand out, gesturing for me to come to him.

My mouth twisted on approach. "I spoke with Gregor and he told me about the hack and photos."

Jonas's face contorted. "I told Gregor that I wanted to tell you." For a moment I thought he was going to rage against Gregor, but then he said, "Never mind. He did his part. This is about your piece of shit ex. Yes, he got out of jail and sent a photo. But I don't want you to worry. He will be going back tonight, I'll make damn sure of that!"

I hesitated. Declan had been in jail? *Good,* I thought bitterly. But then I remember how this all had happened in the first place. I raised my voice and shot Jonas a steely glare. "It was a warning for me! If I hadn't been left in the dark I could have—"

Jonas interrupted. "Could have what? Stopped him? Or me? No. Not telling you was my way of protecting you from what needed to be done to that fucker. We didn't think he would be stupid enough to retaliate after his release with a trial pending. But my team will fix this—"

"It's too late now," I spat and sobbed. "My job is ruined. I mean, what the hell am I going to do now? I'm losing my life," I said miserably.

"He will be back in jail tonight. Trust me, if that piece of shit ever gets out again, he won't have a damn thing to return to. That, I can promise you!" he said furiously.

My anger lost some momentum once I met his now-desolate expression. His voice calmed, a hint of regret filling in around his words. "I didn't let you listen to your messages," he explained, "because they were filled with abuse and threats. I wasn't going to let him hurt you again." His face softened as we looked at each other. "It hurts me to see you in pain, and I wanted to protect you. I want you happy and safe with me."

My gaze was direct as I took his hands and held them firmly. "I am happy. I love you, and it hurts me to see you sad, but you have to give me a chance. I need you to trust that I'm strong enough to handle it. I'm getting better and stronger every day, but I'd be even more with you by my side, instead of trying to carry me. Please, Jonas. Share with me what's going on. Let me in for the both of us," I pleaded.

Jonas bit into his bottom lip as he took my hands and rubbed my knuckles with his thumbs. "I hear you. But I need you to remember it hasn't been long since I came to Arch and found you almost broken. My heart broke seeing you like that." He moved his hands to my hips and slowly pulled me into his arms. I didn't resist, though I didn't attempt to hold him back either. Sure, I wanted his comfort, but I needed him to stop sheltering my life more.

He stared down at me and I met his stare. "Lily, I do see you getting stronger every day and I'm proud of you." He took a long exhale. "You're right. If it was up to me, I would keep you away, but I see that's not possible when *we* are dealing with a man without limits or conscience."

My shoulders dropped. "I realized that too late."

Jonas ran his hands down my arms. "I wanted to protect you and keep you on your road to recovery. But I'll do whatever you need. I'll get you a new job or internship. Even a mentorship. I've already contacted—"

"I want that, and I know you have wanted that all along," I said, cutting him off. I pressed my lips together. "But I planned to work around my job at Arch until I could move on—on my own when I was ready. I didn't want to be pushed out, and Gregor said I'm not, though I don't know how comfortable we will be working together after this." *Especially with Gregor's feelings for me.*

The angles of Jonas's face went hard. "I could kill him." I knew he meant Declan, but I also knew he hated the fact that Gregor had seen that photo as much as I did. This was our reality, though.

"I want to be told everything. No more secrets for both of us," I said. "Can you respect that?"

He took my hand and I reluctantly allowed him to lead us to the couch, where we sat down. We moved to face each other. "Yes," he finally said. "I'll tell you right now all that has been done, and you will know what's to come. No more secrets…from me." He pulled out one of his handkerchiefs and wiped my cheeks. "I should have been here for you. I'm sorry I didn't make it back sooner tonight. You've been crying."

"I understand why you didn't get back earlier. The airport was overrun with press. You're here now, that's all that matters." I was going to stop there, but then thought better of it, realizing that if I wanted him to stop keeping secrets, I needed to do the same. "I got sick. And I started to exercise a little. But I stopped myself," I admitted.

Jonas tilted his head down and my chest tightened. "I wasn't here and you relapsed—"

I clasped his face, my eyes steady on his, which were now shimmering. My powerful Jonas, he loved me so much. So before he went back into protection mode, I spoke up. "I stopped. It wasn't a relapse, it was just a few minutes of trying to exercise away my anxiety. Even if you were here, I may have done the same, but I stopped. That's what matters. I know that's not the answer. I wouldn't have stopped before, but I stopped now." I dropped my hands and took the handkerchief, wiping over my face and damp brow.

Jonas nodded slowly, then picked up his briefcase from the side of the couch and placed it down on the coffee table. "The photo of you is only part of what's going on. With his criminal record…" He opened the case and removed some papers.

My mouth gaped. "He has a criminal record? I knew he had it rough growing up and had gotten into fights, but he has a business. Wouldn't that be difficult with a criminal record?"

Jonas handed me Declan's background check and criminal record. "Yes. It could be difficult, but not impossible with his background."

I let my hair cover my face as I looked over the sheet. 'Public Intoxication, Disorderly Conduct, Simple Assault, and Solicitation.' *Did I ever even know Declan at all?*

"He had a few calls out to his home recently, on domestic disturbance, but no charges were filed," he said.

I sat, dazed, as I touched the side of my face, the place where Declan had slammed it into the car dash. *Heather?* He did it to me, so why had it never occurred to me that he could be hurting her, too? "Heather, his fiancé, approached me at Arch the other day."

"When? Why didn't you tell me?" he said sharply, his voice raised.

I placed my hand on his knee. "I did tell you a woman approached me when we were there together, and that she ran off after telling me her name. Remember? I didn't make the connection until later. She didn't say anything more than introducing herself, so I didn't make much of it," I explained.

Jonas didn't say anything for a few minutes. Then, finally, he sighed and said, "Well, I'll have her name included in our next discussion on your cases. Here are copies of what my legal team has filed on your behalf."

He handed a stack of papers to me as he read aloud from one sheet. "Aggravated harassment and dissemination of unlawful surveillance, both criminal offenses committed by Declan." He placed it on top of my growing pile. "We have reopened your harassment and assault cases, though the police hadn't exactly closed your assault case because of the physical evidence."

I looked down at the filing forms and Jonas handed me a copy of the original file, with the paperwork I had signed for the harassment and assault. "How were you able to gain access to these, or to file cases, without my knowledge? I mean, I did agree to your help, but I should have at least had to sign—"

"It was in the agreement you signed for me when you moved in. My team and firm are on the filings," Jonas confirmed. "His work and home computers will be confiscated. We have contacts that are investigating his business practices, tax files, funding, and accounts. The building housing his business had a surprise inspection. I inquired on his lease..."

My eyes widened and my stomach turned over as

Jonas continued to speak about his plans for going after Declan's life. I suddenly understood why Declan had gone after my job with those photos. But Jonas had exposed his name and company on all the legal filings. *What if Declan goes after him too?*

"Tell me what you're thinking," Jonas said, bringing me back to him and taking the documents from my trembling hands. I closed my eyes and focused on my breath to stop the familiar fear from gaining ground. He breathed with me and waited for my answer.

"I'm thinking he's furious and may try to hurt you. I don't want anything to happen to you," I choked.

"All that you have gone through, and you're worried about me?" He wiped my eyes with his thumbs. Once they were clear, he gave me a look that stole my heart. "My sweet Tiger Lily, I love every inch of you." He paused and kissed my lips. "I'll be fine."

His confidence eased my concerns. And with his display of strength, I found mine. Declan wouldn't get away with anything this time, not if I helped.

"I want to be involved," I said in earnest. "I'll help complete reports, testify, whatever is needed," I said with a glance at the papers. But looking up, I saw doubt on his face.

So I spoke from my heart. "Just because I expressed my feelings doesn't mean I'm too weak to fight. I'm ready and behind whatever *we* do. But *I* need to be involved in ridding him from my life. I admit my stolen possessions have stopped me before..."

"His place was searched, but nothing was found. He may have your things elsewhere. We may not get them back, depending on what he's done with them." He took my hand.

I processed that for a moment, then said, "I wanted…want, my things, but I want *my life* more. So I'll sign, file, and testify. Whatever it takes to make sure he can't hurt anyone else. Even if it means I never see my things again." I sucked in air.

He wiped my chin. "Then that's what we'll work on together. Getting your life back."

Jonas leaned over and kissed me hard on the lips. "I know how hard of a decision that is for you," he said. "I'm proud of you."

I swallowed. "Thank you for telling me everything."

He kissed me once more and sighed. "I wish I could say that was all that was happening. But there's more." He squeezed the hand he was still holding. "The press at the airport…"

I had temporarily forgotten about that. So much had happened since. But a flash of dread ran through me. "Did Declan contact the tabloids?"

Jonas shook his head. "No. It was Melissa. She announced that we're engaged at a charity event tonight. She paired the news with press releases. When we landed, I received numerous congratulation messages and requests for interviews, among other things."

My brows furrowed. "I knew she wasn't done. I told you," I said in annoyance.

"Yes. I know. And every time I tried to reach her, she avoided me. But oh, was she ready to talk tonight. Threatening me with a press and talk show tour about our companionship if I don't marry her," he said and sighed.

"Do you have any idea why she chose now to announce an engagement?" I asked.

He massaged the space between his eyebrows. "No. We're looking into it. I should have answers soon."

It was me now moving to hold him in support. "So, what can we do?"

He looked past me. "I'm going to meet with my lawyers and see how best to move forward. I've only gone as far as releasing a 'no comment' statement. I'll have to approach this with care, especially with the press involved," he said and went quiet.

"What is our plan?" I asked.

"I'll handle it. I'll get this done, once and for all. But I have to be smart about it and not act impulsively. I could stay at the Waldorf tonight, and maybe even tomorrow, to keep the press off of you."

My lips pressed together. "You're leaving me?"

"If I don't, we'll be prisoners here and you'll be dragged into the public press," he said plainly. His plan was shaping into his old pattern and I had to stop it.

"No. I can handle it. I did tonight, and I'll do it again. I need you here with me, and you need me with you. And anyway, wouldn't she be winning by you altering your life?"

"The press is wide, and could uncover anything and everything. Would you want to be with a man that could be vilified? A womanizer, with a history of open relationships, companionships, and kinks? It will follow you. And Dani and Paul," he said.

Jonas wasn't one to cower. And from what I had come to know of Dani and Paul, he had their support, too. This was about me. He was worried about the press uncovering my nude photo. I didn't know if I could face it, as I was still reeling from Declan's mini-leak, but being hurt wasn't going to stop it from happening. While I hoped it wouldn't, I had to prepare for that possibility. *We* had to prepare for that possibility together.

I waited until his eyes met mine and said, "I can't speak for them but yes, I would. Because I love you and I'm proud of you. Would you want to be with the woman with nude photos that went viral, if Declan somehow found a way to do it? Or if the press got them?"

"Yes," Jonas said without hesitation.

I jutted my chin out, "Well, then, they're in for a fight with us."

"We'll fight together," Jonas agreed.

He studied me, but I knew exactly what he was seeing. I felt stronger and brave. I felt like my parents' Tiger Lily. And in that moment, I believed with all that I was that they would have been proud of me and my decision. Just as I was proud of myself and Jonas. He took my face in his hands and brought his own to mine, kissing me. "I'll call Ian and let him—"

The front door opened and David walked in. His sudden interruption and frazzled appearance had us both on alert.

"I apologize for the interruption, but this is urgent. Someone leaked you were here to the press and a crowd of reporters are now outside the building."

"Call Samuel and get him on it," Jonas said and turned to me.

My pulse sped up and my stomach flipped over as I anticipated Jonas leaving me behind to handle this all on his own. It hadn't been but a few seconds, but it felt like time had expanded as he stared at me. I lowered my head.

"We'll meet you in the office, David. Could you check and see if Lin is already on her way or see what we can do about dinner?"

My head lifted and so did my heart as his hand opened and reached out for me. I hurried over and closed mine around it and squeezed. "Thank you," I whispered as we walked off to the office to face what was to come together.

CHAPTER FOURTEEN

THE OFFICE WAS all brick, with mahogany and leather office furnishings, including a six-seat conference table with a state-of-the-art computerized note board between two flat-screen televisions. Like most of the loft space, it had a touch of old style with Asian rugs and clapboard flooring. Jonas quickly seated himself behind the large mahogany desk after sending David off to work with Samuel to get our late dinner and ensure security was in place. I used the spare phone next to the conference table to call Mary. When I couldn't reach her, I called Ian. He answered on the second ring. "Hi, Ian. It's Lily," I said.

"It's Lily," he announced.

Mary yelled out "Lily!" in the background.

"One second," Ian said. I could hear a muffling of the phone. After a few seconds, he spoke again. "Mary wanted me to tell you she didn't realize her phone is dead until now. She can't wait to see you," Ian said with amusement in his voice. "Everything alright?"

I chewed my bottom lip. "Not really. The press is

outside the building and along the block. The police and security have been called, but…"

"Mary will stay over here tonight. Hey, Mary. Oh, one second, Lily," Ian interrupted and left the phone again.

"What's going on?" Jonas asked.

I lifted my shoulders "I don't know," I said as loud laughter rattled my eardrum, and I held the phone away. "I think they may have been drinking?"

"Ian, drunk?" Jonas grinned and returned to his phone and computer. After a minute, Ian came back on the line and said slowly, "Mary is fine with staying here. We'll see you tomorrow."

"Can you put her on the phone?" I asked and smiled at Jonas.

Ian chuckled. "If you insist, but she's naked in the aqua massage," he responded. His voice elevated. I heard a scream of "no" and more laughter. *Yep.* Mary wasn't a big drinker, so it wouldn't take much.

"No. That's okay," I replied quickly. "Thank you, Ian, we'll see you both tomorrow." He hung up. I looked over at Jonas.

"The final statement to be distributed to all media contacts and channels will read, 'Jonas Crane is not engaged to or dating Melissa Finch. They are and remain lifelong friends,'" he said as he motioned for me to take the seat across from him.

I yawned and stretched before occupying one of the two empty chairs before the desk.

"I didn't realize the time before I sent David out for dinner, but he has picked up something fast and will have it here soon," Jonas said and rubbed his eyes. It had been a long day. "I've got a couple more calls, but we can work on the rest in the morning."

I nodded and he returned to the phone. After twenty minutes, David entered the room with Thai curry, which we both ate at the desk. Jonas's phone buzzed before we finished and his face lit up, which led me to believe it was Paul calling. "Just a second." He looked at me a twinkle in his eye. "I need to talk to Paul a little more about the plan he shared with us at dinner."

I gave him a toothy grin as I recalled Paul's announcement that he intended to lose his virginity. And soon.

My chest swelled at how Jonas tirelessly worked to please all of us. I met his gaze and answered the curious look on his face as he studied me. "You're amazing, my superman," I said jokingly and walked around the desk to kiss his cheek.

"Don't tell anyone," Jonas kidded and kissed my lips. "I'll be up soon." I gave him a quick hug, my own offer of assurance that I understood and he needn't worry. I would be there when he did.

"We'll go away together, just the two of us, soon," he said softly after I released him.

"I'd love that," I whispered and strolled out of the office and up to the bedroom, where I cleaned up and climbed in the bed, falling asleep fairly effortlessly.

The first thing I noticed when I woke up was that the blinds were drawn. Had the press been able to look in? We were up on the top floor, but this was a renovated factory with only seven floors, two of which were part of this bi-level house. The possibility of a long scope lens taking photos of us in here had me grateful for the darkness. Putting on my robe, I vowed never to walk around unclothed again. Not when we both had enemies.

Declan and Melissa had shown themselves to be cunning and impulsive. Both traits that meant you wouldn't fare well if you left yourself unguarded. I peeked through the binds and lowered my eyes to the street below. It was cleared, but only as far as a barrier at the end. I watched in dismay as one of the reporters with a camera approached a car pulling up at the end.

Jonas had released his announcement last night. Why were they still here? Had they found something else? I suppressed the sinking feeling and returned to the bathroom, where I showered and brushed my hair and teeth. The possibility was there, but I wasn't alone. I had Jonas and my best friend Mary, who was going to start her visit with us today. Was she on her way? Returning to the bedroom, I was surprised to find clothing left out for me to change into: a dress, underwear, and thigh-high stockings on the bed, as well as a handwritten note:

Mary and Ian will be over soon. Come on down to the office when you're ready.

I put on the underwear and stockings that he left out for me and thought on this simple act and what it had come to mean. Without doubt, there was his will and control in laying out my clothes. However, I realized now, it didn't end there. There was also attention and care, as well as assurance. His actions assured that I was his, that I was special to him and his heart. I exhaled long as I pulled on the dress. I was Jonas's and he was mine.

The sound of the door had me running to the bathroom to brush my hair quickly so I could see Mary. As I walked down the hall, the uneasiness I had when I woke up returned. At first, I didn't understand what had prompted it, but the answer became clear from the high-pitched cackle that soared up to me on the stairs. It halted me in my tracks. My face drained as I looked down toward the living room and saw who was now standing by the door. It was Melissa. She was arguing with Jonas. While I dreaded her presence and considered rushing down to bring a quick end to the unwelcome intrusion, I stood still for a moment and observed. Jonas had warned that we needed to be smart about this to find out just what she was up to. I needed to trust him to do that, so I moved myself out of their direct line of sight and listened in on the conversation.

"You can't be serious. You'll be ruined—" Melissa was saying.

"So will you. Give me the name of one person who released a tell-all book who wasn't ruined afterward," Jonas replied.

"You'll lose all your public appearances, endorsements—" she warned.

Jonas let out what sounded like a scoff and a laugh. "I *give* appearances and endorsements, I don't *need* them. I lead. I rule. Try again."

She laughed. "You're cocky for a man who stands to lose everything. Admit defeat. I'll be asked by all the major networks for interviews about you."

"We'll see, once I pull everything I have and sue them," Jonas said.

"They stand to make billions off my interviews. They can cover their loss of revenue from you. Once the world learns about your kinks, orgies, open marriage, and companionships, you'll have no friends left," she said.

"Media and the public can be fickle and cruel. I'll be an eccentric playboy with a past, but like most men in my position, I'll become lovable in less than a year. You'll be a whore forever, though."

She raised her hand, as if she was going to slap him, but he grabbed it in mid-air. "I don't think of you that way, but you're not the only one with things to share. I know you, too. Your psychology practice will be ruined. Who'll invite you to anything and risk you exposing or tarnishing their reputations?"

Melissa stared back at him.

"The media will play both of us, but I still have a business, and people still love making money. Or have you forgotten my father? And what about yours? How will Arthur feel about having his name tarnished and his privacy stripped? Not to mention every joint venture, sponsorship, and endorsement we have together."

"He'll stand by me," she said, though her face hinted at doubt. They looked at each other, her head tilting down. Jonas lifted a hand toward her, almost like he was about to offer her comfort, but he quickly let it drop back at his side.

"We both know better. Stop this now," Jonas said in a calm tone.

"You told me Dani was your one and forever. You said it was impossible for you to love again, but that if there was a way, you would love me," Melissa said dejectedly.

"I said I would never leave myself vulnerable to love and I didn't believe I was capable of loving again, which was true…until Lily. I never said I would love you," Jonas said. His tone didn't match the pain that his words elicited. I rubbed my chest. Hearing my name jolted me out of the trance I had fallen into while quietly watching them. I walked the rest of the way down the stairs and up to Jonas, reaching my hand for his. Melissa squared her shoulders as Jonas reached out and clasped the fingers I was offering him. That was when she walked away and stood before the elevator. "He won't marry you," she said.

"Or you. Good thing I didn't announce it," I said. My words were cruel and I could feel Jonas's eyes on me, but I kept mine on Melissa.

"You're no longer worth my time, gold digger," she

said dismissively to me as she pressed the call button.

"And you're not worth Lily's. Or mine," Jonas said. "You're not welcome here. So don't come back again."

The elevator doors opened. "You leave me no choice," Melissa said to Jonas and stepped inside.

"You don't leave me one, either. Good luck," Jonas said as the door closed. Once she was gone, he hugged me to him. "I know you were on the stairs listening."

I ran my hand over his back. "Yes. She doesn't seem to care what happens."

"If she was acting like the women I have known for most of my life, I would say she was posturing, but not this time. I wish I had seen that part of her before. She hid it well," Jonas said.

"I know the feeling," I said quietly. My pulse jumped as the elevator opened again and we let go of each other. I let out a sigh of relief when the high red ponytail and horn-rimmed glasses belonging to Mary came into view. She was wearing her twin of our green "Stages of Man" t-shirt and a pair of boot-cut jeans and sneakers. She was followed by Ian in his tailor-made business attire, carrying a briefcase.

"NuqeH!" Mary shouted out upon seeing me. "Wow, look at you. Where is Tiger Lily?" I ran in for a hug, and we twirled around each other. "You look so sophisticated in your fancy clothes. Strike a pose?"

I did an exaggerated vogue pose and, of course, Mary had to do one of her Elvis-esque ones. That had Ian and Jonas chuckling, while Mary and I both stifled our own giggles.

"I'm so happy to see you," I said and hugged her again. "Sorry about not meeting you, and the delay in getting back."

Jonas walked up and shook her hand. "Hi, Mary, and welcome. Glad you could make it. I'm sorry you didn't get my message in time."

"I missed the message, but thank you for inviting me," she responded.

"Thank you for hosting my friend," I said to Ian and grinned.

"It was quite a hardship," he teased, looking at Mary. She swiped his arm, rising to his bait. He caught her hand and released it slowly.

She blinked at him for a couple of heartbeats before she turned back to me. "Did you arrange brunch yet?"

Ian responded before I could. "We can order that pizza you devoured over lunch yesterday."

She snorted. "That was barely a slice. How that place passes that for a whole pie is a problem created by you pretty boy hipster types."

Ian stared at her before joining us in laughter.

I felt as though I had just entered a new space and time and was about to ask Mary to clue me in when Jonas chimed in, "Lin's bringing over lunch and should be here soon."

Mary rocked on her feet, hands clasped together excitedly.

I mockingly did the same and we beamed at each

other. "So, what would you like to do besides…?"

"Old movie night," we said in unison.

"Well, actually, we've planned to watch Star Wars episodes four, five, and six tonight, since we are staying in. I hope that's okay with you," she said and looked over at Ian, who confirmed with a nod.

I wasn't bothered, being that I had watched old movies with Gregor not long ago. I was more curious about the way Ian was looking at her, as well as how Mary was pretending not to notice, though I could see she was struggling not to laugh. She finally gave me a pointed look to get me to stop staring, but that only had me bursting with laughter. Jonas and Ian were looking at the both of us, so I asked, "What happened last night when we called?"

"We were only relaxing," Mary said, answering for the both of them.

Ian looked through her now and walked over to Jonas.

Mary adjusted her glasses and put on a smile. "If things settle down, how about we go to karaoke tomorrow night?"

That wiped the smiles off both mine and Jonas's faces.

I gave her a pained look. "Please, no karaoke."

"You'll have fun after a couple of drinks like you *always* do," Mary said and elbowed me.

"Oh, I would love to hear about that," Jonas teased.

I shook my head. "Once, Mare Bear. Not always."

"Mare Bear?" Ian repeated and laughed. "I'll be calling you that from now on."

Mary adjusted the rim of her glasses and lifted her chin. "You most certainly will not, or you're uninvited from our marathon tonight."

"They're my movies, so you can't un-invite me…Mare Bear," he said.

Her smile evaporated and I cursed myself for mentioning her nickname. "Please don't call her that," I spoke up.

Mary cleared her throat. "It's fine." I moved to take her hand, but Jonas slipped his arm around my waist, holding me back as Ian tugged the sleeve of Mary's shirt and she reluctantly followed. His voice was too soft for us to hear, but whatever he said into her ear had her laughing.

I looked at her questioningly, and she waved her hand, announcing, "He can stay."

The elevator opened again and Lin stepped and greeted us. "I have rosewater custard."

"My favorite," Ian said, giving Lin a smile that had her grinning and patting his arm before walking off. He smirked at Mary, who turned her head.

"Excuse us, ladies," Jonas announced, giving Mary *his* winning smile and throwing a wink to me. I ran my tongue over my lips, and Jonas walked up to me and pulled me into his arms and gave me a possessive kiss that he deepened enough to leave me panting once he let me go. He leaned over my ear, "I'm fucking you later."

While my face flamed, he kissed my forehead then walked off to join Ian, who I spotted turning into the office.

Mary linked arms with me and we walked off to the kitchen. "Ian warned me that you two were all loved up, but I must say," Mary mockingly gagged, which made me laugh.

I gave her a sly smile. "Speaking of, you and Ian seem awfully chummy."

She gave a quick shake of her head. "Hardly. He was nice on the call when I landed, but I could tell he wasn't all that impressed once we met up in arrivals."

My lips thinned. "Was he rude to you?"

She looked away. "Yes. No…well not exactly. He was all dressed up like today, pressed business suit and all. And…I was me." She gestured to herself.

I linked arms with her. "Perfect."

"That's right," Mary said with a jut of her chin as she pulled me in a tight hug. "You are too. Do you know I haven't slept well since we talked? I was so worried about you." She ran her hand along my back. "I couldn't wait to come down. I told Jonas I would just show up because I needed to see you for myself and make sure you were okay. I couldn't be shut out again. I love you and I'm here, my friend."

I swallowed and eased away. "I'm happy you're here," I said hoarsely. Our arms were still linked as we walked off to the kitchen.

"Come try my rosewater custard," Lin said, calling

Mary over with a tub and spoon.

Taking a taste, Mary moaned in delight. "This is delicious."

"Ian's favorite," I said to Mary.

She sighed in exasperation. "I greeted Ian in Klingon. Can you believe he corrected my pronunciation?"

Mary was awfully proud of her mastery of the Klingon language, so I sided with her and empathized, though I suspected Ian may have been teasing her. "I didn't realize he spoke the language."

"He didn't say much, but enough to flex his geek card, as if I was impressed," she rolled her eyes.

I pursed my lips to cover my grin. *She was so impressed.*

"I see two protein shakes marked for today still in the refrigerator," Lin sung out to me.

I reached in and took one out as she patted me on the shoulder. "You're looking better, Lily."

"Thank you," I said, the corners of my mouth lifting. We took our respective treats and walked out of the kitchen and up the staircase. "You seemed happy when I called yesterday," I said to Mary as we walked.

"We talked about Star Trek and Star Wars. You know I'm insatiable when it comes to discussing both with just about anyone who knows what they are talking about. He was making conversation, being polite. He didn't expect to have to spend the day and night with me," Mary replied once we reached the landing at the top of the stairs.

I frowned as we entered the spare bedroom. "I really am surprised. You seemed like you were having a good time last night."

When she didn't say anything more, I added, "Are you back together with Hans?"

She gave me a sour face as we walked into the spare bedroom, confirming all that I needed to know, but she answered anyway. "No. Hans and I are officially over. I'm done with college professors. I want someone that won't try to compete with me at every turn. I got an article published. So Hans announces he has two articles—"

"You didn't tell me!" I said, shocked and disappointed that I hadn't known she'd been published. I squeezed her shoulder then plopped down on the bed. "We must celebrate."

"I'm sorry, you just had so much else going on. It was only a small publication, but yes, I got published!"

Looking in her suitcase and finding it empty, she switched gears. "Where are my things?" I pointed her towards the closet, and then reached over and opened one of the dresser drawers at the same time. "Lin probably put them away for you. She did the same for me."

Mary smiled. "She's very nice. This place is beautiful. Ian's place is ultra-modern. I stayed up half the night just trying out some of his gadgets."

I gave her a goofy grin. "Oh really?"

She rolled her eyes. "Stop it with Ian. He doesn't like me. Besides, after Hans, I want a fling. No strings, preferably someone I will never see again. And I suspect I will be seeing plenty of Ian in the future, seeing as you and Jonas are committed. Right?"

I smoothed my dress. "Well, yes, I suppose."

"You suppose?" she said, frowning.

"I love him, and Jonas just told me he loves me, too. But I don't know what we will be beyond that given all the problems we are both experiencing lately. Plus, he's recently divorced. I doubt I'll be getting a proposal anytime soon," I replied, my voice nasally.

"Do you and Jonas have a plan for dealing with Melissa?" Mary asked, changing the subject.

I shrugged. "He released the statement, and he's meeting right now with his advisors. The media will move on soon." I turned and watched Mary pick up her laptop and turn it on. "Do you mind if I check my email? I have a couple of assignments I turned in that I want to make sure my professor received."

"Sure. By the way, is there anything you want to do besides movies and going out?" I asked.

"Get a haircut," she said.

"I'll call Dee." I walked off to the master bedroom and collected my phone from the bedside table. Dialing Dee's cell, I asked for an appointment for Mary.

"I can get…Marco to set yours, but if you want me to do her hair, it will have to be after my last appointment. So, 4:00 tomorrow?"

"We'll be there. Thank you, Dee. See you tomorrow," I said quickly and hung up as I returned to Mary. She was done and sitting back on the bed. "Would you mind if I check mine too?" I asked. She motioned for me to go ahead, and I discovered a new one from Gregor. "It's Gregor. Do you mind if I answer it?"

"Of course not. Gregor must be beside himself with the stunt that asshole pulled yesterday," Mary said, turning her head and picking up a magazine to give me some privacy.

Lily,

I'm really sorry for calling and telling you about what happened. My timing was off, but my intention was to let you know that we stopped and reported it immediately. We used discretion at Arch and I know Jonas's legal team will make sure it's handled with care too. So please don't quit over this, and let me know how you are…as okay as you can be under these circumstances, I hope. Sorry.

Gregor

I frowned. "Gregor's worried I'll quit over the photo."

I typed out "I'm humiliated," but quickly erased it. I was humiliated, embarrassed, and angry about the photos, though I worried that saying all those things would make Gregor feel bad. *But lying makes me feel bad.* I sighed and replied.

Dear Gregor,

I'm humiliated and upset, but I'm grateful you stopped the image from spreading. Thank you for telling me the truth. Mary's visiting.

Lily

I paused. I always included Gregor in movie nights, even when Mary came to visit. However, after what had happened with the photos, I wasn't ready to see him. Normally, I would try, but not this time. "I feel weird not including Gregor in movie night, but after what happened, I'm not ready to see him."

"I didn't expect you to, but I'm glad you told me what *you* wanted to do," she said with conviction. "No one would blame you if you decide to quit, but I hope you don't. At least not over this. I'm sorry about what that asshole Declan put you through. What are you leaning towards?" she asked.

I finished up my reply to Gregor with "I'll be in touch soon," and sent the email. Then I turned around and responded to Mary. "I don't know. I'm embarrassed, but I'm not in a position to quit. You know what a nightmare I experienced trying to find any work after graduation. I've been looking into options for running the Love Legacy program. And I will still eventually have to find my own place."

"Did Jonas mention you moving out?" Mary asked in a softer tone.

I shook my head and tilted it away from her.

"Well," she said. "I was thinking of doing an internship in New York City this summer. Maybe we could live together? I could help with the deposit on your new place. And you would have my income for half to help float you for a bit. Then I could help you find your new roommate, too, assuming you and Jonas don't decide to just get a place together."

Ignoring the hope her last sentence filled me with, I simply said, "That sounds great." She touched my hair, but didn't say anything. A new message caught my eye. Its subject line read:

> *Please Read. It's Heather.*

"What the hell is she writing me for?" I huffed.

"Who?" Mary asked.

"Heather. Declan's fiancé," I said.

Mary snorted. "What the hell. How did she get your email?"

"Declan had it," I reminded her.

"Delete and block her," Mary said as we both looked at the now-open message. But my curiosity wouldn't let me do that. I clicked on the subject line as Mary leaned over my shoulder to read.

> *Lily,*
>
> *I tried your phone, but it only goes into voicemail. I didn't get a chance to talk with you on the street. Declan was arrested at work on Monday. They came and arrested him again early this morning. He can't handle being in jail. He's talking about harming himself if he has to spend another day in there. I'm scared for him. He can't run his business. He's losing all he worked hard to build. He won't be able to pay his bills if he stays in jail.*
>
> *Dec said he's sorry for the mistakes he made with you and just wants to move on with me and our family. I'm pregnant. Dec has sworn to me and God he will never contact you again. Please drop the charges.*
>
> *If Declan has any of your things that he was holding*

for you, I can get them back. You can even come over to our place and search for them. Please just send me an email or call me. My number is 555-4348.

Sincerely,
Heather

"No way!" Mary said, her voice elevated. "Too fucking bad he's in jail. He deserves to be in there for all he's done to you! How dare she try to make you feel sorry for him? Dangling carrots in front of you! Tell her too bad and block her."

I glared at the computer screen. Marriage and family. Declan was giving her the marriage and family he had once used to woo me. Would he marry her? Declan wasn't a man of his word, so I had my doubts. I no longer trusted Declan and wouldn't be fooled enough to help him again. "I have no intention of dropping the charges. And even if I tried, Jonas said they had enough to go after him without me. Too bad he can't handle jail."

"Good, I can feel your anger…your journey towards the dark side will be complete!" she said in a poor impersonation of the Emperor Palpatine from *Return of the Jedi*.

I groaned and laughed. "Is this what I get to look forward to today?"

"Sorry, I couldn't resist. I am happy you want Declan to suffer," Mary said wickedly.

Did I want him to suffer? I thought about her words as I stared at Heather's message. I didn't want him to suffer, but I did want him to pay for what he had done to me.

I moved the cursor on the mouse to delete it and hesitated. I could be deleting my best chance at getting my book and photos back. I could be done with Declan once and for all *and* have my things.

"What are you thinking?" Mary asked.

I averted my eyes. "Heather is delusional, but she did say she would let me into their place to search for my stuff. I know his apartment. Maybe when they searched they missed it. I could look—"

"Absolutely not," Mary said heatedly. "Surely you don't believe her? She lays with the devil, she's a minion."

"But you don't understand," I said, raising my voice back at her. "You have your parents. This is all I have left of mine. I want it all back. I went through so much to get that stuff back. I was ready to let it go earlier, but with Declan in jail, I at least have a chance to get everything."

"I'm sorry I yelled," Mary said. "I know how important the photos and your book are to you. And I know how much they loved and cared for you. I loved them too, and it broke my heart when they died, but I don't trust anything that is linked to Declan. He's trying to manipulate you through her."

I hunched my shoulders. "I know that." I swallowed hard. She was right. But still, I couldn't help the heartache that followed when I deleted the message. It was like saying goodbye to my last chance at getting my things back.

"I should change clothes," Mary said.

"I have a shirt and jeans that I think you would look great on you," I said. Mary followed me into the walk-in closet. She eyed me speculatively as I searched through the clothes for the outfit I had in mind.

"How about this?" I said and handed her the new pair of jeans I had bought before my weight loss and a pale green shirt.

She immediately went about trying them on. "I know what you're trying to do. I'm not Ian's type. Trust me on this," she said as she smoothed the shirt in place.

I smiled admiringly at her in the clothes. Mary was pretty, but when she dressed up, she was stunning. And as far as Ian, nothing Mary said was convincing me I should give up on trying to hook them up.

"You look great." I grinned.

Mary turned a few times and a crease appeared on her cheek. "Thank you. Don't you want to take off that dress?"

I blushed. "Well, Jonas likes it."

"And wants to take it off?" Mary said, causing me to blush even more. "Then by all means, keep it on," she teased.

I lifted my chin and she lifted hers as we laughed together. We returned to the guest room to brush our hair, passing by Lin as she was heading into the master bedroom. "Lunch is on the table," she said.

"Thanks, Lin," we said. After putting our long hair into ponytails, we went downstairs and into the dining room area. The large oak table had been set with four sets of covered plates and a bottle of wine.

Ian walked up and we discovered Mary wasn't the only one who had changed clothes. He was dressed in a light blue button-down shirt and jeans. I looked over at Mary and saw she had also noticed, though she pretended to be very interested in the place settings.

"I thought we were hanging out here tonight. You two look good enough to take out," Ian said. He was staring at Mary.

"We looked good enough to take out with what we had on earlier, too," Mary chided.

"I meant that as a compliment," he said playfully, pulling the seat out for her.

"I can do that…thanks," Mary said as she took the seat.

Ian sat down next to Mary and started filling the glasses with wine.

"What's the name of the place in the East Village that has karaoke on Sunday nights?" Mary asked.

"The Blue Room," he said. "I've never been," he added, when he heard my giggle.

Jonas walk in to join us. I let my eyes roam over his dark shirt and jeans. I thought he looked amazing in suits, but he was mesmerizing in casual wear. He gave me a peck on the cheek.

"So, what did I miss?" Jonas asked, taking the seat

next to me.

"Nothing. We just started," Mary responded as we all uncovered our plates of paella.

"How about a toast? Anyone have a quote?" I asked, looking at Jonas just in time to see the corner of his mouth turn up.

"To new friends and new beginnings," Ian said and hit Mary's glass. It wasn't a quote, but his sentiment felt perfect for the four of us. We clicked each other's glasses and started eating.

"What movie are we watching tonight?" Jonas asked.

"Star Wars. An 'extra special exclusive edition'," Mary said with a bit of suspiciousness in her tone.

Ian gave her cool confidence back. "It is. Very few have ever seen this version."

They launched into a deep discussion, and Jonas leaned closer to me and asked, "Everything alright?"

I focused on my glass. "Yes. We were just catching up. We're going to Dee's Salon tomorrow."

"We're thinking of getting short haircuts," Mary said with a straight face, adding to our conversation.

I shook my head at her and laughed, knowing this was one of her social experiments. "I was thinking of getting a pixie," I teased. I had no intention, of course, but the look on Jonas's face was priceless.

"No. You won't," he said and sipped his wine. "That's too much of a drastic change."

"Don't cut your hair short," Ian said to Mary.

"I wasn't really planning on it," Mary said. "Though

I will get a trim. This was merely a short experiment, gentlemen. And you have proven that men are addicted to long hair."

"Fine," Jonas said, squeezing my thigh. "I prefer longer hair."

Ian scoffed. "That's not true, though. Not about all men. My last girlfriend had short hair."

"*Last* girlfriend," Mary repeated with a smug expression on her face.

"Shoulder-length and, if I recall, she cut it after you got together and again before you broke up," Jonas said, stirring the pot. Ian gave him a pointed look and I covered my mouth to suppress my giggle.

Mary was not letting go of her thesis. "Studies have shown there is a high percentage of breakups over an alteration of the physical elements that initially brought on the attraction. Any drastic changes could, and may, end a relationship. I believe men who are obsessed with appearances are especially quick to end said relationship, with the maximum time being three weeks after the haircut occurred. Would you care to share when the haircut occurred, compared to when your relationship ended?" Mary asked, eating her paella and ignoring the daggers Ian was giving her between bites of his own.

"We didn't end over hair. I'm not shallow. She was a bit of a know-it-all and I got sick of her dribble," Ian said, actively choosing to ignore Mary's snorts.

"Mary, tell us about your program," Jonas asked, ending their standoff. Mary eased into a discussion about her Sociology Master's program at Boston College, which led Ian and Mary off on another conversation about continued education.

My thoughts shifted back again to Heather and the possibility of collecting my things from Declan's. *Maybe if someone came with me during my search?*

Jonas studied me, finally asking. "Something happened? Tell me."

I nodded. "I was going to wait until later. I received an email from Declan's fiancé, Heather."

"When? How? Give me details," Jonas said, his voice cross. Mary and Ian stopped talking and looked over at us.

I sighed. "Today. The email was sent to my personal account, not work. Declan must have given it to her. She was asking me to drop charges and help him get out of jail. I won't. So that's it."

Jonas stroked a finger under my chin, getting me to meet his eyes. "I want to know right away. Anything that affects you is too important to wait."

"It was right before we came down here. I was there when she read it. Heather making grandiose offers to Lily," Mary added to the conversation. "She actually said Lily could go over to Declan's and search his place while he's in jail."

I looked over at her to avoid the weighted stare I was getting from Jonas. "I was going to share that part with you, but Mary beat me to it."

"You swore in your affidavit that you had no relationship with Declan. If you go over there and search his place, it will ruin your theft allegation and compromise your other cases. Tricky bitch," Ian said hotly.

Mary nodded at Ian as they bonded before my eyes. "I knew it! She's Declan's Siren, trying to ruin your progress," she declared.

Ian gazed at Mary for a few heartbeats before turning to speak to the rest of us. "Abusers are often master manipulators. They play upon weaknesses. If a person is still with them, they are under their influence and can't be trusted. Sorry, Lily."

I stared down at my food. *Like me.* Ian's words stung, but they were true. I had been under his influence for a long time, and had covered and lied for him many times. Heather was probably experiencing the same.

If so, she had also been asked to get a response. And I knew what happened to me when I didn't give him answers. "He could hurt her and her child. What can I do?"

"You don't know that, and it's not your place to get involved," Mary replied.

"If you still have the email, we'll give a copy to Diane. She is heading your criminal case," Ian said, looking at Jonas. He next turned to me. "We'll get Diane to send a referral to Heather for the local domestic violence organization, but you are not to have contact with her until after your cases are closed. That is, if she will want to talk to you after he is convicted."

I felt a queasiness in my stomach. "I won't compromise my case. So can we move on and talk about something else now?"

"Of course," Mary said, and Ian agreed. They went back to their discussion of Boston.

Jonas touched my hand and leaned down by my ear. "I'm happy you told me, and I also know it's hard for you, but our intentions are good. We all care about you and want you safe."

I nodded. "I know. I didn't see that I was being manipulated by him again. The offer Heather made was too good to be true, I guess."

"You're more important than your possessions," he reminded me. I took the kiss he placed lightly on my lips and we all ate the rest of our lunch, engaging in light conversation between bites.

Afterward, we went in the living room, where Ian put in the movie and Mary helped flip the television to the right channels to play it. Jonas and I sat down on the couch. Mary sat next to me, and Ian sat down next to her as the movie started. After we had watched for twenty minutes, Mary admitted. "Okay, Ian. You do have a version I've never seen before."

Ian grinned at her and they started talking together through it.

"You're not interested in this movie," I said to Jonas, leaning over to his ear.

"I'm interested in you," he said.

My body warmed and my pulse sped up as I scooted in a little closer to him and tried to focus on the film.

When the first ended, Mary got up and came back with a tray of the rosewater custards. She placed them down on the table, handing them out to all of us as we delighted in the delicious taste.

"Why are these portions so small?" Ian griped after polishing his off with a few spoonfuls. He sought Mary's small bowl and she twisted away, giggling. "Not a chance, Unger." He had her by the hips, but Mary twisted away and scooped the rest in her mouth. Some of it had smeared around her lips. He pinned her and licked off what little was left there and let out a triumphant groan. Mary, to my surprise, was speechless for the first timc all night.

After watching their show, I finished mine and placed it down. "I think it's my favorite, too," I said, turning my head toward Jonas.

"You can have mine," he said lifting his last spoonful before my lips. I ate it and he kissed me, our cold lips heating up as we deepened the kiss. No words came from Ian and Mary. Were they sharing a kiss too? When our lips parted, they were sitting closer but watching the movie.

My eyes lingered on Mary as I collected the bowls, but she was giving the credits rolling past all of her attention. So I moved on to the kitchen and cleaned the bowls before returning to the living room. I sat down as close to Jonas as I could get, though I wanted to be closer. Without a word, he lifted me into his lap and a shiver went through me at the thought of how well in tune Jonas was to my desires. He ran his hand over my head, willing me to place it down on his shoulder, to which I complied. He cuddled me close. *He's my home.*

Whatever was to come, this was where I wanted to be.

CHAPTER FIFTEEN

"SO HOW WAS last night with Ian?" I asked Mary for the second time at breakfast in the kitchen the next day. I had dozed in the middle of the second film and was carried away to bed, where I promptly fell asleep—well, after making love. Yes. Jonas and I made love. Whether it was quick, slow, hard, or soft sex, there was love between us.

"What do you want to know? I told you we watched a few episodes of Star Trek after you and Jonas went to bed. We made bets, which Ian lost, and we devoured the rest of rosewater custard we found in the freezer," Mary responded between bites of French toast.

I smirked before eating a bite of the toast off of my plate. "I want to know more than that."

Mary sighed loudly and opened her laptop. "We didn't have intercourse last night. Okay?" she said. Her tone was a bit snippy, and she quickly added an apology.

Frustrated? I mused to myself and opened my laptop.

"He's off-limits," she said and sipped her orange juice.

"If you say so," I said, my voice light as I ate the rest of the toast on my plate.

"I do," she said quietly. Her lips turned down as she stared at her screen. "Everything okay?" I asked.

She gave a wave of her hand. "Hans being childish again. He hasn't signed off on the independent project I did with him last semester, but I'll handle it." She went back to eating, so I opened my laptop and logged onto my email. Checking my new messages, I discovered one from Ian. "Ian sent me a message. I didn't know he had my email."

Mary looked up from her laptop. "I gave it to him last night. So you can forward over that message from Heather."

I opened and read his message.

Forward the message from Heather.

Thanks,
Ian

A man of few words. I opened my delete folder and recovered the message, just as I noticed there was a new one, too. I sent the one from yesterday to Ian, then read the new message.

Hi Lily,

I went to visit Declan in jail and he gave his blessing in having you over to find your stuff. He said he was out of his mind at the time and has no idea where they could be. I searched myself, but I really don't understand what I'm looking for. Maybe you can tell me?

Did you know he's suffering from an addiction to

pain medication? He also was diagnosed with impulse control problems a long time ago, but couldn't afford to get help. Now with his business closed during his busiest season he may not financially recover. He's been in prayer and wants to do the right thing. He told me to tell you his first act of penance is to apologize to you. He's willing to do it in person. I'll be there so I promise it will be okay. I work near your office. If ever you want to talk, I go to Sophie's for my lunch pretty much every day. He's getting help, now all he needs is a little help from you.

Sincerely,
Heather

I moved the cursor to hover over the reply key. Did she know Declan was manipulating her or was he different with her?

"Lily. What's wrong?" Mary asked, frowning.

I blew out my breath. "Another message from Heather."

Mary moved my laptop to read it and let out a huff. "He's coming up with a medical excuse to use as a defense," Mary chided. "Please don't believe him. She has some nerve trying to make you feel bad for him."

I tilted my head. "He's probably pressuring her to keep trying to get me back under his control. I know that, but I still feel sorry for her." Mary watched as I forwarded the new message to Ian and shut down my email.

"You can't save her. Ian said the best thing for her right now is Declan in jail. So if you want to help her, help him stay there." Mary moved her cursor and turned her screen around to show me a view of a website. "Ian recommended a new spa he uses called Verses on Bleecker Street. His skin is flawless close up." Her eyes flicked to the computer screen. "Anyway, he said the facials make your skin as soft as a newborn. He lost our bets last night, so we get his appointments, or something like that." She waved her hand. "It's a short subway ride. What do you think? Or do you need to tell Jonas?"

Jonas had left earlier to take Paul to their rescheduled baseball game at Yankee Stadium. The building had security and the street was free of press. Jonas was their target, so I didn't see any reason why we shouldn't. "I think it will be fine. I'll just send a message to him." *After we leave.* I thought.

"Great. I'll go get my handbag and we can leave for the spa right away," she said, firming up our plan.

"Alright. I'll just change quickly and we can go." We ate the rest of our brunch and cleaned the dishes before getting up to get dressed. I changed into a silk jersey t-shirt and cargo pants with low heels. Putting my hair in a messy braid, I grabbed my handbag and phone before going downstairs to meet Mary, who was at the door waiting for me, and we left.

The sunshine had finally returned, coupled with a cool breeze that blew our jackets and hair as we walked down the sidewalk. Passing the security guard outside of the building, I peered down to the end of the block and noticed the barrier was moved aside. There was no sign of the press. I let go of my breath and fell into pace with

Mary as we walked past the factories and galleries in the area until we reached the Chambers Street subway and descended the stairs.

Although I had caught the subway hundreds of times since moving to Jersey City, I hadn't realized how much I'd been spoiled by the smooth, spacious rides of the car. Digging out my old subway card to add funds and waiting with the passengers to board in the cramped space was exhausting. The Bleecker Street stop couldn't come quick enough.

Mary, on the other hand, soaked it up, adding change to the jars of subway performers and complimenting a woman's crocheting. I stood rigid by the door, holding on to the metal pole as passengers bumped into me to rush to an available seat. The car soon filled up and we were sandwiched together as more boarded the car, making it oppressively hot. When we finally reached our subway stop, I rushed up the flights of stairs, not stopping until I reached outside, where I gulped air to catch my breath.

"Are you okay?" Mary asked.

I nodded, catching my breath. Once I calmed, I looked around to get my bearings, and that was when my heart stopped.

"Isn't that bastard's shop over here?" Mary asked, wrinkling her nose. The sign for Verses Spa was on the beginning of the next block. The direct route passed Parco's and Declan's import-export shop.

While I was deciding what to do, Mary moved with

purpose towards his shop, leaving a trail of curse words behind her. The path was set, and I took tentative steps in the direction of two places that held some of my worst memories. Clutching the strap of my handbag tightly in my grip, I walked down the almost empty sidewalk, reaching Parco's first. My mind said to run as I replayed the sequence of Declan slamming my head against the dash of his car. My breathing quickened as I passed the door. I couldn't stop myself from looking inside and staring at the small tables, some with patrons chatting and eating. I cupped my hand over my mouth, the normality of the scene leaving a distaste on my tongue.

I shifted my gaze to the sidewalk and moved forward, closer to his store, half expecting to find him standing outside smoking a cigarette, something else he had lied about giving up a while ago. But to my relief, there was only Mary peering in the darkened window.

"You're lucky it's closed, asswipe," Mary said ardently.

The store *was* closed, just as Heather had said in her email. From the dust and fliers outside, it had been closed for at least a few days, though I couldn't be sure. Nonetheless, Declan wasn't there and Jonas's plan was moving forward. I clutched my purse and stared at the closed sign. I couldn't help but think on the years he spent building it. Seeing the work possibly destroyed was disheartening.

"Declan hit you and was hateful to you. He stole from you. He's the reason you're on stress leave. He tried to ruin your job. Didn't you say he showed his coworkers the photos, too?" Mary said, uprooting the twinge of guilt that was trying to plant itself in my conscience. She was harsh, but she gave me what I needed, a dose of reality.

"I lived it. I know all that. I'm still scared. When will I stop being afraid of him?" I said to myself as much as I said it to Mary. *Will I always feel this way?*

"Give yourself some time," Mary said softly. Linking arms, she and I walked to the end of the block and crossed over to Verses Spa. Mary opened the door and asked. "So, what did Jonas say about the subway? I'm sure he probably spoke to Ian. I hope he didn't send David."

I moved back from the door and fumbled with my phone. "I didn't tell him." I pressed reply on an old message and typed in.

Mary and I took the subway to Verses Spa. Hope you're both having fun. Got to go.

My phone beeped immediately with an incoming reply.

David called and told me you left. I'm not happy.

"You're in trouble?" Mary asked biting her lip.

I felt a pain in my chest. "A little," I said before writing back.

Declan's in jail. His shop is closed. I sent the new email from Heather to Ian. I'm with Mary. I'm not alone.

Jonas sent a response.

With everything going on are you seriously arguing with me? David will pick you two up.

He had a point. I responded.

You're right. Talk to you later.

I followed Mary inside the building. Verses was filled with white and grey décor with soft chrome accents. I peered up at the lit sign on a series of screens that listed the selection of services as Mary gave our names to the female receptionist.

"Great. Everything is set. You can both take a seat and someone will be with you shortly."

Mary started to walk away, but I asked. "I didn't have an appointment and I was going to see if I could schedule a manicure and pedicure?"

She stared at the computer screen before her. "The appointment was changed to two this morning and services were added for Mr. Unger?" She glanced up and I nodded. "Full facial, body scrub rejuvenation, wax, massage, manicure and pedicure. I'm sorry, but it's too late to alter the services now."

"Oh. Thanks," I said and nodded.

Mary laughed "Ian lost a bunch of bets with me last night. He really shouldn't gamble. I mean, can you believe he didn't know the real name of Whorf?"

I smirked. "Absolutely not."

"Exactly," Mary said and looked away. "I played along with his game to pretty me up."

I had started to suspect as much as well, but it hammered the point home to hear her acknowledge the reality of these appointments out loud. She gave a handwritten card to the receptionist and I followed her to the waiting area. We sat down next to each other in two of the available white cushioned chairs.

I pursed my mouth. "You're beautiful Mary. You don't need Ian Unger to tell you so." I took my phone out and texted Jonas.

Ian is playing Mary with the spa. I'm not happy.

Jonas wrote back.

He's not playing, but now we are both unhappy ;) Got to go.

I grinned and put the phone away. After a few minutes, we were escorted into a locker room to store our things and put on robes. Déjà vu, though they had chocolate-covered strawberries here. I clinched my robe and went to sit with Mary, who was tucking away a few magazines along the long chrome coffee table. I reached out to see what she was hiding and was struck immediately by the cover photos. Jonas Crane and Melissa Finch stared back at me. Picking up one of the magazines, I sat down in the seat next to her and flipped through it to the article. *Crane and Finch: Empires Unite For Love and a Whole Lot of Money.*

"Don't read that crap. They know nothing," Mary whispered.

I read on anyway. The page had a chart highlighting the similarities between the two of them. They both were from old, wealthy New York families and at the top of their careers—though Jonas was described as 'a business deity,' well established, influential, and good looking.

The article had Jonas linked to a few starlets I hadn't known about after his marriage, with a chart showing how long they had lasted before he moved on—an average of two months. All except for Melissa. She was in his life for many years. She had, according to the article, "What it takes to get the illustrious divorcee too settle down again."

While I was sure of Jonas's love and that he wouldn't be marrying Melissa, I wasn't sure of how long we would remain together. I had him for now, but knowing all that he was, I couldn't imagine keeping him forever.

The thought sunk my heart and left me feeling less than refreshed as our appointment continued.

When David picked us up, we went through a drive-through for a late lunch and still made it in time for our afternoon appointment at Dee's Salon. The lights were all on, but the sign in the window read 'closed.' Dee had warned me that we would be the last appointment of the day. We walked through the glass door and a bell sounded. Mary's phone buzzed just then and she answered it while we waited in the empty reception area.

My mind drifted over last night with Jonas and the many ways he continued to show me how much he loved and cared about me. Love was what I had and could give, but would that be enough for a man that had everything?

"Oh, yes. Better. Definitely better. You look exceptional. What are you wearing? Marc Jacobs?" Dee questioned as he broke through my thoughts and gave me a hug. Dee was standing there wearing one of his signature outfits, designer jeans, printed t-shirt, and leather shoes. He eyed me from head to toe and whistled.

"Yes. I believe it is, but I'm not sure," I mumbled

against his shoulder as I reached up and touched his ponytail.

"Like it? I'm growing my hair out," Dee said, releasing and turning me as he lifted the collar on my dress. "Yep. I'm good. He pulled my ponytail out and fluffed out my hair. "Well, someone did their job on you. Your skin looks better too. Getting sleep, and what else?" He let me go and I blushed and laughed. "Oh lord. She's getting some too. Must be good with that laugh," he said and laughed with me.

I motioned Mary to follow us back to his station as Dee took my hand. "You can go short with your hair now, if you still want to do it," he said, motioning for me to take a seat. I tried to suppress my laugh. *That won't be happening anytime soon,* I thought.

"Dee," I said, pulling Mary up next to me. "This is my best friend Mary. She's here for a new style today."

Mary held her hand out, which Dee took as he did one of his polite assessments. "Red. Curvy. Cute glasses, though I bet she's hiding some beautiful eyes behind them. Clothing has patchouli oil college girl all over it. Send that back and pick up *Dolce and Gabbana* fragrance today. I'll give you a sample. I promise, you'll love it." He turned to his Assistant Marco and me as he said, "She's a swan. I can work her into a...Mad Men Maven."

Mary's bow mouth broke into a wide smile, and I could have hugged Dee again. She turned to me. "Mad Men?" she mouthed.

"Oh, I'm Dee's Tim Burton Beauty," I said, taking the spare chair.

"Films and television references for style. I love your ideas. Please make me a Mad Men Maven," Mary said. Dee motioned for his assistant to come over and take care of me. He started spraying my hair as Dee fussed over Mary.

Removing her glasses, Dee said, "Look at these pale green eyes. Mascara on these long lashes will bring him to his knees. Push up bra, burn the one you're wearing. Show off that cleavage, and please, no more baggy t-shirts."

"Oh, I plan to show more than just cleavage this break," Mary trilled as Dee put on a cape over her clothes and took her over to wash her hair.

"Oh, what're you planning?" Marco asked Mary, suddenly curious as he sat me down at the station next to her.

"A holiday fling," she said with a sly grin. "I just have to find a guy."

"Oh, I like her," Dee said and smiled at me.

"What kind of a guy do you want?" Marco asked. "I'll tell you where in the city you need to travel to get him. Do you want a dominant businessman?" That had my face warming. "Hipster? Motorcycle man? Hell, I can even tell you where to get yourself a cowboy in New York."

Mary tried to lift her soapy head, but Dee put her back. "Just talk."

"No suited hipsters. I don't even want him to talk too much. He has to be sexy, though," Mary said.

"You want the Three G's—grab, grunt, and grope?" Dee said and we all laughed.

"Volte Bar. No muss, no fuss," Marco interjected. "But don't go tonight, it's private. You can dance there, too. But don't hold a blue light to your dress later. It'll light up like Christmas."

I gave her a smirk she couldn't see. No matter what she said, I highly doubted Ian would watch her cozy up to someone else tonight. "You haven't shared how you plan to meet this fling while you're out with me, Jonas, and Ian?"

"We're all friends. Ian and I are not together," Mary responded, shutting down me and Ian in the space of a few words. "So what was that you said about a dress, Marco?" Mary asked.

"Throw it away and never tell anyone you went there," Marco said and rinsed my hair.

Dee scrunched up his face. "Don't listen to him, ladies. These two are not ready for that kind of wild aggression. And I doubt Lily's man will let her go there, unless he's a sleaze bag." He picked up a magazine and flipped it to show Mary some of the latest fashions. "Wear stilettos like this, Mary. You don't need to go to a desperate dive bar. Everyone wants to get laid. Just go for quality. Shake your butt in a castle, you'll be asked home. You understand? We'll go over your colors after this." Dee rinsed Mary's hair. "Lily, what does your man look like? Because your last one wasn't even cute." He wrinkled his nose. "What's his name again?"

"Jonas... Jonas Crane," I said with a bit of a stammer. "I've got photos."

"Let's take a looksee," Dee said as we all moved back to the seats. When Marco toweled my hair I took out my phone and found a photo and handed it over to Dee.

Dee fanned himself. "Whoa! He's yours? Exceptional."

I touched my face and grinned as Marco started trimming and rolling my long black hair to my now normal large curls that fell a few inches past my shoulders.

"Oh she has it bad," Dee said, cutting layers into Mary's hair.

"Yep. Loved up. Jonas has the look, too," Mary said as she glanced at the picture.

"He looks familiar," Marco said when he looked at the photos. "Is he an actor or celebrity?"

"No. He's a businessman," I said and put the phone away, my face falling as the highlights of the article from the spa came to mind again. *I have him for now.* I attempted to remind myself.

"He's more than a businessman. He's a mogul. Celebrated in the business world," Mary said. "Lily's worried some hag will steal him away, but she needn't worry. He's absolutely crazy about her."

Dee looked over at me and lifted his chin. "Listen. He can't be stolen. If he's yours, he's yours. You're gonna have to learn to adjust. Exceptional men like us need an understanding partner."

Marco dried in my curls and I beamed at Dee. "You are exceptional." He gave me a broad smile.

When we were done, Mary kissed Dee on the cheek. She was thrilled with her new look. I was also happy to see what Dee had done for Mary. He had added a part to her scalp, making her hair fall across her forehead into curls and waves that flowed in layers down her shoulders and back. He threaded her brows and added a little pencil, making perfect arches over her pale green eyes, which were now enhanced by shadow and mascara. A little blush accented her cheekbones, making them more prominent in her angular face. The high gloss to her perfect bow lips set everything off beautifully. She truly looked sensational.

Dee went on to make up my face, adding the smoked colors he liked around my large silver eyes and a couple of layers of mascara on my thick lashes. My cheekbones got a light skim of pale blush. They stood out prominently on my heart-shaped face, more so since my weight loss. He added a pale gloss to my full, lush mouth, and beamed, pleased with his work. So was I, though I always wished I could make it look exactly like he did at home.

I texted David to let him know we were ready to go.

"God, you both look good. Mary, get over to Bloomingdale's and get some clothes," Dee said as he walked us to the door. "Keep it up, beautiful girl. Whatever it is you're doing, keep doing it. He makes you happy, the rest will work out."

My eyes watered and he tutted. "You're ruining your makeup." We hugged each other. "Oh well, put it back on later," Dee said.

"Thank you, Dee. See you soon."

"Take care of your friend, gorgeous," Dee said to Mary.

"Always. I love my look. Thank you again, Dee," Mary said. He unlocked the door and with a wave, we left the salon.

David pulled up and I quickly climbed in. Mary followed, closing the door. I reached inside my purse and started to send a text to Jonas, but stopped myself. I put the phone away and smiled, joining in with Mary on praising the salon and spa treatments. After a brief stop at Bloomingdale's, we went back to the loft.

We walked inside the loft to the sound of the piano and I recognized this time that it was Paul playing the music he had shared last week. Mary and I quietly removed our shoes and padded over to the living room, where we found Jonas standing with Dani next to the piano. Their arms were resting casually around each other as they watched Paul so absorbed in his performance. Jonas saw us first and, as our eyes connected, the air charged between us. He broke away from Dani and came up and brushed my lips. The music stopped and I looked over at Dani, whose face lit up. She walked over to join us.

"Lily," Dani said and gave me a hug. The fabric of

her blue cashmere turtleneck was soft against my cheek. "You look beautiful." She turned her head and looked at Mary and smiled. "The both of you."

"This is my best friend, Mary," I said in introduction. "This is Dani." She let go of me and surprised Mary by giving her a hug too. "Nice to meet you, Mary. I'm Jonas's best friend," she said, borrowing my words.

"Yes, she is." Jonas confirmed. "And my ex-wife," he added without animosity or wistfulness in his tone. "We were just enjoying Paul's piece he will be performing at a recital soon."

Paul strolled up, his hands in his pockets. "Hey," he said in greeting.

"Hello Paul. You play beautifully," Mary said enthusiastically. He raised his shoulders and glanced back at the piano. "Thank you," he said softly. His eyes flicked over her then down to the floor, where they stayed.

Jonas, Dani, and I looked at Paul and back at Mary.

"I'll just go put my things away and get ready for tonight. Nice meeting you both," Mary said and walked off to the stairs. Paul's eyes followed her before he walked back to the piano.

"Did something else happen?" I asked.

Dani and Jonas smiled. "No. Nothing since our press statements," Jonas said and walked over to Paul.

Dani motioned for me to take a seat with her. "How are you doing?"

"I'm alright..." I said.

"Considering all that is going on," Dani finished for

me. "Well, if the press moves forward, things will change for all of us. I've made my peace with the past," she said and took a deep breath. "Anyway. I wanted to tell you how much I admire you and your strength."

I looked at my hands. "Strength? I'm still afraid of my ex and what could happen with Melissa and the photos."

"Admitting you are afraid takes strength. Going forward with your charges takes strength. Going out with your friend today takes strength. I admire your strength," Dani said.

I looked up into her face and found nothing in her expression but seriousness. Her words and admiration touched the pain and negativity I had about myself. "Thank you, Dani," I said, my voice thick.

"I agree," Jonas said, walking up with Paul. Dani rose. "We are on our way to an evening meditation."

"You alright, Paul?" I asked, bringing his attention back to us as he stared off.

"Yeah. Everything's good. Your friend staying for a few days?" he asked.

"Through tomorrow, but she's looking at coming up for the summer. We're looking into a place together," I said and chewed my lip.

"Oh. I thought…" Dani looked at Jonas and me, then took Paul's arm. "I'm sure you will see Mary again." We all walked over to the elevator and said goodbye and they left.

"Paul alright?" I asked. "He seemed unusually shy."

He chuckled. "Yeah, hormones. I think he might have been a little smitten with Mary."

I giggled. "Sweet." I turned and started walking toward the stairs.

"Speaking of Mary." Jonas added. "I'd have liked to have known your plans to move in together." His voice was light as he followed me.

I stopped walking and averted my eyes. "She made the offer yesterday. I'm sure you'll want to get something permanent."

"Yes. Dani gave me a few places to view," Jonas said, his hands pushing through his hair.

I nodded, unable to speak.

"You okay?" Jonas said, placing his hands on my hips. I wrapped my arms around his waist and hugged him.

"Yes. I'll go check on Mary and take a power nap before getting ready."

"Alright. Ian will be picking us up in a couple of hours. I have a few things to do too. Maybe I'll crawl into bed with you after I'm done," he said.

I didn't answer, but took his kiss before heading up the stairs.

CHAPTER SIXTEEN

WE WALKED INTO the small bar in East Village. A woman that looked the spitting image of Bettie Page took our cover charge as we listened to a Janis Joplin wannabe do a gritty version of "Me and Bobby McGee." Ian was staring at Mary. In fact, other heads turned her way when we walked into the main room as well.

There was a small stage along the center with dark velvet curtains and small circle tables for seating. I talked Mary into wearing a pair of my stilettos with dark denims that hugged her curves and a v-neck silk shirt in light green she bought from Bloomingdale's. Her red curls swept in waves just past her shoulder, and though she had on her glasses, she kept Dee's makeup style he showed her. She was looking hot.

I beamed at her as Ian managed to get to her seat before she sat down and held it out for her. I wore a black fitted silk dress with flared skirt and stilettos. My hair was down in the loose curls Dee had put them in. My eyes settled on Jonas in one of his dark designer suits, no tie. Reminiscent of the way he dressed at Sir Harry's bar. Was it the same suit? I wasn't sure, but I found myself staring at him and getting many winning smiles back from him. The man had me.

"Would you like something to drink? Cosmopolitans?" Ian asked, standing up. He was wearing a blazer shirt and jeans, and I noticed Mary giving a few lingering looks his way.

"Yes," Mary said, pulling out her purse. Ian walked away before she could give him the money in her hand and headed to the bar. She got up and followed him.

After a few a few minutes, Ian and Mary came back with drinks. Cosmopolitans for us and Scotches for them.

"I put our names in for songs you all told me to request." She winked at Jonas.

I looked at him and he gave me a blank face. "What?" I teased.

He shrugged and sipped his drink. I listened to a male's risqué performance of "Ride My Pony." Mary and Ian knew all the lyrics and decided to sing along at the table. I giggled as I sipped my cosmopolitan, but I was getting nervous about singing. I hadn't sung since before my parents died. I didn't know if I could do it in front of the audience, but then I looked around at the tables and saw multiple drinks on them. No one would remember anyway. I gulped down the rest of my drink.

"Pace yourself. I don't want you slurring through your performance," Jonas said.

"I'm nervous," I said.

Jonas took my hand in his. "You'll be fine."

Mary's name was called and she strolled up to the stage. The guitar chords of Elvis's "Suspicious Minds" started and Mary, who had memorized his Las Vegas performance, started with a thrust of her hips. Ian looked like he wanted to crawl under the table, though his eyes didn't move off of her during the performance. Mary's enthusiasm won the crowd over and they cheered her on with me.

Jonas laughed hard. I clapped along and called out when she finished. "Yeah Mary!"

She strutted back to her seat. "Top that, Unger," she purred.

"Oh, I wish I had gotten that on tape," Ian said. He took a sip of his Scotch.

"How about a round of shots?" Mary asked, ignoring Ian's slight.

Jonas shook his head and placed his hand on my knee. "After the song."

"Gotcha," she sat down and we listened to a woman with a good voice sing "Killing Me Softly." Mary and I swayed. Mary finally turned to Ian, whose gaze was fixed on her. He leaned close to her ear, and I was sure I saw his lips brush her neck.

I turned my head to Jonas and he leaned over and kissed my lips. Ian's name was called and he got a few catcalls on his way up the aisle.

Justin Timberlake's "Rock Your Body" started and

Ian began singing and dancing so intensely you would have thought he was the man himself. The crowd was certainly convinced, the way they carried on. Ian could dance, and his singing was good too.

Mary was like a cat watching a fish. Maybe it was the poured-on jeans he worked with rolling his hips. The moves were hardly subtle, and she practically leered, leaving little doubt he could have had her naked by the end of his cover.

When Ian finished, he left to a few pretend faints and loud applause. He sat down with a well-deserved smugness and Jonas and I clapped for him. Mary did as well, though she was quiet for the first time since she arrived.

The good singing ended with an ear-splitting version of Rhianna's "Only Girl" by a young female who had clearly consumed one too many.

"Our turn is next," Jonas whispered at the end.

Mary, finally awake again, turned to us and clasped her hands together. "I can't wait."

"Our?" I asked.

"A duet," Jonas told me as they announced our names. My heartbeat increased as we walked up to the stage. The notes of Nat King Cole's "Unforgettable" started playing and my heart leapt. Jonas gazed in my eyes and started singing. "Unforgettable, that's what you are. Unforgettable tho' near or far," Jonas serenaded me. "Like a song of love that clings to me, how the thought of you does things to me."

I was supposed to sing too? I was sure my heart was

too big for my chest, so overwhelmed I was by the sound of his rich voice and the look in his eyes. I felt tears in mine.

I started singing and Jonas went quiet, watching me as I put my whole heart and emotions into the song. "Never before has someone been more…Unforgettable in every way, and forever more," Jonas sang the last notes.

Then I sang to him, "That's how you'll stay."

We sang to each other. "That's why, darling. It's incredible that someone so unforgettable could think I'm unforgettable too."

His eyes teared up and he grabbed me around the waist and kissed me passionately. We were in our own bubble of happiness. We turned and there were people cheering in the audience. Jonas took my hand and we walked back to our seats.

Mary's cheeks were wet. "That was so beautiful, Lily and Jonas."

Ian clamped his hand on Jonas' shoulder. "You sing lovely, Lily."

I dipped my head and said, "Thank you."

Jonas had me in his arms and wasn't letting go. So I moved to straddle his lap and he held me. I was madly in love with him. The brief thought of moving out and being away from him crushed my heart and I teared up as I rested my head on his shoulder.

Just then, his phone rang. He sighed long and reached inside his jacket and turned it off, then wrapped his arms back around me. "I'm here with you."

His choosing me and our night out with our friends over whatever business was beckoning him had me abandoning all social decorum. I clung to him, and he let me, silently holding me as we listened to more singers. Meanwhile, Mary and Ian chatted away and sang along with the performers on stage, offering occasional shots in their amusement.

Eventually, Mary turned to me and said, "I told him that would make you cry." She winked.

Jonas kissed my lips. "It was the only song that came close to how I feel about you."

"Oh stop it, Crane. You're going to make her cry all over again," Mary said, half-joking.

"I'll take my Tiger Lily whatever way she comes," Jonas said and wiped my eyes with his handkerchief.

Mary and Ian groaned together and laughed. But we didn't care. Jonas was not holding back.

"I love you so much, Jonas," I said.

He rubbed my back. "I know. I love you too."

Mary bounced on her seat and clasped her hands together excitedly. You could almost see the light bulb go on above her head.

Ian chuckled. "Oh, this should be good."

"Are we hungry? Can we have breakfast food? I have a craving for strawberry crepes," Mary said with added enthusiasm.

Ian put his arm along her shoulders. "Yes. There is a place a couple blocks down from here."

I smiled when I noticed Mary didn't try to remove his arm as we got up and walked out of the bar. I snuggled into Jonas's side as we followed behind to a small crepe vendor a few blocks ahead on Orchard Street. We ordered then stood outside eating crepes.

I laughed when I looked down at my watch. 1:17 a.m. "It's odd to eat here in the middle of the night."

"It's New York," Ian said with a shrug.

Only in New York can you dare to dream and have a wish granted, I thought with a smile on my face.

After we finished, Ian's driver pulled up to the curb to drive us back to Tribeca.

Ian stepped close to Mary and fixed the scarf around her neck. "Why don't we give them the night and you come home with me. What do you say, Mare Bear?"

She scrunched her face. "If you never say my nickname again."

Ian gave her a mischievous grin, leaving little doubt he wouldn't keep his promise.

The driver opened the door and we all got in, headed back to Tribeca. The street barrier was moved aside and we didn't see any reporters as we pulled up to the loft. Once we stopped, I caught Mary's eye and gave her my "are you sure" look.

She returned her "nothing will happen" eyes. I glanced at Ian. "Nothing" wasn't the impression I was getting from him. But Jonas's hand was out for me to take, beckoning me to get out of the car.

"See you tomorrow, my dear friend," I said with an

emphasis on the last two words as a protectiveness rose within me.

Ian took my now-vacant seat next to Mary and I watched her scoot closer to him. Before the door even closed, they were all over each other. The car pulled off before I could say anything.

Nothing will happen? So much for off-limits.

Jonas wrapped his arm around my waist and we moved past the security guard and into the building. We took off our shoes and walked straight upstairs to the bedroom.

"Sit here and wait for me," he said, shifting to command mode. He rose and walked into the bathroom and I heard the tub filling.

An anticipatory thrill went through me. I could get him to compromise on other things, but I understood this was our domain. This was where we could let go.

He was nude from the waist up. He stalked back up to me, seemingly larger than before, and stopped in front of me. He bent down and unhooked my bra and I lifted my arms for him to remove it. He then hooked the sides of my panties and worked them down my legs. "Lay back."

I laid back on the bed with my legs dangling on the sides. As Jonas bent down, he eased the nylon fabric of my thigh highs down my legs, then gripped my thighs and opened them wide. "I want your legs and arms open. But will you be able to keep them that way for me?" Jonas asked.

"Maybe." *Probably not. Just touch me.*

Jonas rose and walked away. My gaze followed as he moved to stand at the bottom of the bed, his hands holding onto the posts. Nothing he did was without consequence, and my pulse went up as my mind guessed his plan.

"I've been thinking about us sharing this experience for a while. When I replaced the bed, I chose this one for a reason. I'd like to tie you down," Jonas said.

My brows lowered. Yep. Tying me down. Something he had mentioned before, but we hadn't done together.

I didn't respond, but I watched as he left the room and returned holding a small black case. Sitting down on the bed facing me, he opened the lid toward me. Nestled between the inner black velvet castings were four leather cuffs.

"These two are for your wrists, and these are for your ankles," Jonas said.

I absently picked up one. The padded cuff had some weight and a couple of belts on it that I gathered would adjust in size. There were also metal rings hanging off, I assumed for attaching to keep the submissive in place. I had seen as much from a few videos online. From what I saw, the acts that followed were acts that frightened me.

I dropped the cuff back on the bed and moved my legs up under my chin, my arms tightening around them. "You want to hurt me?" I said in a small voice.

"Please look at me," Jonas said, moving the case away and tugging my hands down so that he could kiss the back of them. His eyes were soft when I met them. "I wouldn't hit you, Lily. Not ever. Especially after what happened to you. You are so special, so precious to me. Do you honestly believe I would harm you?"

I said without hesitation "No…not on purpose. But why do you need to do this?"

He smiled at me. "I don't need to, I want to. But only if you let me. Bondage, or binding you, isn't to hurt you. It's another way for us to connect and deepen our trust in each other. I won't gag you, and I'll remove them if you don't enjoy it."

I held his hands as he waited patiently for my answer. My mind circled over why he would want to try this now. I knew he cared for me, but this was a leap in trust. And, honestly, I didn't know where I stood on it. But this, to Jonas, was a way to try. And I wanted to for him.

"I'll try," I finally conceded.

He kissed my lips tenderly. "Thank you."

He didn't waste another minute and started fastening the cuffs around my ankles and wrists. He then pulled something from under the bed that looked like leather straps and walked around the bed, hooking them on the posts, leaving a lead with a hook on the end from all four corners.

"Pull back the covers, and move into the center of the bed," he instructed and I did. He set about hooking my cuffs to the lead. First he secured my ankles to the corners, making my legs open wider than I had ever been with him before.

I looked down my body and blushed. "This is too open. Can you adjust to close them more?"

Jonas's face filled with amusement and he laughed, fitting a pillow under my body, baring me further still. "If this is my only chance at seeing you this way, no. I'm going to enjoy looking at your body completely open and exposed to me."

I closed my eyes. My breath caught and I shuddered.

Jonas ran his hand over the bottoms of my feet and found a tickle spot that made me giggle and instantly relaxed me, though as he did it more than once, annoyance crept in. "If you're going to do that, forget it," I grumbled.

He kissed and caressed my instep until I squirmed a tremor that went up to my core. "Like that?" I moaned in response, though the swell of my breasts and wetness on my thigh gave him the answer.

Climbing off the bed, he moved to the headboard, securing my wrists in place next as he had done with my ankles. He checked and adjusted the restraints to make sure they weren't too slack or constricted. My arms and legs were all open toward the four posts and secured to the bed.

"Try to move," he commanded.

I turned my head and tried to pull against the restraints on my arms and couldn't. I tried to move legs and my arms again and started to pant. He cupped my face and kissed me.

"Relax," he whispered. He then massaged downward,

starting at my head over my shoulders, and all the way down my legs until I was relaxed. "I'm turning off the water in the tub." Jonas started moving away from the side of the bed.

"Jonas, don't leave," I cried out. I was trapped and completely at his mercy. What was he going to do to me?

He came back to my side in less than a minute. Leaning over, he caressed my face and kissed me to calm me, then said. "I'm right here. I'm not leaving. I won't keep you bound long. I'm going to touch, lick, suck, and fuck you. You'll come for me. After, I'll take them off and we'll bathe. Then I'll hold you the rest of the night."

I quivered and moaned against the throbbing ache in my clit as his plan lit my senses. I arched my back in the restraints. He let out a groan as he stood up and moved to the end of the bed, removing his jeans and freeing his cock that was fully erect. His gaze was bold as it traveled over my body, burning everywhere it fell. "You look stunning," he said, his voice rough. With the view of his ripped, toned physique, I could say the same about him.

Jonas climbed on the bed and settled between my thighs. He then rested back on his knees. His pupils dark. His lips parted. His chest heaving. Seeing me bound and open did it for him.

He moved his hands up to the crease at the top of my thigh and ran his finger across my clit. I arched. The barest of touch had me desperate for more. He let out a long hiss as he stroked over my folds, then commenced with light brushes on my clit again. He leaned close and inhaled as I arched, willing him to do more. But he moved back up and was now pumping my breasts in his hands, rolling the nipples and sucking hard on them. Pushing them together and pinching the tips. I was gulping air as they swelled. I mewled as a trickle of sweat passed close to my eye. Jonas looked up at me and wiped the sweat away with a cloth I didn't see he had, then went back to my breasts. They ached.

"Jonas, please," I rasped. He squeezed and licked the tips and I moved my head. I was still in my head. He finally let go and kissed down to my belly button, dipping his tongue inside. I quivered as the sensation went straight to my core. Fuck. I shook.

"You're doing good," he said and moved down to my mound, kissing then moving down to lay flat on his stomach. Placing his shoulders between my thighs, he ran his tongue over the hood and around the sides of my clit as I cried out and tried to arch. It felt good. *Fuck.* I grunted. He did it again and again. I shook, not being able to touch him or put him where he could finish me off and give me that orgasm that was rising and falling. He had me completely and I couldn't do anything but take what he was giving to me.

"Jonas, please, make me come," I pleaded as anger rose in me. He knew how to finish me off so easily, but he wouldn't. He continued the slow, light licks and flicks of his tongue through my folds and held onto my shaking thighs. My mind faltered. But still he held on to my quivering form with the torturous strokes of his tongue, making me hotter and swollen. I felt desperate and started to beg again. "Jonas, please."

"Let go, I've got you," he whispered and went back to his light strokes. My teeth scraped my bottom lip. Sweat was covering my body and tears hurt my eyes. *Never have I felt so desperate before.*

"I. Need. To. Come," I gulped between pants. He started lapping faster and fingering, but still it wasn't enough. Climaxing was all I could think about now, and I felt about ready to burst. Then I fell.

I couldn't think and I made incoherent words as my body trembled. I felt delirious with need. I was chaotic, incoherent left in his hands.

Jonas finally showed some mercy and drew on my clit, crooking a finger inside me right on my g-spot. I came, screaming. Climbing my body, he thrust his cock in all the way to the hilt as I contracted around him. His hips bucked against my pelvis as surges of pleasure filled me.

"Ohhh, Lily. I love you," he growled out as he moved faster, slamming hard and deep, brushing against my womb. I felt that sweet building again, knowing I was going to come once more. Through the blubbering mess that I was now, there was my Jonas. His gaze fixed on me. His smile. His love.

"Come with me." He shifted, angling his hard strokes right up against my clit, and I exploded again in climax. I kept on screaming as Jonas moved his fingers down to press on my clit, dragging out my orgasm. He had taken every piece of me until there was nothing left, and that was when he came, filling me with his cum as he panted above me, his sweat dripping down my body. He leaned down and kissed my mouth as I continued to tremble hard in the restraints. He eased out, then freed my wrists first and massaged the circulation back into them. Then he repeated the action down by my ankles. I was too tired to move, and I didn't need to. Jonas was here. Massaging my legs, arms, and shoulders, then picking me up gently and hugging me.

"Thank you for trusting me, my beautiful Tiger Lily," he said.

My eyes were heavily lidded but fixed on him as he lifted me up and carried me into the bathroom, where he eased us both into the warm foamy water in the tub and held me in his arms.

He was whispering soothing words as I relaxed in the lavender-scented bath. With my back against his chest, he kept an arm around my waist as he lathered up a sponge and quickly washed me. I was too exhausted to be of much help, so I silently drifted in his arms, surrendering to the intimacy of his support and care.

After rinsing me off, he lifted me out and set me down on a large bath sheet and dried us off, then carried me back to bed and placed me on top of his chest and cuddled me.

"Jonas, how long can I stay with you," I mumbled, my eyes closed.

The words *forever* floated through my mind as I slipped into the most peaceful and contented sleep.

CHAPTER SEVENTEEN

"YOU HAVE BEEN leaked to the press," Jonas said.

My eyes popped open and I sat up with a start. With the blinds drawn, the bedroom was dark, though my internal clock placed the time at early morning instead of night. The bedside lamp flared to life and so did my mind as it sought to understand just what Jonas said to me.

"What was leaked exactly?" I asked and held my breath.

"Our relationship. The press is linking our trip to Miami and the end of my fake engagement to Melissa," he handed me some clothes to put on. "I've set up an emergency meeting in my office now. We'll be discussing how we will communicate our response and introduce you to the world." Our eyes met then. His were dull, though he looked handsome as ever in a dark blue suit, pressed shirt, and tie.

I also wanted to be covered before we went any further with this conversation. As if he was able to read my thoughts, Jonas gestured toward the dark blue shirt and matching A-line skirt he had given me, along with dark lace lingerie and silk stockings.

I quickly put on the undergarments and went into the bathroom, where I cleaned up before returning to put on the remainder of my clothes. The whole time, Jonas stood in place, though his eyes followed me. After I brushed my long hair and put on a smidge of gloss, I came back to stand before him. Our outfits went together. *Like us, right?*

The way Jonas was staring at me had me fidgeting now. I knew he had something he wanted to share with me. "What is your plan, Jonas?" I asked.

He gave me a smile that didn't reach his eyes. "My plan is to announce you as my *girlfriend*," Jonas said, his voice steady.

Girlfriend. We gazed into each other's eyes and our connection flared between us. Wasn't it only a week ago that I reveled in the title of Jonas Crane's girlfriend? Jonas had said the title didn't express the depth of his feelings for me or mine for him. Not after all we had shared together. I truly believed in my heart I was his, and he was mine.

"I thought we were going with calling me 'mine' and I could call you 'my man'?" I teased.

His arms went around my waist. "We've been public anonymously, but now you'll be in public *with* me. Things will change for the both of us. But in private, and to those that are close to us, everything will stay the same. You're mine," Jonas said.

"And you are mine," I replied. His lips crushed against mine possessively and I gave myself over to the kiss, feeling the same need to seal our bond in that moment. When we broke apart, I placed my hand in his and we walked down to the office.

Jonas didn't stop holding my hand even as he headed over to the head of the table and had me take the vacant seat next to him. A small group was seated around the conference table. The ones I recognized were Ian, Samuel, and Diane. The others, I didn't. There was a deeply tanned male with highlighted blonde hair and light blue eyes and a female with a prominent widow's peak and close-set brown eyes.

Everyone was similarly dressed in the latest designer business wear, making me feel comfortable in my selected style of clothing. They sat in uniform, briefcases at their sides and folders at their place settings, with only a slight difference in their choices of pastries, fresh fruits, coffee, and juice from the platters in the center of the conference table.

"Lily, you know Ian, Samuel, and Diane," Jonas said. "I have also asked Ava Mills and Patrick Stollwater, heads of my Public Relations and Communications, to attend this meeting."

He paused for a minute, smiled, and said, "This is Ms. Lily Salomé, my girlfriend." Ava and Patrick's four eyes assessed me as we briefly greeted each other.

"Reports on the leak?" Jonas asked, addressing the group.

"Our sources informed us that Melissa Finch is responsible for your flight and location leaks," Diane said. She passed a report to Jonas. "This is from one of our private investigations into the announcement. Press at the airport and your home are all linked."

"Here are the latest newspaper articles. The one on top is the only one with leverage," Ava said as she pulled out folders for Samuel to hand to everyone in the group. "Unfortunately, Ms. Salomé's disguise at the airport plays into Melissa Finch's jilted, ex-fiancé story, which has grown legs since our press release stating you were never engaged."

"Surprised Phil chose to embarrass himself," Ian said, his eyes scanning the article. "We could get him for nondisclosure and privacy violations."

"Everyone knows Phil's done," Jonas replied.

Phil? I opened the folder to a newspaper clipping of a tabloid article. There was an enlarged portrait of Jonas and Melissa together. Someone had Photoshopped a jagged rip between the two images, with currency burning in the gap. Below the flaming money was a photo of me in the flight uniform at the terminal building and one of my graceless crawl through the driver's door of Jonas's car. The last image was one of Jonas getting out of the same car. The blood drained from my face as I continued on to the tabloid headline: *Mile High in Miami: Mysterious Mistress Revealed.* My stomach soured as I read the article.

Our exclusive story on why heiress Melissa Finch was

ditched by billionaire Jonas Crane. "Jonas introduced her as Lily Salomé, his personal secretary," said Phil Keane, head of KeanexTech Studios, who watched the secret lovers attend a 'business meeting' at his company. "Jonas had never flown in a 'secretary' in all the years of doing business with me," he revealed, giving us rare inside scoop on New York's most eligible divorcee.

A source says Jonas and the lush Lolita stole intimate moments in an office before jetting off to their secret love nest in Tribeca, New York, 'without mentioning' his leaked engagement announcement by blindsided ex, thirty-nine-year-old Melissa. "I feel sorry for her," Phil said when asked.

KeanexTech recently parted ways with Crane Holdings.

Phil using me to get back at Jonas for closing his company wasn't surprising after what occurred between the two of them at KeanexTech. I wasn't sure any news of closing would have come across better. Still, Jonas had known Phil for years, and the man he had helped in business had turned on him. That alone must hurt. Reaching under the table, I squeezed Jonas's thigh, wishing we could be alone so that I could hold him.

His eyes shifted to me and he leaned over to my ear. He understood and said the only thing he could in his meeting, "Thank you." Then he cleared his throat and addressed the group. "Samuel?"

Samuel picked up the small stack of papers in front of him. "I have created a profile on Ms. Salomé." He handed it out to the group.

My face heated as everyone looked over the few sentences that captured my life history, mostly revolving around my parents. I made a vow then and there to do more with my life.

Lily Geneviève Salomé

Mother: Jane Schafer, born in Dorchester, Massachusetts. Occupation: Marymount First Grade Teacher

Father: Randall Salomé, born in Auteuil, France. Immigrated to Quincy, Massachusetts. Occupation: Principal Viola Player for the Boston Symphony Orchestra.

Both deceased from tragic car accident.

B.A. in Anthropology at Boston University, Magna Cum Laude. Honor Student.

Publishing Assistant at Arch Limited.

Head of Love Legacy Program, a cross-cultural youth art program.

Recent recipient of grant from Arthur Finch and Jonas Crane Joint Partnership in Annual Finch Fanatic Fundraiser.

"Ideas?" Jonas asked, addressing the group.

"We can introduce Lily Salomé as a hardworking, independent Bostonian. We say her tragedy touched the heart of Jonas through her Love Legacy Foundation. We can tie in your presentation at the Finch Fanatic Fundraiser last month," Ava suggested.

"Maybe photos of the two of you together at a local event?" Patrick suggested.

Samuel shuffled through his e-pad. "The New York School of Business How to Succeed panel Wednesday afternoon." His voice dropped an octave. "There is also the New York Art Alliance Auction at Killian Gallery Wednesday evening?"

"I'll get back to you on the gallery," Jonas said. "Any other ideas?"

"We could move up your announcement of the publishing house you're using for your book?" Patrick offered.

My pulse jumped as I nervously waited for the name.

Ava shuffled through her papers and pulled out a sheet. "Are you sure you want to go with an unknown? I have confirmation that Melissa has started to shop her ideas for a book to a couple of the top publishing houses."

"We'll get to Melissa later," Jonas said.

He glanced at me. "Yes. I've spoken to Gregor Worton of Arch Limited. We will move the announcement and press up to this week."

Oh my god! I was practically bursting in my seat in wanting to call Gregor and share his joy in the news.

Jonas leaned over to my ear and whispered. "I need you here for the rest. You can call him soon."

"Thanks," I whispered, and he winked at me.

Patrick was pulling out his iPad as he said, "Arch Limited can work. Jonas Crane is the savior of up-and-coming business. Lily will be a part of his joining with Arch. We can get photos of you both together. Maybe do something casual now, and more at the press announcement for the event. Are you doing anything together today?"

"Mr. Crane has to leave for business in Texas tonight and Seattle on Wednesday. He won't be back until early Thursday morning," Samuel answered for Jonas.

"Yes. We'll be starting our vacation later this week," Jonas announced, grinning at my wide eyes and mouth. "Surprise," he said softly to me.

Patrick cleared his throat then said, "We can call a press announcement for the book? We'll get the team moving on Arch for early Thursday afternoon or Friday."

"We'll release statements to all media. I'll need more on the Legacy program, Ms. Salomé."

I cleared my throat. "I can send information."

"Maybe connecting her with some of our philanthropy groups could expand her profile?" Ava said.

"We're working on it," Jonas said and looked at me. I nodded.

"That could work. We can use the information on Ms. Salomé's backstory to promote her art program," Patrick said with enthusiasm.

"If Lily's assault case and photos were leaked, we could use it to promote domestic violence awareness and have Lily—" Ava said.

"Absolutely not," Jonas said, cutting her off.

"We'll prepare something just in case," Patrick said in a hushed tone.

"We'll take a break and move on to the legal issues with Diane and Ian. Ava and Patrick, I'd like a word," Jonas touched my arm. "Alright, Lily. Go on and make your call, but come back. We'll be moving on to the criminal case soon."

I stood in the most casual manner I could and walked out of the room, then ran to my phone to call Gregor. "Yay!" I yelled into the phone when he answered.

"He told you. I wanted to," Gregor said and we laughed. "Yes, we discussed the terms, and it looks like we may be moving up the announcement."

"Congratulations!" I said excitedly. I watched Ava and Patrick leave the office. Their faces were pinched but morphed into smiles to me as they rushed out.

"I couldn't have done it without you," Gregor replied, bringing me back to our conversation.

I looked down at my feet. "You deserve it. And thank you again for what you did for me."

"I'm sorry. If there is anything I can do, let me know," Gregor said and sighed.

The line went silent. Finally, I said. "Well, I should go. Congratulations again."

"Yeah. Tell Mary I said hello. Thanks again. Goodbye, Lily…" Gregor said, his tone crestfallen.

I hesitated. Was this really goodbye? We had accomplished our goal we set out for in the beginning. Jonas was publishing his book and I shared in that achievement. However, with the circumstances and changes in my life, I couldn't say with certainty that I would return to Arch Limited.

Stop being silly, I thought. *Gregor will always be my*

friend. "Goodbye, Gregor. See you at the press conference." Tucking my phone in my pocket and wiping the corner of my eye, I headed back to the office. Once I sat down, I felt Jonas's hand on my thigh. I looked at him. "You alright?" he said in a hushed tone.

"Yes. Thanks," I said and plastered on a smile. He turned back to the group. "On the other matter, Diane."

"Nothing on the leaked workplace photo. The assault is public record, so there is a chance the photos may appear," Diane said, her gaze on me brief. "On a positive note, Declan Gilroy was arrested. The investigation of fraud in his business trade practice will continue. His bank accounts have been frozen, so I doubt he will be able to make bail this morning. Assuming it were even to be granted. He was assigned a public defender, who from our conversation, gave me the impression he would be making a plea." She turned to me. "Here are a few papers I need you to sign. I'll also need your statement on the email photo at the end of this meeting."

"Did you get the emails I sent from his fiancé Heather?" I asked.

Diane smiled wickedly. "Oh, yes. He was requesting a visit and apology?" she said sarcastically.

Ian snorted. "He can forget it."

"I was also against the visitation at first," she said to Ian. "But if she goes, we may get a confession out of it. It could strengthen our case." She looked between the three of us.

My heart skipped at the way Jonas looked at me. The

daggers his expression was sending to Diane were deadly. And I could see he was about ready to turn her down, throw me over his shoulder, and lock me in his bedroom. He was my warrior and she was, in a way, using me as a lure for the greater good, to keep Declan in jail. But while I was admittedly scared, I was more frightened that I would never get past my fear of him, leaving myself vulnerable to his control.

I wanted to do it, but I was also willing to compromise for us. "I think it's a good idea. Diane could come, and you. We could wait until you return. But I think it could help with my recovery, too," I said and placed my hand on his.

Jonas wouldn't look at me, though he didn't move my hand away. He wasn't ready to let go just yet. "We'll come back to the visitation. Leasing and building contracts," Jonas said, shifting the discussion.

I wrote my statement and signed the papers for my case and handed them to Diane. At the end of the meeting, Jonas finally looked at me. My heart constricted at the raw emotion I found on his face. "I don't want him verbally abusing you, but if your therapist approves it, we'll go together with Diane." He then turned to Diane and gave her a pointed look. "Let me be clear, and you make this non-negotiable. One negative word on his part ends the visit. I don't give a damn what you think you can get to further the case."

Diane blanched. "Yes, Mr. Crane. I'll check into it and get back to you both soon," she said and wrote on her notepad. "I'll give you a copy of this statement to sign again later. I must get going to court."

"We'll meet again after I return," Jonas said, concluding the meeting.

CHAPTER EIGHTEEN

I TURNED TO Ian, who was packing up his briefcase. "Is Mary alright?"

A ghost of a smile appeared on his face. "Yes."

I waited for him to elaborate, but he didn't. He just strolled toward the door.

"Is she on her way back here?" I called out. He looked at Jonas and they shared an exchange. Before I could ask what was going on, Ian replied, "I'll have her back by the time you return this afternoon. See you in Midtown, Jonas."

I pursed my mouth as I watched him power walk the rest of the way out of the room. When he was gone, I said, "He's annoying."

Jonas scoffed. "He's annoying because he doesn't want to gossip about your friend?" Jonas replied.

I shrugged. *Yes.* "No."

Jonas leaned over and kissed me, sucking on my poked out bottom lip. "My sexy little liar. I'll have to get Samuel to add that to your profile," he said and winked at me. And that was when it hit me. I was now, officially, the live-in girlfriend of highly successful business guru Jonas Crane.

I eyed the tabloid article. *The young temptress gold digger that stole a committed man from heiress Melissa Finch.* "I think we can leave that off. I'm already a 'lush Lolita temptress," I said.

He grimaced and started packing up his papers. "I'll make Phil regret being connected to that trash."

I gave my profile an once-over and sulked. "I haven't done much. I mean, compared to you and Melissa. Or even those you dated before. I understand why they might question what you are doing with me. I'm not even working right now."

Jonas moved the paper from my hands and touched the side of my face. "You didn't stop working, you're on stress leave. And we are together now. Anyone I've dated in the past is in the past for a reason. The public gets to know you're my girlfriend, but they will not dictate our relationship," Jonas said. He took the folder out of my hand and closed it. "Now, kiss me."

I leaned in and gave him a peck on the lips.

Jonas rose and moved to his desk. We had no time to spare if we were going to make it to our next appointments for the day. So we collected and packed up our things then left the loft.

I cupped my hand to block the brightness of the sunlight once we arrived on the sidewalk. The barriers and security guards remained in place outside the building and at the end of the street, though that wasn't a guarantee a photographer wasn't taking photos. Jonas paused before the car and brushed his lips against the side of my face. A flutter went through my chest. He was all in and ready to claim me.

Jonas had his arm around my shoulder the second the door closed. "I'm sorry I won't be able to take you with me when I leave town today. I don't want you to miss therapy."

I pressed close to his side. With all that had occurred, it felt like a lot of time had passed since my last appointment. Nonetheless, I didn't want to miss therapy either. There was a lot to talk about, and I wanted to garner her support in getting closure with Declan.

"I agree," I said. "And I understand. Besides, Mary will be here at least for another couple of days."

"Dani and Ian are here too, and I'll be just a phone call or Skype away," he added. A salacious grin spread across his face. "I enjoyed our last Skype session. We can do that together tonight."

"With everything going on?" I said and clucked my tongue. "What if someone hacks into our session? No way."

"That's not possible," Jonas declared, but I detected doubt in his tone. I wasn't sure it could happen either, but I wasn't willing to risk it. He moved his hand up my skirt. "I'll look into it, just to be sure."

I clamped my legs together, trapping his hand. "The car too. Do you want someone with one of their fancy cameras filming us?"

"Through tinted glass in a moving car?" Jonas said, his voice elevated. He worked his trapped hand higher and my breath hitched. We both knew I wasn't able to resist him, but if we could, I'd rather avoid more bad publicity.

"Come on, Jonas, please. Just until things die down," I said, cursing the huskiness in my tone.

Jonas let out a derisive noise and removed his hand. He went further still by moving away from me. My lips parted as I stared at him. *Jonas Crane, pouting?* He'd never let me get away with that, so I scooted closer and leaned my head on his shoulder. "Will I see you before you go?"

"I've got a lot to do today, but I'll do my best to see you before I leave," he said and returned to holding me. A crease appeared on my cheek. He wasn't able to resist me either.

We rode in comfortable silence the rest of the way uptown and parked in front.

"If Isla approves, you can go to the jail, but not without me. I mean it, Lily," Jonas said, his tone authoritative.

"I won't. I promise. I need Diane to go too, and she won't go without your approval anyway," I reminded him. His face softened. I leaned over and kissed him before getting out of the car. "See you soon." I said as I ducked out of the door, heading to my appointment.

After the short meditation at the beginning of our session, I 'checked in' by sharing all that had occurred since our last appointment, ending with the possible visitation with Declan in jail.

"What do you think will happen if you go to this visit?" Isla asked.

I pressed my lips together. "I think Declan won't apologize. He will insult and threaten me. He will try to manipulate me by promising to return the things he stole if I drop the charges against him."

Isla nodded and wrote on her notepad. "What would he gain by doing that?"

I sat and thought about her question before answering. "He would get the satisfaction of hurting me one more time."

"Do you think that's enough to sustain him in the long run? From what you shared, that wouldn't move him toward his goal of getting out of jail. Even if you drop charges, there is enough evidence against him to proceed anyway, right?" Isla prodded.

"Yes, but Declan would still think I have some way of stopping it," I said.

"But you don't and he would still remain in jail. Let's pretend he knows and accepts this as fact. What if he wants to apologize to you?"

I frowned. "You think he will actually apologize?"

"I think you need to look at all sides of the situation and prepare yourself," Isla replied "What if he *does* apologize to you?"

I folded my arms. What if he did say he was sorry? If Declan apologized, I knew I wouldn't believe him. He had apologized in the past, and I forgave only to have him hurt me again. "I don't think it would help me because I wouldn't believe or trust him. His apology wouldn't mean anything." I thought for a moment more and then said, "So are you saying I shouldn't go?"

"No. I just want you to think through how and what you want to gain from visiting him in jail," Isla responded.

The bile of bitterness rose within me and I clenched my mouth. "Part of me wants to stop being afraid of him and hopes to get closure on the past. The other wants to see him suffer and hurt like he hurt me. Then I guess I expect he will offer to give me my things he took back. But I won't be there to make things good for him. I don't plan to drop the charges or help him. My motivations are not altruistic," I spilled out and covered my mouth with my hand. They weren't the words of the woman my parents had raised to be or indicative of the type of person I would ever want to be.

"I'm not here to judge," Isla said in a calm tone. "I'm here to help you. Seeing Declan weak, paying for his crimes, and possibly suffering may empower you. Being heard when he has no choice but to listen may be healing, too. But have you considered forgoing any hope of an apology from him and reading a statement instead?"

"Could I do that?" I asked.

"Why not? It's *your* visit," Isla said.

My face lit up. Her words were like a weight coming

off my mind. Declan may have asked me to come, but that didn't mean he could dictate what he would get from the visit. The visit would be my choice. I could use the time for myself, to get what I needed.

I knew Declan would freak at not being able to control the way the visit would go. But he was no longer my concern. I was doing this for myself to move on.

"I hadn't thought about the visit that way." I said. "But I like it."

"I'm thinking this visitation may help you gain insight into yourself, which we can discuss again in future sessions," she added. "You'll have the safe environment and support with you. You can go share what you want to say. What do you think?"

I beamed at her. "Yes. Jonas will be there and so will my attorney. I think reading a statement would give me a chance to say what I need to in order to move forward."

"Be careful with your expectations," Isla warned. She wrote on her pad. "I want you to take this with you. Think about the visit and write out the pros and cons of going. Prepare your statement ahead of time. If you want to work through more, contact me. You have a lot to digest, so we will end here today and I'll see you for your appointment tomorrow. After tomorrow, your appointments are two sessions a week. With your consent, I'll speak to Dr. Steinman and Jonas to recommend the visitation."

"Great," I enthused. "Thank you."

We ended with a short meditation and I left her office. I took out my phone to text David about the early end to my session and found two voicemails as soon as it beeped to life. One from Jonas and one from Diane. I played Jonas's message first.

"Wednesday night's charity auction is set, as well as my book announcement with Arch later this week. We will have a public lunch together at Gramercy Tavern today. I'll have to leave town afterwards. I'll see you there after your appointment. I miss you already."

I sucked my bottom lip. *I miss you, too.* I next played Diane's message.

"Hello, Lily. Declan's bail was denied, but his public defender put in an appeal. He may be released before trial, but not anytime soon. I've informed Jonas the visitation is available on Thursday morning, hopefully before your vacation plans. Thanks."

I peered at the passing pedestrians on the sidewalk as I waited for David to pick me up. Was someone watching? He arrived a few minutes later and I climbed inside the car before he opened the door. *Paranoia has set in.*

I took a deep breath and went through the few contacts on my new phone, hovering over Mary's number. I was surprised not to hear from her and pressed the button to connect a call to her. She answered and spoke before I even had a chance to say hello.

"Sorry I didn't call. I was up late, but Ian said Jonas is taking you for lunch and he asked me to a show tonight on Broadway. I hope that's okay?"

"Of course it is," I replied. "I'm just amazed you got

Ian to commit to anything. He's tight lipped these days."

"Oh. Sorry." She giggled. "I think he's trying to protect my virtue, but I'll tell you know. Yes. We had sex." The phone muffled. "She's my best friend, of course I will tell her. Alright. If you're too uptight." She whispered into the phone, "We'll talk later."

I giggled. "I look forward to it. How long before you need to get back to Boston?"

"I'd like to get back by Wednesday morning. I'll leave tomorrow afternoon, I suppose." Her voice trailed off. The car slowed and I looked out the window. We were on Twenty-Third and Park Avenue, only a few blocks from the restaurant.

"Anyway, well," she broke into a deep throaty laughter. "Stop Ian, or I'll tell her what you did to me," she threatened then screamed with laughter.

I laughed. "We've arrived and I have to go. I'll see you later." From the noises they were making in the background, I suspected she hadn't heard me.

CHAPTER NINETEEN

I PULLED OUT my brush and quickly raked through my hair and touched up my makeup, not wishing to get any more saucer-eyes photos like the ones in the tabloid. David helped me out of the car and informed me Jonas would be here shortly. I stood before the beautifully carved stonework and red awning and couldn't believe how much my life had changed in such a short amount of time. I went from eating chicken salads at my desk to waiting for *the* Jonas Crane to join me for lunch at Gramercy Tavern. *Heady.*

"Why are you standing on the street?"

I turned and found Jonas and he took my breath away. He still had that effect on me, and from a shift of my eyes at the passersby gaping at him, he had the same effect on everyone he met. He was oblivious, of course, his gaze steady on me.

"I was just…uh, waiting," I answered, suddenly tongue-tied. I spied a cameraman a few feet away and my smile tightened. Jonas placed his hand on my lower back and moved us toward the front door, which David was holding open for us, and we made our way inside the restaurant.

Jonas's entry caused the same sensation as he had on the street. He was even stopped a few times, though he took it in stride and was kind to each and every person that approached him. But he kept me close to his side, and I felt myself falling in love with him all over again, just from all I knew about the man.

We sat down and Jonas ordered for salads and red snapper for us, as well as scotch for himself and a pinot grigio for me. "You like red snapper. I remember," he said as a preemptive response to my disapproval of him ordering for me. It wasn't coming. I did, indeed, like his selection. "Sounds good." I said, taking a sip of the water that had just been brought out to us.

"We'll be attending the New York Art Alliance Standing Up for Mental Health Art auction on Wednesday. Samuel will be sending you information. I want you to pay particular attention to director Penelope Carmichael."

I took out my notepad and pen from my handbag and jotted down the information. "I'll look at it when I return. Is there any reason her in particular?"

"Penelope is the director at New York Art Alliance, which is a longstanding staple of the art community in New York. She also heads art programs and charities in the Tri-State area. She would be a great contact for your program. Samuel will be dropping off cards on your Love Legacy. I think you need to work on improving your brand, but that will come," Jonas said.

"I always wanted to do so, but I was hoping to hire someone with the raise I was to get from landing you at Arch," I said and took a sip of water.

"I want to help," Jonas said and tensed, clearly waiting for another protest by me. The program wasn't about my ego though, and I wasn't about to pass up assistance from one of the best business minds in the world.

"Thank you, Jonas," I said.

His mouth formed a broad smile. "You're welcome, Lily." The waiter returned with our drink orders. After a sip of my wine, I told him, "Isla approved the visitation."

Jonas grimaced. "I'm still not happy with the idea," he said, drinking his scotch.

"We talked about it. She suggested I simply read a statement," I said. "It would give me a chance to say what I need to without expecting much from him in the form of an apology. I don't know how well that will work, though, with the way he usually behaves with me."

"You won't be alone. I'll be there and so will Diane. I just don't want you to have unrealistic expectations. It sounds like Isla helped with that some," he said, buttering a piece of bread from a basket on the table and placing it on my plate.

"Yeah," I said. "I think we'll need to visit Kate again, to go up a size in dresses. I know I've gained weight," I said, eyeing the bread.

"Sounds good to me," Jonas said, giving me a flash of his perfect teeth. I blushed for him and ate the bread.

"You're still shy after all I've done to you," he said pointedly. That only made me blush more and I scowled at Jonas.

Our salads were brought and we started eating them. I paused between bites. "Any news about what's going on with her book?" I asked and looked around the restaurant.

"Legal delivered a few reminders today to her and her father. I expect to hear something soon," Jonas responded and took another sip of his drink. "I think that will clear that up."

"I'm really sorry about Phil. He and Dottie seemed so nice," I said, reaching over and putting my foot against his leg.

He lifted the corner of his mouth. "Friends make the worst enemies. I'm not bothered. We stopped seeing as much of each other after they moved to Florida, and even less when we backed his company. What are you doing?"

"I'm giving you support without disrupting your meal," I said innocently after the waiter removed our salads.

"I thought it was called footsie," he said, lifting the corner of his mouth.

I moved my foot a little higher up the leg of his trousers.

Jonas gave me a dark look. "I really don't have the time, but I'm willing to forget about the cameras and we can continue in the car?"

I blushed and quickly removed my foot, swiftly putting my shoe back on. "You're right. I don't know what I was thinking."

"I did enjoy your *support*," Jonas said. I glanced at him and his gaze was fixed on me. I gave him a small smile and we ate our main course before sharing a Gramercy cookie plate for dessert. Silence fell between us as the time approached for him to leave. I glanced at him between bites. "Can I come to the airport?" I whispered, staring down at my plate.

"I think it would be best if I drop you off first," Jonas said softly.

I took in a shaky breath and dipped my head. "Oh."

"Tiger Lily," he said. I wouldn't look at him. I couldn't.

He asked for the bill and settled it, then took my hand and moved us quickly out of the restaurant.

Jonas ran his hand over my back. "Is it wrong to love how much you want to be with me?" He kissed the side of my head then helped me into the car. I inadvertently crawled into his lap and froze, having forgotten about the photo possibilities.

"I don't care," he whispered and cuddled me. I placed my hand on his shoulder and pressed my lips against his neck before closing my eyes and resting my head on his shoulder. He didn't say anything, just held me close and occasionally gripped my waist or caressed my thigh as we rode back to Tribeca. The ride was short. Too short. And when we stopped, so did my heart.

"I'll call you later," he said. "The second I can, I'll head home. And then it will be the two of us away together soon." Jonas pressed his lips against my forehead. He moved back and tilted up my face, stopping the progress of the tears on my cheeks with two kisses.

"My smile. I need it," he requested in a gentle tone and waited for me to compose myself and wipe my tears away. I looked into his eyes that shone back at me.

I swallowed hard, my mouth quivering up into a smile. "I love you," I said.

"And I love you." He gave me a hard kiss on the lips. Then he knocked on the door for David to open it. "Go inside quickly," he commanded, his voice faltering.

I let out a sob as David opened the door and helped me out of the car. I followed his instruction and hurried to the building, not stopping until the front door of the loft was pressed against my back. There I allowed the rest of my tears to fall.

I got up early the next day and set up my own mini workstation in the living room. With Jonas gone, and not needing to go out anywhere myself, I let my hair down. Or, rather, up in a messy pile on top of my head. Between that and my favorite tank top and sweats, I was happy and homey.

I researched Penelope Carmichael and the New York Art Alliance for Jonas over breakfast. And then I worked on editing changes to an updated version of the manuscript Gregor had sent me last week over lunch.

Mary didn't come back, but I didn't begrudge her

that. I wasn't really up for hanging out after Jonas left anyway, and I had a feeling I knew what it was she was swept up in.

Jonas did send me a text letting me know he had arrived safely the night before, and another this morning to let me know he would be working hard all day so he could return to me tomorrow. I couldn't wait. I missed him already.

I tried on the dresses Kate had delivered and found they fit—just barely. Like I suspected, I had gained weight. I was one step closer to moving forward with my life.

Next on my list was to pen the statement I wanted to read during Declan's visitation. What exactly did I want to say to him? *No.* What did I want to say for myself?

I spent a couple of hours trying to figure it out. On my third draft, and after I devoured reheated pizza, the front door buzzed. Before I could jump to answer it, in walked Mary, doing a stride of pride with a sheepish grin on her face. She was followed by Ian, who walked with a bit of a swagger.

I raised my hand. "No apologies. It's all fine. I understand, Mary," I said, cutting her off before she said anything. She simply smiled my way.

"Ian." I nodded his direction. "Thanks for driving Mary back." I wasn't even being nosey, but I still got a tense jaw from him, followed by a one-word response. "Yeah."

"I'm here for the rest of the afternoon. I can get my

flight tonight," she announced.

I sighed and smiled. I was going to miss having her around. "I wish you could stay longer."

"I told you I can drive you back," Ian said to her, tugging on her scarf.

She grinned at him and swiped his arm. "You ride, you don't drive."

"Then I'll ride you back," Ian said with a straight face.

I was just about to gag at Ian's cheesy pick up line, when Mary gave him a husky reply. "I'd like that." She was eating it up and asking for seconds. I turned my head back and watched Ian pulled her against the front of his body and do a two-hand lift of her ass.

I covered my mouth to suppress my laugh. I couldn't wait to tease her good about it when he left.

"Okay. Uhm," she said, pulling herself back from his kisses. "See you in a few hours?" she sounded breathy.

Ian gave her some kind of grunt in response and kissed her in a way that made me want to give my eyes a shower. She was groping him too, like she couldn't get enough. *He's sexually intoxicated her.*

Ian practically strutted to the door, with Mary getting more kisses and gropes in before it finally closed. When it did, I decided I had held it in long enough and burst into a fit of laughter. She resisted at first, but then gave in and joined me. "Laugh it up. I guess I deserve it," she said after we stopped, plopping down next to me on the couch. "I'm going to need a vacation from this break."

I smirked at her. "So much for Ian being off-limits, eh?"

She covered her face with her hands. "I don't know what I'm doing." She positioned herself to face me. "Neither of us is looking for anything but fun, so it's still a fling. You don't have to worry, though. We're going to be friends, or friendly, after we end things tonight. We'll still be fine to stand as your best persons in your wedding. And to be joint God parents of your children."

"I wish," I muttered and stared off dreamily. Mary knew me well. I always wanted to fall in love, marry, and have children, just like my parents. In my heart, I wanted to marry Jonas and have his children. But would Jonas ever want that? I wasn't sure.

I let out a puff of air and tilted my head down. "I'm not sure he will want to marry again," I finally said. "Or have more children."

Mary looked at me for a moment, and then said, "I would normally say it's kind of early in your relationship to discuss marriage and kids, but you are living together now. Maybe you should at least have a conversation about what you both want before saying he doesn't?"

I laid my head on the couch. "I guess I'm afraid. It wasn't that long ago he wanted me only as his sex companion. He's divorced and has a teenager. He told Melissa…" I stopped myself. *He also told her he didn't think he could love again, until he met me.* Could it be possible he would marry me?

Mary came close and put her arm around my shoulder. "I've seen him. He absolutely loves and adores you. You can give the both of you more time. But if I'm wrong and he doesn't want to marry you, then you'll know soon enough and can choose to move on. It's not good to leave your dreams behind to fit someone else's. So, think about it. And then bring it up with him when the time is right."

"I will," I said and swallowed. She hugged me.

When she released me, I looked at my laptop and moved my cursor. I didn't want to discuss this anymore.

"So, what are you working on there?" Mary asked, taking the hint. Her jaw dropped open as she read over my statement. "Declan? Now you're writing to that loser?" There was disgust in her tone.

"Not exactly." I replied, filling her in on the upcoming visitation.

Her top lip curled up. "I have a few words I'd like to say to him. It would be worth missing classes just to tell Declan what I think of him."

I shook my head. "He's not worth it."

"True." Mary stood up.

"After I read this statement," I said. "I'm putting him, and everything that happened, behind me."

Mary nodded. "I'm glad." Then she stood and said, "I'm going change and pack. Then we can talk and watch an old movie?"

"I'd like that," I said. As she left the room, I went back working on my statement. After a while, Mary returned, dolled up Dee style. Her hair and makeup looked flawless, and she was even wearing a V-neck that totally highlighted her cleavage.

"Must be good," I teased.

Mary put on her glasses. "Yes. It is. Too good," she admitted. "But please keep that to yourself. I'm trying to play it cool."

I hid my incredulous expression. I was happy to see Mary letting her hair down and enjoying herself, as she usually spent her time doing homework and research during our visits. I pointed out as much to her as we went into the kitchen to get snacks for our movie.

"It has been a stressful semester," she acknowledged. "I took too many courses to try to finish my degree program early." We looked through the refrigerator, and Mary took out a shake for me and a bottled water for herself.

I pulled out the container of fruit and started filling up two small bowls. "How were your grades after the mid-terms?"

"Good," Mary said, grimacing before adding, "Though I've got a feeling that when Hans finally signs off on our independent project, I'll be lucky if I get a B." She said it like it was a curse word. And for Mary, it was. She prided herself on her top honors and record in academia. So I knew this wasn't something easy for her to share or admit.

"When did this happen?" I asked, coming over to stand next to her.

She hunched her shoulders. "He sent an email today indicating as much. He suddenly has a problem with everything I submitted." She collected spreads and muffins on the counters and we walked them back into the living room.

"What can I do to help?" I asked once we were seat-ed.

She shook her head and flipped through the movies on the rental list. "I'm handling it. Now let's watch…Notorious."

I wanted to press, but I could see she didn't want to discuss it. I also knew if she was in serious trouble, she wouldn't be sitting here. So I let it go. At least for now. "Alright, but if I can help, let me," I said and popped a grape in my mouth.

"I will," she said, facing the TV. "How many times have we seen this movie?" she asked, changing the subject.

"Not enough," I said, giving our standard answer. We laughed.

We spent the rest of the time eating and talking through the movie. The time went by fast. Before we knew it, Ian had returned and was ready to take Mary back to Boston.

"I'm a call a way if you need me. I love you," Mary said and let out a sob.

I hugged her tight. "I'm here for you, too. Thank you for coming to visit. I love you."

After she left, I finished up on the computer and ate

dinner. I found a link from Gregor in my email of a group of cats dancing to Queen's "We Are the Champions." Arch was celebrating, and now so was I. I replayed it and danced along. The kind of dancing you only do when you know no one else can see you.

The front door opening stopped me mid-chicken dance. Jonas had returned early and was laughing at me, clearly having seen more than I would have liked. But I didn't care. I closed the distance between us and yielded to his arms, which were open and waiting for me to fill them.

CHAPTER TWENTY

WE ARRIVED WITH a few minutes to spare at Arch Limited. The media had descended on the Midtown building to cover Jonas' book announcement. At least that's what the morning was supposed to be about, though it was also our first official public engagement as a couple.

We were both pressed and dressed, Jonas in a fashionable black suit and white shirt with his freshly trimmed hair coiffured back. As for myself, I was dressed in a black knit dress and pumps and wore my hair in a ponytail. Walking hand-in-hand, we made our way through flashing lenses across the stone courtyard and up to the glass-door entrance of the lobby, where the announcement was set to take place. It was packed with smiling staff. A small aisle led up to a podium with three banners, one each with the logos of Crane Holdings and Arch Limited. A central banner draped in a sheet remained covered. I imagined it would be revealed at the start of the press event.

My eyes darted across the faces of my peers and

found mixed reactions to my being at Jonas's side, but I didn't have time to dwell. Gregor stepped up, his usual tweed with patches replaced by a charcoal gray suit. His parted hair was pulled back in a tight, short ponytail. Even his goatee was gone. His mossy green eyes flicked to me, and he gave me a small smile before showing off a set of white teeth as he shook Jonas's hand to cheers and claps from the Arch staff. The banner revealed:

> Arch Limited presents: *Driven: An Autobiographical Reflection on Success by Business Titan Jonas Crane*

Gregor stepped up to the microphone at the podium. "Arch Limited is excited to present our newest client, Jonas Crane, and his autobiographical story, *Driven*, his brilliant account of how he triumphed in business." Jonas stood respectfully to the side as Gregor shared a brief biography of him and read a long list of his achievements and all the companies that he had brought to the top ten over the last ten years. I was proud of Jonas, but hearing his accomplishments out loud, I once more couldn't help but wonder about myself. Why was he with me?

Once Gregor finished, we all clapped. Jonas took the podium next and spoke eloquently and humbly on his decision to write as gratitude for all those who were a part of his success and as a way to help inspire others who were working to achieve their dreams. He ended his speech by saying. "I'm excited to be a new member of the

Arch Limited team. I'm also very happy to share this occasion with my beautiful girlfriend and member of Arch, Lily Salomé."

My face pinked and my lips parted. I was speechless, but I didn't need to say anything. He walked over to me and gave me a light kiss in front of everyone. The flashing lights exploded. I leaned up to his ear. "This is Arch's moment," I admonished. He shrugged and kissed me again before returning to the podium. Gregor announced they were open for questions. Not surprisingly, the questions that should have been about the book and Arch shifted to his relationship with me.

Ms. Salomé is here as an employee of Arch Limited?

Gregor answered. "Yes. Ms. Salome worked—" He cleared his throat. "Works as my Publishing Assistant. Arch expects to devote a team to Jonas Crane's *Driven*."

How long were you seeing Ms. Salomé before signing with Arch Limited?

Jonas answered this one. "Lily was a part of bringing Arch to my attention, but ultimately it was my decision to choose Arch Limited after meeting with Gregor Worton. The meticulous attention to detail and client-focused approach made Arch the forerunner and ultimately the best choice for my book."

Was this before your engagement to Melissa Finch?

"I was never engaged to my friend Melissa Finch. No more questions will be answered on my relationship," Jonas said authoritatively.

I understand Ms. Salomé is on stress leave. Could you

explain why?

My face drained and my stomach churned. Someone had disclosed I was on stress leave. What else would they uncover? Even if they didn't learn anything more, I was already a distraction.

"We will not be discussing Ms. Salomé at Jonas Crane's book announcement. If you have questions related to *Driven* and Arch Limited, we would be happy to answer them," Gregor said in a crisp tone.

Our relationship was ruining Jonas's book announcement and Gregor's media attention for Arch Limited. I was stuck between wanting to be there and wanting to run away. Someone touched my arm.

"Want to get some air?" I turned my head and was relieved to find it was David.

I nodded appreciatively. David took my arm and I followed him as he blocked any approach in my direction up the aisle and out of the building. I ran my hands over the goosebumps on my arms that came from the chilly breeze in the courtyard. Outside, members of the press, camera people at their media vans, and curious passersby were gathered along the sidewalk.

"Want to sit in the car?" David offered.

I peered through the glass front at Arch. The press conference had continued, but I didn't want to go back in should the questions turn back to our relationship. I wasn't sure how long the announcement would go, but I didn't want to go sit in the back of the car, either. "No. Thank you. I think I'll just go have a coffee at Sophie's until it's done." I knew it to be the closest restaurant to the building.

"Best I drive you," David said. Looking around once more, I noticed a cameraman snapping photos of us a few feet away from where we were standing.

I sighed and followed him to the car. We rode around the block before he dropped me off to join the crowd a block away from Sophie's. I hurried down the street and walked inside the restaurant, sitting down at the counter facing away from the door. I ordered a coffee and a muffin and exhaled long, relaxing back into anonymity, though my thoughts raced at what was to come if this was only a small press event.

Did Jonas have this much celebrity or was it the sordid scandal that made us appealing? I didn't know. But my thoughts were preoccupied with worry over it. So much so, I didn't realize someone was tapping my shoulder hard enough to make me want to soothe the spot once I became aware of it. "Yes. What is it?" It came out snippier than I wanted it too, but I rubbed my shoulder where the person's pointer finger dug in as a visible explanation.

"Oh, I'm sorry!" the female voice said. I swiveled my chair around and looked at my apologetic intruder and my face fell. *Heather.* She was dressed in a suit that was at least two sizes too big for her. Her bobbed hair was half covering her face, but not enough to hide the purplish circles around her dull, red-rimmed eyes. The marks stood out against her pale, peeling skin. Her teeth were nibbling on cracked lips that looked painfully shredded and sore.

"Hi, Lily. It's me, Heather," she said, unaware of my recognition.

"I know. Listen, I was told I can't speak with you—" I said.

"I'm sorry for approaching you," she said, speaking over me. "I know what you were told, but I'm not like what your lawyers think. I'm not trying to mess things up for you. I'm just trying to fix my life with Declan." She sucked in air and touched her neck.

"I can imagine," I muttered. My eyes followed and I saw the faded bruise, while she quickly moved her hair forward to cover it.

"I know you don't care," she snapped accusatorily.

"I don't care about Declan, but I don't want you to get hurt," I said.

She eyed me coolly, then coughed. I offered her my water, which had appeared with my coffee.

"I'm sorry. I'm not mad at you. I know your boyfriend is putting you up to it," she sipped her water. "Declan knows, too."

My lips parted and I wanted to argue, but her appearance had me holding my tongue. "Did Declan cause that bruise? He used to beat me too. He called me names like fat—"

"I'm not going to listen to you bad mouth him. That was his past. He will get the medication he needs to help him once he is freed from jail." She held up her hand

and I gasped. The tips of her fingers looked painfully chewed down past their mark.

"I'm not dropping the charges, Heather. And even if I did, he has other things that he could get in trouble for that have nothing to do with me," I responded.

She worried her bottom lip and I turned my head away.

"If you could open your heart to his apology, I know you will see things have changed. This stress has made me spot."

Her baby? I looked back at her and watched her rub her belly. It looked flat. "How far along are you?" I asked softly.

She hesitated and blinked. "I'm not sure. Dec did the test with me and it was positive a few weeks ago, but he said I had to wait until after he is granted the appeal and comes back home before I can go see the doctor. He wants to be there with me."

"Oh, please don't do that Heather. Please go to the doctor and check on your baby." I said. The plea was out of my mouth before I could think on what I could say to combat the dangerous cruelty Declan was wielding over her.

She smiled wide, making one of the sores on her lip open. "See, I knew you had a tender heart. Dec can only love those that are good."

I stared at her. *He preys on those that want to be good.*

He preyed on me. I had been just as gone as her. I was willing to do any and everything for him. I lied and hurt myself and those that cared for me. I needed help. *And so does she.*

"Heather. He could get in trouble for keeping you from a doctor if you don't go get yourself checked out by a physician." I wasn't certain that was true, but I acted as if I was, and I could see the doubt and worry spark her eyes. I hated to use his brand of manipulation, but it was the only thing that would have worked on me when I was under his power and control.

She gave a little nod and took a drink from the water glass. "I've been praying on this and I know we can heal what's going on between you and Declan. You will see when you talk to him how much he has changed and wants our family."

"Do you have family here Heather?" I asked. I ran my hand over my sour stomach.

"Not here," she said quietly. She tucked her hair back and adjusted the collar of her shirt. "I've been looking around for your stuff. I think I found some things I can return to you."

"Lily."

I turned toward the door and watched Jonas walk in with Gregor trailing behind him. I glanced at Heather. She was answering her phone, which was now chiming in her hand.

My pulse jumped as I turned my head to her. "You found my stuff?"

She held up her index finger for me to wait, as I hadn't realized she was still on the phone. "I'll go right now. I'll catch a cab."

"This is Heather, Declan's fiancé," I said when Jonas stopped in front of me. He gave her a hostile look. Heather ended her call, but didn't offer her hand in greeting. Neither did Jonas or Gregor.

Jonas looked down at her. "Apparently she didn't understand the communication she received from our attorney," he said, speaking at her. His tone was sharp.

Heather glowered at Jonas. "I'm not doing anything or asking for anything. I was just telling Lily I think I have something for her. Please don't sue me for daring to speak," she spat out to him, but it had no affect since Jonas looked through her as if she wasn't there. She then turned to me and said, "I've got a problem back at my apartment, so I've got to go, but I can bring it tomorrow at your visitation."

Heather walked out and over to the curb to try to flag a taxicab.

"Did you hear her, Jonas? Heather said she found my stuff," I said, a lift to my voice, hoping he wouldn't be upset he found me speaking to her.

He placed his hands on the side of my face. "Please don't get your hopes up there. I didn't hear any guarantees. Remember what I told you?"

I ran my tongue over my lips. *I'm more important than my possessions.* "I know, but…" The stony expressions on Jonas's face let me know he wasn't willing to listen anymore. I sighed and quickly settled my bill. Afterward, Jonas kissed me tenderly and gave me a hug, which I returned. When we parted my gaze landed on Gregor, who I found staring at us. His arms were folded and his lips were pressed together. When he noticed I was staring back at him, he turned his head and moved toward the exit. Jonas placed his hand on the small of my back and moved us out of the restaurant and stopped a few steps in front of Gregor. We stood looking at each other for seconds, though it felt like minutes.

"How did the rest of the announcement go?" I asked, ending the silence.

"I think overall it went fine," Jonas said with a glance at Gregor, whose head was slightly turned, his eyes fixed on something other than the two of us speaking to him. He responded, "I agree. Sorry about what happened back there. I will find out who leaked the information and they will lose their job, but I assure you the photo is gone and alerts are out for anyone who tries to market the image."

"Thank you Gregor," I replied politely. *He can't look at me.* I had somehow been so distracted that I almost forgot about Gregor seeing that photo. Now that it was brought into conversation, I didn't quite feel like I could look at him, either. My cheeks warmed and Jonas moved his arm around my waist.

Gregor stared at me and there was something else in his gaze. The feelings he had for me were there. I knew what that look meant, because I had seen a similar one daily on Jonas's face. It was love. Jonas was right. Gregor still had feelings for me. I couldn't look at it anymore and dropped my head.

"We've got to go. Talk to you when we get back from our vacation," Jonas said. I looked at him. He gave his business to Gregor and Arch Limited despite disliking the way Gregor felt about me. He did it for me.

"Thank you again, Jonas," Gregor said and shook his hand. He then reached out for mine.

My head lifted up to him and I clasped his hand. "Thanks for giving me the work from home, and congratulations."

Gregor kept my hand well past politeness and I felt the stir of Jonas behind me, letting me know he was about to end it. Gregor let me go, and Jonas's arms closed around me, topping it off with a hard kiss on my lips. *Yep. His and his alone.*

"Goodbye, Gregor," I said. And with a wave, Jonas moved us down the sidewalk and into his waiting car and we left.

I slumped in the seat. "I'm glad that's over."

"We still have the art auction tonight," Jonas reminded me.

"Oh yeah," I muttered as I stared out the window at Arch Limited. "I always thought of Arch as the one thing I had going for me," I muttered.

"You have a lot more ahead of you, Lily." Jonas tugged my ponytail. "Get over here." I moved close and settled next to his side as he placed his arm around me. "You will find your way."

"Gregor," I said softly. *Still loves me.* I didn't want to

say the rest aloud.

"Yeah, I know," he said in a crisp tone.

"I don't love him. You know I don't." I peered at him through my lashes. "Just give me some time to think—"

"What is there to think about?" Jonas cut me off. "I *chose* Arch to help *your* friend. I ended my friendship with Melissa. You need to do more than think. You can't deny what we both just witnessed. I won't have him rhapsodizing over you at Arch." We sat in silence for a few minutes.

My stomach sunk as I met the stern expression on his face. Why was I making it difficult for him? My need to look for a new job was clear, though I hated to admit it. "I'll leave Arch. It was difficult to get that position, which is the only reason I've had any hesitation. I will have to send out a bunch of resumes, but I will resign.

"You will accept my help with that too," Jonas said, a look of relief on his face.

I chewed my lip as thoughts of my run-in with Heather at Sophie's returned. "Speaking of, Heather needs help. Declan has brainwashed her. He's manipulating her from jail."

"He is trying to manipulate you through her," Jonas scowled. "She may need help, but she has to be open to receiving it. You can't fix her."

I couldn't help but see the similarities between us. "I could have easily been her."

"But you're not and will never be. Not if I have anything to do with it," Jonas said.

I looked out the window. Perhaps Jonas was right about her, though she seemed genuine.

"Samuel's dropping off cards to pass out tonight on your art program," he reminded. "Did you get a chance to look over the New York Art Alliance between dancing yesterday?" he said, changing the subject.

I giggled. "You surprised me."

"You surprised me too." He gave me a peck on the cheek. "I've got to go back to work, and you're at therapy?"

"Yeah. I think it will help with preparing for the prison visitation tomorrow."

Jonas tucked my hair behind my ears. "We fly away tomorrow."

"Where are we going?" I asked, but got a suddenly busy Jonas staring at his phone. "I need to know what to pack," I complained.

"Nothing," he responded.

"Vacation at the loft?" I kidded.

"I like that idea, but no. I think with all the publicity we'll have to face soon with my book, a real trip away from here would be better," he said.

My brows knitted. "We never talked about your book. I work at Arch and I never asked for details. How could I do that? I'm interested in what you plan to put in your book."

"I've shared more with you than will ever go in that book," he said ruefully. I kissed and held him.

"Please continue to share with me. I want to know everything about you," I said.

A ghost of a smile formed on his mouth. "That's one of the many reasons I love you," he whispered.

CHAPTER TWENTY-ONE

THE NEW YORK Alliance Art Auction at Killian Gallery was close enough to walk to from the loft in Tribeca. Nonetheless, David picked the two of us up and joined the queue of cars lined up before the building. The gallery was in yet another one of the renovated warehouses with imported glass and modern accents so common in the area. What weren't common were the strobe lights and gated, carpeted runway leading to the front of the building. Suit-clad security guards kept back the press that lined the velvet-rope sidelines. The event called for the type of press that would cover any major celebrity event. From the fireworks of flashing lights, I was sure there were some stars attending along with New York's elite.

Like Jonas. I glanced at him on the phone, looking mesmerizing in his black tuxedo, and realized I had been awfully naïve in the beginning when Jonas mentioned the type of events we would attend as part of our companionship. Looking around, I doubted I would ever fit in. Even in the embroidered organza eye-lit black dress

Kate had sent for me, none of this was me.

Jonas ran his hand over the length of my long hair that I had flat-ironed straight for the evening. "Try to relax," he encouraged.

My eyes darted over the spectacle going on outside the window as the car crept forward. I was trying. I could feel my pulse in my ears. David pulled up the curb and one of the car doors opened. I froze. Jonas's hand closed over mine and pulled me out of my haze and on my feet. We walked up the runway and stopped at the press line before the gallery. I nervously plastered on a smile, willing it to end quickly.

Your book Driven is already slated as a best seller just from your announcement today. Care to comment?

"I'm looking forward to the release of *Driven* with Arch Limited," Jonas answered.

Who is your date tonight?

"Lily Salomé," he moved me close in his arms to an explosion of flashes from camera lenses.

Is Crane Holdings parting ways with Finch Enterprises now that you ended your engagement with Melissa Finch?"

"Crane Holdings and Finch Enterprises have a longstanding relationship," Jonas's reply was vague, but the proposer didn't attempt a follow-up question.

Is it true Melissa Finch has been rumored to be penning a book on your relationship?

"You will need to ask Melissa," Jonas answered. "We must go in. Thank you." Ignoring the questions that followed, he turned and guided us through the entrance.

"Now it's time for work. Members of New York's Arts and Philanthropy will be here tonight. I want you to mention your Love Legacy program to everyone I introduce you to," Jonas instructed.

I nodded as Jonas stopped to shake hands.

I stumbled over my words, but quickly got used to introducing the Love Legacy Art program. We stopped before a regal female in sequins with an elaborate twist in her blonde hair. "Lily," Jonas said, "This is Penelope Carmichael, director of New York Alliance of the Arts. This is Lily Salomé, the woman I spoke with you about."

My nerves jumped. Of course, Jonas had planned this all along. I was pleased I had some knowledge of her from the website. She was one of the major contacts in New York Arts. She had a dream list of philanthropic contacts and had her hand in most of the major fundraising events.

Her wide mouth curved upward. "You have a youth art program?"

"Yes. It's the Love Legacy Art program. Artists participate in a weeklong art exchange with local and international future artists and raise funds to further encourage and support their artistry."

"How many years has the program been around?" Penelope asked.

"Twenty-seven years. It was formerly Art for Art Sake and was created by my mother. My father, a viola player with the Boston Symphony, was the first to participate. It has since been renamed the Love Legacy in their memory," I said evenly. Penelope listened and repeated pieces as if adding to memory.

"It was recently one of the recipients of Finch's Fundraiser," Jonas added. This news brought an arch to her brow. "The program is in need of structure, branding, marketing, and partnerships."

"I understand you personally take on diamond-in-the-rough programs for evaluations," I said.

"Not often, but I can be persuaded," she said to me and grinned. She then turned to Jonas. "You knew I wouldn't be able to pass this up, didn't you?"

Jonas grinned at her. "Yes, I did. And you won't regret it."

"If Jonas Crane is sold, then who am I to doubt it?" Penelope trilled. Reaching inside her clutch, she handed me her card. "Do you have a card to give to me?" I reached into my own clutch and began to hand her one.

"Wait," she instructed. "Give me a few more so I can hand them out too."

"Thank you," I smiled.

She looked the card over. "Your assistant is in Boston?"

I hesitated. Ms. Parker was working on the Legacy with me in her spare time. I had used volunteers. But truly, I couldn't afford to hire someone part-time.

Jonas spoke before I could. "She's hiring a new assistant. Have your assistant coordinate through mine."

"I'll have them use me as their contact, but you'll need a New York assistant or you'll be exhausted before you start," she joked and laughed. We politely joined in. "Now, before you have me organizing an event, I'll leave you both to enjoy the auction."

"Thank you very much," I said with enthusiasm.

"Thank you, Penelope. I won't forget this," Jonas said.

"No, thank you, Jonas. It's a pleasure, Lily," she said and sauntered away.

I wanted to throw my arms around Jonas, but I settled for a bright smile and a squeeze to his hand. "Wow. Did that just happen? Thank you so much, Jonas."

"I didn't do anything. You sold your program. So now you can't blame me for taking over," Jonas teased.

"You still helped. I know I've resisted your help in the past, but thank you," I replied.

"We all need help. My father helped me and his father helped him. We don't get anywhere on our own," Jonas said.

"You're right," I said. He leaned over and gave me a peck on the cheek. "Good. That means you won't fight me with hiring assistants." He covered my mouth with his before I could protest. "It's for selfish reasons. I want you around me. With what Penelope and I can bring to your program, I'm confident you will be able to cover it."

I stared down at his polished shoes. "I'd love you even if you didn't…"

"Lily, I know you," Jonas spoke over me and kissed my lips. "Now, let's meet some more people before we sit down for dinner."

Jonas didn't have to approach anyone. Everyone seemed to gravitate toward him once we walked further into the hall. He introduced me, and I stumbled at first, but found my stride in talking about my art legacy program and passing out cards. The lights eventually flashed off, followed by an announcement that dinner was being served in the main hall. It was decorated with black and white "NYAA" banners and artwork framing the center stage, with a couple of display cases in the middle.

We were met at the entryway by a hostess who escorted us to the front circle of tables. Above the stage was a large projection screen displaying quotes and art images on what it means to stand up for mental health by the charity organizations that were the recipients for the night's event. I was so busy reading one of the quotes that I hadn't noticed Jonas wasn't moving us to sit down. When I realized we weren't moving, I followed his gaze and eyed the approaching couple. It was an elderly male with oiled gray hair and a waxed mustache standing with a pretty middle-aged woman with shoulder-length, wavy hair. They were both dressed formally, the male in tuxedo and the female in a flowing black velvet gown. Something about them was familiar, and Jonas confirmed this when he said, "Arthur Finch and Rita Wallis."

They halted at the seats across from us. We all stiffly shook each other's hands and forced smiles to the strolling photographer before sitting down at the table.

"A friend would have warned me, Jonas. We are still friendly," Arthur said smiling.

"I was friendly when I called you about the incident last week. A friend would have warned me, too, before I flew back to New York," Jonas replied.

"No need to recount," Arthur said and looked at his Rita, who excused herself. Our champagne glasses were filled, though Jonas and Arthur placed additional drink orders for us.

"I was just as surprised as you, though I often said I wanted you two to marry," Arthur responded, glancing at me.

I busied myself with my champagne, since I wasn't "ordered" away like I suspected Arthur had quietly done to Rita.

Jonas sipped his champagne then replied, "We both know that's not going to happen. Did you get a copy of Melissa's papers from my legal team?"

Arthur sipped the brandy he was given as the wait staff placed the salads down, though Arthur ordered them to bring Rita's back when she returned. "Yes. You have her on nondisclosure violation. The defamation and slander would expose you, so we know you won't use it."

"If my hand is forced," Jonas said, then ate his salad. I focused on the screen on the stage, but started eating my salad too.

"So we are in negotiation now?" Jonas asked after taking another bite. "I could sue her for malpractice and invasion of privacy. Her behavior at my home would call into question her mental competency. That would expose her and your family if I were to go forward."

"We all know I'm not one for public scrutiny or tabloid fodder," Arthur said with irritation in his tone. "Melissa's not using her brain, forcing me to clean up her mess. She's been given an ultimatum. She gets on the plane tomorrow morning for Spain or she's on her own."

"I'm sure that went over well," Jonas replied.

"As much as expected. Trust me, though. She may love you, but not enough to stop being a Finch and lose everything," Arthur said between bites of his salad. I felt a twinge in my chest. From the way he said Finch it was clear that meant more to him. "Now, let's enjoy the rest of this event. No more talk of dissolving partnerships," he added.

"Not by me," Jonas assured. Rita returned to the table as if on cue and we ate the rest of the dinner and smiled when cameras came forward to take photos of us at the table. When we were done, Jonas turned to me. "I'm going to speak with Arthur for a bit. How about taking a look around at the paintings up for auction."

"*Now* you send her away," Arthur said lightly. He looked me over then turned to Jonas. "She's quiet, no fuss. Perfect." They smiled at each other and Rita laughed. Jonas didn't correct Arthur's assessment, but from all I'd heard, this was part of repairing their business relationship. I now understood what Jonas meant by business friends.

I plastered on a smile for Jonas. "Nice to meet you, Mr. Finch. Ms. Wallis. If you would excuse me."

I walked away and into the gallery room labeled Artwork for the Auction, where I looked at each of the items up for bid. They were all good, but one stood out amongst the others. It was an abstract of vibrant colors, but the feeling that rose in me caused warmth in my skin. Looking at the label, I understood why. It was called, "Uninhibited Desire." In smaller print, "Monique."

"Like this one? It's one of my favorites," a male's accented voice said, stopping next to me.

"Yes. I'm not an artist, but the feeling I get when looking at it…It's captivating. I don't know," I said, glancing at him. He was wearing a dark suit as opposed to a tuxedo. It stood out from his white-blonde curls that framed his chiseled face. His full lips spread into a smile.

"It sounds like you do," he said. "Monique, the artist, outdid herself. I've enjoyed it long enough. I thought someone else would enjoy it. Perhaps you?" His eyes were a unique shade of blue, so similar to the cerulean in the painting.

I shook my head. "I couldn't afford it," I answered frankly, then dipped my head.

"I'm not an artist either, just an accountant," he said.

My eyes flicked over the Rolex watch on his wrist. I was now certain that I was in the wrong profession. I looked back at the painting. "You know the artist?"

"Sometimes I do," he said. The sadness in his voice

had me looking at him again, and I found his gaze was on me.

"I'm Sergio Caro. You are?" he asked.

"Lily Salomé," I held out my hand for him to shake, but he lifted it to his lips. "Je suis enchanté de faire votre connaissance, Ms. Salomé."

"Nice to meet you too, Mr. Caro," I said, taking a step back when he let go of my hand.

"I'd love for it to go to someone who enjoys it," Sergio said, gazing at me.

I felt an arm around my waist and a kiss on the side of my face. "Mr. Caro. You've met *my* Lily," Jonas said.

"Mr. Crane," Sergio said and looked between us. "We were admiring the painting. Nice to meet you, Lily. I wish you both a good evening." He walked away.

I looked up at Jonas. "We were only talking about the painting."

"You were, but not him," Jonas said and kissed me again, this time a possessive one.

Jonas jutted his chin. "I don't like this one. Let's look around." He said and placed his hand in the small of my back and guided me through the paintings again. We chose a small beach house one, but I didn't tell him that it was by the same artist. We returned to our seats for the auction. Ours went for ten thousand, driven up by Arthur. It seemed as though he was intentionally making it a competition, though they had both agreed to donate more to the charity event.

At the end of the auction the podium was cleared

and desserts were being distributed to the tables. I looked at the watch on Jonas's wrist. It was close to midnight. We had to leave for the prison early. Before our table was served, Jonas announced to Arthur and Rita, "I must be going. Good to see you again, Rita. We'll talk again soon, Arthur."

"Of course. Have a good evening. The both of you," Arthur shook Jonas's hand and paused for a cameraman to take a photo of the two of them together.

Jonas texted David as we walked back into the gallery. "Did you know Arthur was going to be here tonight?" I asked.

"I took a chance. It was something we attended together in the past," Jonas said.

I looked around at the glamorous crowd around us. "Is this how your life has been and will be?" I asked.

"Sometimes it will. My book will require publicity. I get invited to attend events fairly regularly," he said.

I looked at my shoes. "Now I'm embarrassed taking you to karaoke. I don't fit in here."

Jonas clasped my chin. "You don't need to focus on fitting in. You focus on spending time together with me. That's what I did when we went for karaoke. And tonight. I thought about how much I love spending the evening with you."

I was again undone by his charm and the tender kiss he placed on my lips.

Glancing around the room once more, my eyes connected with Sergio Caro, whose sad eyes were on me. He was standing behind a female with light brown curls slumped down in a chair. She was dressed in a simple white cotton tunic. *No shoes. The artist?*

A little smile appeared on his face. I turned my head and snuggled against Jonas and he led me out of the gallery.

CHAPTER TWENTY-TWO

I WAS UP hours before I had to be at Rikers Island for my visitation with Declan. I used part of the time to dress simply in a white button-down shirt and jeans. I spent the rest polishing the statement I planned to read during the visitation. My lack of sleep the night before had more to do with anticipation than fear, though I knew it was still there. I believed it to be residual fear of the powers he used to control me: physical, verbal, and material. I now realized they were all powers I gave to him. *Not anymore.*

I was ready to remove Declan and close this part of my past. I was ready to let go and live in the new life that was beginning. The one with the man I had fallen in love with and loved with all my heart. Jonas Crane.

He was laying on the bed on his side with a pillow in his arms. My heart swelled. It was like he was still holding me. Crawling onto the bed, I gently kissed over his face until his eyes opened up for me. And when they did, a flutter went through me as I took in his beauty.

"You my alarm?" Jonas asked, replacing the pillow

with me. How long had he been mine?

I ran my hand over the soft hairs on his chest. “Yes, today I am.”

Pulling me close to stare into my face, he studied me. “Something on your mind?” he asked. Something was. Both the publicity we were receiving and this visit had me worried.

I licked my lips. I hated to give him news he wouldn’t like, but after yesterday with the media, I wasn’t sure about what we had planned. “I’m not sure if you should go to the prison with me today.”

“Why not? Tell me what you’re thinking,” Jonas asked.

He patiently waited, and I took a deep breath and told him. “What about what happened at your book announcement yesterday? They asked questions about our relationship. If they connect you to my cases, it could become a trial by media.”

“If it comes to that, it’s beyond our control,” Jonas responded. He got up off the bed and I was temporarily distracted by his nudity before he went into the bathroom. A few moments later, the shower turned on, marking the end of the discussion. For now at least.

I straightened the bed, though I knew Lin would change the sheets, and waited for him. Jonas returned twenty minutes later and I watched him get dressed. I tried again. “I know you’re right. I’m worried your involvement will put us under scrutiny.”

“I understand your concern, but my legal team is on

all the criminal filings," Jonas responded as he tucked his shirt into his denim jeans. He came over and cupped my face. "The media will find out anyway. We'll handle it like we're handling everything else that happened. It'll be okay." He took my hand. "Now, let's eat before Ian picks us up." We went down for breakfast and I muddled over what Jonas had said to me. Some things were beyond our control. Even the threat of losing a job hadn't stopped someone at Arch from leaking my stress leave.

Still, I went through the pros and cons in my head as we quietly ate our breakfast of poached eggs and fruit salads. Finally, Jonas commanded, "Come over here."

I took a deep breath and walked over to his side. Jonas pulled me down on his lap, his hand sliding to cup me on the outside of my jeans. A tremor went through me at the contact and his claim. I had come to understand that this was his way of reminding me that I was his and he would have a say in what happened to me.

"I don't stand on the sidelines, Lily. I need to be sure he won't hurt you. The only way I can do that is if I'm there with you. I am who I am and I will not allow the public to dictate my life. You're not alone. You're mine. I will be there to care for and support you," he tightened his grip between my thighs, making me squirm on his lap. Brushing my hair away, he sucked on my neck, marking me.

I closed my eyes and my throat closed. He was being playful, but this was Jonas. Nothing he did was without purpose. Truly, I was touched by the meaning. He claimed me and I was a part of him. Yes. I knew he was controlling with his heart. Jonas shifted me around to straddle his lap. "All in, together. No matter what," he said.

"Yes," I murmured. Our agreement. We would stand together.

We quietly held each other until the doorbell sounded. Jonas got an alert on his phone and I sat back for him to check it. "Arthur," he said. "Melissa left."

I kissed him. *Good.*

He tapped his phone again. "Ian's downstairs. We need to leave. We won't be coming back here, so make sure you take everything with you."

"I still haven't packed anything for our vacation," I said, my voice going up an octave.

That earned me one of his mischievous grins. "Trust me. You won't need anything but your passport."

My brows rose. "Passport? Please tell me."

"Seychelles, North Island in the Indian Ocean," he said, finally relenting.

My face lit up in surprise and he kissed me. I wasn't familiar with the place and didn't have time to look it up, but I dutifully went upstairs and collected my passport and a few things from the bathroom and bedroom to take with me.

My curiosity was piqued about the vacation. I found it a welcome distraction as we left the loft and got into Ian's car for the ride over to Rikers Island in Queens. Jonas kept me close as he and Ian discussed business, then Ian had his driver put on music for the rest of the distance to Rikers Island. Once at the gate, Ian gave his attorney pass and paperwork for our visit at the building marked Registration. We then gave our identifications and did security checks before moving on to the main building of the prison, where we were to go for the visit.

"It's best to leave everything but your ID and the statement in the car," Ian instructed before we got out. Once outside, it all hit me. The steel barbwire fences running the length of a virtually windowless brick building really set the scene. We were going to prison.

We walked inside, where Ian's attorney pass granted us passage to skip in front of the long line of men, women, and children there for visits. Still, we had to go through the security checks. Thorough security checks. I felt a little worked over by the pat down, mouth, and hair checks. Jonas and Ian seemed to have taken it in stride when we joined up again.

We were next led into the visitation area, where we found Diane waiting for us in one of the brightly colored wooden and metal chair rows. Like Ian, she stood out in her expensive business suit.

She rose when she saw us, along with a thin male with wiry hair and glasses who introduced himself. "I'm Tim Waters. Declan Gilroy's Public Defender. We are waiting here until they collect him from his cell."

Diane looked at me. "The officer will escort us through those doors," she pointed to the one open with a uniformed officer standing outside of it. The room is small and will be divided. You on one side and Mr. Gilroy on the other. Both sides will have a desk with microphones to speak. There is a large plastic wall between you so he will be visible, but you will be protected."

"And where will you be?" I asked, no longer wishing to be alone in one of the rooms.

"I, along with Jonas and Ian, will be in the chairs right behind you. We have been given half an hour, but I don't think we will need to use it all. What do you think?"

"I've prepared a statement that I'd like to read before anything else. That's all I'd like to do," I said, glancing between the three of them.

"Yes. Jonas informed me," she replied, glancing at Jonas. "We will have you speak first, and then Mr. Gilroy will be allowed to speak."

"He has things to say, as well as an apology," Tim spoke up.

Jonas and Ian gave him a hard look. "You're also aware if his apology is abusive, we will end the visitation."

He nodded and we sat down. After a few minutes, a number was called out that had Diane, Ian, and Tim rising again, with Jonas and myself following. We were escorted into a plain drop-ceiling room with noisy overhead lights. Other than that, the room was just as Diane had described, two-sided with a long shelf and a plastic wall dividing it. I was brought to sit on a wooden chair in front of a built-in microphone. Jonas, Ian, Diane, and Tim took the seats on the row of chairs behind me. I stared across and noticed the same setup on the other side. I wiped my hands on my jeans and took out the sheet of paper from the folder with my statement. A bell sounded and my pulse sprinted as Declan was brought in through the door on the other side. His wispy, reddish-blonde hair was in disarray and a few days' growth of beard appeared on his face. He was in dressed in an orange jumpsuit and white t-shirt. His green eyes were sharp and immediately zeroed in on me. A smug smile spread across his face.

I tightened my jaw as I peered at him. He looked past me and seemed to realize I wasn't alone. His facial expression morphed, taking on a softer appearance. One I also found familiar. It was the face of the man I had fallen in love with years before. He slumped his shoulders as he sat down in the seat.

"Alright, Lily, you can say what you have prepared," Diane said.

"What? This is my visit. Aren't I the one who gets to speak?" Declan argued. "Tim?" He turned to his attorney for support.

"Turn off his microphone," Ian said.

Diane motioned for the guard and they muted Declan's microphone. His face reddened as his mask slipped, showing the monster we both knew lived beneath.

I cleared my throat and started reading.

"Today will be the last day that I will voluntarily see you, Declan Gilroy. The next time we are in the same room, I will be testifying against you in court for assaulting me outside of Parco's Diner—"

"Objection," Declan yelled, loud enough to be heard without his microphone.

Diane rose and walked over to the microphone. "This isn't court. This is a visit. You can't object to it. You can end it. Do you want to end it now?" she growled.

He gave her a harsh look. "This is—" He tapped the microphone, and Diane requested that it be unmuted for him to continue speaking. "This was supposed to be a visit for me to apologize to her."

"You can't both speak at the same time. Lily is speaking first. You will have your turn after she's done, or do we need to mute you again to behave?" she said, her last words dripping with sarcasm.

He sneered at her, then gave me a hard look and my pulse picked up. Tim rose and came over to the microphone. "You will get your chance to speak, Declan."

Declan puffed his chest out, but gave Tim a nod. They took their seats again.

"You may continue, Lily," Diane said.

I lifted my chin. "I will also testify against you in court for harassing me with threatening calls and for distributing pornography to my coworkers—"

"Alleged. You have no proof," Declan interrupted and lifted the corner of his mouth.

"I'll end this visit now if you can't control yourself," I said authoritatively.

His eyes widened and his lips curled up. He didn't speak, but placed his hands on the surface of the desk, then closed and opened them.

Sweat broke out all over my body as my eyes narrowed on his hands. The hands that had hurt me over and over again. *Never again.*

I took a deep breath and continued. "My only regret in all of this is not contacting the police when you first beat me. I lied, protected, and supported you because I believed in you. I brought you to my family in hopes—"

"In hopes that you and your snobby parents would change me, try to turn me into someone who would spoil you like they did," he said, cutting me off again.

"I wasn't spoiled, I was loved and cared for by my parents," I interjected. "And they weren't snobs, they just saw in you what I didn't see. That you never loved or cared about me." My voice was calm, but passionate.

"I did. I do. I always will. You are the love of my life," he said and leaned his body over the desk, closer to the glass.

I pressed my lips together. "I don't believe you even know what love is. If you did, you wouldn't have hurt me. But I'm here to let you know that your immature and feeble attempts at ruining me didn't succeed. I'm thriving. I am loved and happy. I doubt you even know what love is, or empathy beyond yourself. But hopefully, during the years you stay in jail for whatever additional charges are to come, you will use that time to better yourself."

"I'm not staying in jail," Declan said defiantly and cursed. His skin turned red. He was breathing hard into the microphone. We were quiet for a few moments that seemed like hours. "My turn yet?" he gritted.

"Are you finished, Lily?" Diane asked.

I turned and nodded my head to her.

Tim walked over to the microphone and said. "Go ahead, Declan."

Declan glowered. "I was going to apologize, but since you decided to act like a stupid bitch, you can fuck off you—"

"We're done," I said loudly into the microphone on my side. Then I stood up, squared my shoulders, and took a step away from the desk.

"She can't leave. It's not time," Declan yelled. "Lily, stop! Sit your ass back in that chair, damn it. Don't do this. I'm losing my job, my place, everything. You have to help me. I'm sorry."

I walked over to Jonas, who was beaming at me. "I'm ready to go."

"I didn't mean it. I love you." I could hear Declan yelling. "What about your stuff? I can give everything back to you the second I leave…"

Jonas kissed me possessively, and a loud bang filled the space. I startled and turned my head toward the sound, only to find Declan punching his fists against the divider wall. Two correctional officers quickly grabbed hold of him. He was swearing and flailing, but I didn't stay to watch more.

I was done with Declan Gilroy.

"Excellent, Lily," Diane said. "His violent outburst will be on record for this visit."

I hadn't set out to get that, so I had no response. However, I did thank her.

We re-entered the visitation room and found Heather in the waiting area. Her face was a cheery mask of heavy makeup. I wasn't sure she would still be able to visit with Declan today, but I didn't want to damper the smile on her face as she rushed up to greet me. "I'm sorry I rushed away yesterday. There was a flood in the basement of our apartment building. I had to spend the rest of the afternoon clearing it out," she said.

Jonas touched my arm. "We have to go, Lily."

"I'm sorry. I hope you were able to salvage a few things," I said.

"Oh, I did thanks. But poor Declan. He's going to be so mad. I was able to save most everything, except for his old leather jacket, his helmet, a box of tools, a DVD called Atuelle—"

I dug my nails into the center of my hand. "Auteuil, France," I said. *Where my father was born.* He had one of the missing videos of my parents from our vacation.

She darted her tongue over her cracked lips, her hand going to her neck. "Was that yours?"

"We're leaving," Jonas barked. I took a couple of steps.

"Wait," Heather called out.

My gaze followed after her as she rushed over to a chair and snatched a medium-size manila envelope. I stopped moving. Her hands were shaking as she tried to hand it to me. "The stuff was soaking in water. I don't know how long. I only discovered it when it slipped out of a book."

"I have to go," Diane said.

I took the envelope in my hand. "A book. Do you know the name of it?" I asked, ignoring Jonas's tugs on my arm.

Heather chewed her mangled lip. Her eyes dilated. "Was that yours too? I threw it away. It was molding. I think it had a drawing on the front of it. Green." She said to my apt face. "It wasn't a college book that you left. It damaged some of the photos. I think some of the words imprinted on the photos," she jabbered.

"We should leave," Ian said with urgency.

"Lily," Jonas said softly.

My fingers scrambled inside of the folder and took one out. A photo of me at five years old with my parents. It was damaged, like Heather said, and I tried to decipher the letters.

"d r e n one grow up e"

All children, except for one, grow up. Peter Pan.

"Was that important to Declan? Do you think he will be angry with me?" I think I heard Heather say.

But I couldn't see or hear. I could only feel my heart breaking into a million pieces.

"You're worth more. Your life is worth more," Jonas cooed as he held me in his arms in the back of the car. How we got there, I wasn't sure. My consciousness had burrowed under memories.

It's the night of my fifth birthday. I'm wearing my angel costume. "Can I wear it to bed Mommy?"

My mommy giggles. She tugs on the wings that are hanging off the back of the white lacy dress that's coated with paints and punch stains. She untangles the halo she made from the tangles in my hair. "Yes."

"Yippee!" I run and jump on the bed and she laughs again.

Daddy comes in the door. "You're not flying without pixie dust, little vagabond," he jokes.

I giggle as he lifts me up and flies me in his arms. He places me down and reaches to the side of the bed. "I have your present."

My head tilts and I try to think. "Mommy said the party was my present."

"Yes, but you were so good, Daddy has another one," Mommy says and sits down next to me. He places a leather-bound book on my lap. It's heavy. I run my hands over the gold letters. "P .e .t." I say.

My eyes widen and my mouth forms an 'o'. "Peter Pan!" I cry excitedly.

He opens the front cover. "It says. 'Ever the vagabond, Tiger Lily. With Love. Your father, Randall Salomé'."

I place my hands on his cheeks. "Why you crying, Daddy?"

"Happy tears," he says.

I tilt my head. "Like happy thoughts?"

"You're my happy thought," he says.

"Mine is a secret." I lean up and he tilts his head down so I can share a secret. "You and mommy are my happy thoughts," I whisper.

"Our beautiful Tiger Lily," Daddy says and they cuddle and kiss me. "Let's read it together."

"All children except one grows up."

Jonas lifted my head. "Ian's dropping us off at my plane. David can bring anything from the loft you might want to take along." I blinked at him and gave a little shake of my head. It didn't matter.

I'm lying on Jonas's chest in the loft. He's reading Peter Pan to me.

My book was gone. My parents were gone. Memories shifted again.

I open the door at Franklin Street. A police officer with watery eyes says, "Can I come in?"

"My parents are sleeping..." It's quiet. I step outside. Where is their car?

"Please. Can we talk inside?" he asks.

I closed my eyes as tears tunneled down my face. *I'm holding it together. I'll make it.*

I sit on the front pew of the church where the community memorial service is being held for my parents.

I'm holding it together. I'll make it.

"Oh, they tell me of a home far beyond the skies. Where my loved ones have gone," the gospel soprano sings out before the caskets of my parents.

I drop my head and sob.

A small, warm hand touches my arm. "Don't be sad, Lily." I lift my head to find Erica Higgins, one of my mother's first graders. She hands me a drawing. It's my mom and dad with angel wings flying above the elementary school. "See. They will fly back to see us."

"Lily, we're getting out to board the plane," Jonas said gently.

We walked out of the car and onto the tarmac. "Thanks, Ian," I heard Jonas say. My vision was blurred. We moved up into the cabin. Jonas fastened me in and cupped my face. "I'm proud of you, Tiger Lily. I know you're hurting right now, but it's over. You have your life and you have me. I love you."

Memories clouded my vision again.

Jonas is reading the inscription of Peter Pan aloud on my bed in Jersey City. We are talking about it and he's holding me. We are standing in the rain and he whispers in my ear, "I love you, Lily."

I'm lying on Jonas's chest in the loft. He's reading Peter Pan to me.

Jonas held my hand as the plane taxied down the runway and lifted off into the sky.

We flew away.

CHAPTER TWENTY-THREE

JONAS HANDED ME a warm cloth at my bedside and I wiped over my face. “Thank you,” I mumbled. My throat felt like sandpaper.

He handed me a water. “I know how much that book meant to you. I’m here when you’re ready to talk about it.”

He went to rise, but I clasped his arm. “Where are you going?”

“After I put the towel away, right next to you.” He stroked my hair back from my face. I closed my eyes and waited. But I knew I wouldn’t have to wait long, because I wasn’t alone. Jonas would be by my side, helping me through my grief.

Jonas had quietly took me back to the suite the second the emergency lights were turned off. I went quietly. I had calmed down. How Jonas had managed to get me out of the prison, I did not know. It was something my mind had mercifully tucked away for the moment—the only mercy afforded me after finding out what happened to my book. A gift of love and a story straight from the heart of my father, marking the loving bond we shared as a family, was gone forever.

Truly, that book worked as a talisman, inspiring and guiding my life. My most precious memories were imprinted on its pages. I strived to be a Salomé, their loyal and brave Tiger Lily, who worked hard and never gave up on her dreams. It was my reminder of love and family. Because I was the last of the living Salomés, I had shared the story with the man I loved and told him my dreams of sharing it with our child. I told him how I hoped it would become our tradition, our legacy.

Despite all that the book meant to me, I knew I had been willing to sacrifice it and all my stolen possessions to remove from my life the man who had controlled and hurt me. And just like fate, the book became my ultimate offering. From its destruction came the last leverage Declan had over me. His violent aggression at the jail may have caused him to remain there until trial. This year? Next? I wasn't certain when that would be, nor did I care. I wasn't afraid either. I was completely done with him.

The mattress dipped, marking Jonas's return. He molded himself to my side, placing his arm around my waist. I took the warmth and comfort of his arms.

I RESTED FOR most of the 17-hour plane ride to Seychelles. I ate when Jonas encouraged me and stretched outside the plane when we stopped to refuel, all the time meditating on my memories. Some memories felt like grooves were being carved into my heart. The pain was intense and part of me wanted to shut it down, run, or try to numb the feelings away, but from what I went through up until now, I knew that wasn't the answer.

I believed I would reach the other side of grief.

I was strong and I would be stronger still.

This became clear as the hours passed on the flight. I found that I had to put effort into finding the painful memories. They were being broken apart by the support from the amazing man I fell in love with, Jonas Crane. He talked about nothing and everything with me. He encouraged, held, and caressed me. I thought I couldn't love him more, but he showed me I could and did. I loved him utterly.

"We are almost there," Jonas said, kissing me awake.

"Do I have anything I can change into?" I asked.

He rolled my trolley case from the side of the bed and set it down.

I opened it up and my nerves frazzled as I eyed the bikinis. I lifted the strings and tiny fabric and let out a short laugh. "I doubt I can fit these, have you noticed I've gained weight? Dr. Steinman will be amazed when I go back to see him."

Jonas lifted one the tops. "I'll judge if it's too small. And our villa is secluded, so you could easily wear nothing," he replied with a roguish grin.

I searched through the bag and was pleased to find a light blue, full-piece swimsuit that I held up. "Thank you, Kate."

"Actually, Mary helped," Jonas said.

My lips parted. "Thank you, Mary. She didn't tell me. How did you get her to keep a secret?"

"I think Ian helped with that," he said, and we both laughed. Ian certainly kept her attention. I went into the bathroom and washed my face and brushed my teeth. My eyes were still rimmed red, but I felt better and said as much to Jonas on my reentry to the bedroom.

"Good," he said and kissed my forehead. He had a carry bag open and was rummaging through it. "Samuel prepared what he called an essential travel pack." He held up a box with a video camera, underwater camera, and a digital camera.

"We can capture the whole vacation," I said. He picked up the digital camera, turned it on and took a picture of me.

"Come here," he said and I came closer. He put an arm around me and held the camera out and took one of us together, then kissed me. *New memories.* I exhaled and sat down on the bed. "I'm not familiar with North Island."

"This should help." He reached inside the side pocket of the case and handed me a brochure.

North Island Honeymoon Escape. I sat down on the bed and gazed at the glossy photos and images dreamily as I looked through the brochure. It was a wish of my heart and born from the love and care that grew every day I shared with this wonderful man. I wanted it to be us getting married. I wished I could spend the rest of my life with him.

"Find something you like?" Jonas asked.

My gaze shifted to him before I had a chance to cloak my expression. He took in a sharp breath and I quickly turned over on my side. "The place looks like a tropical paradise."

"We both know that's not all. Please turn around and tell me what's on your mind," Jonas said, abandoning the suitcase and moving closer to me on the bed.

I sighed and did as he asked, though I chickened out and stared at his chin. "I love you and you love me. I know that. I just…" I licked my lips. "I mean it's all good for now. But we've never really talked about, or I haven't shared, what I hope for in the future." I took a deep breath and then continued. "I loved my family. And I want a family of my own." I stopped babbling long enough to catch my breath and peered at him through my long lashes.

His face was blank and he folded his arms, which had my heart beating faster.

"I knew—" He got out, but I interrupted him by saying. "I don't expect *you* to marry me."

He lifted the corner of his mouth. "You don't want marry me?"

"I do. I would if you do, but if you don't that's fine," I sputtered. I took a breath and tried again. "I love you very much and I'm happy being your girlfriend. I just thought you should know, as part of our relationship, what I hoped for in the future."

After a minute, Jonas asked. "Can I speak now?"

I nodded.

"I knew you wanted a family before you told me. As for marriage, as you know, I wasn't planning to get married again after my divorce."

I swallowed and nodded, then flipped back over. "I understand. It's fine."

"Tiger Lily. I'm not finished speaking. Would you turn around for me?"

"Just give me a minute," I said, my voice thick.

He crawled on the bed and turned me over, pinning me on my back. His eyes glimmered. "First, I was in my early twenties when we had Paul. He wasn't planned, but I love my son. I believe I've grown in the fifteen years since he was born. I don't think you were listening. I said I didn't plan to. I didn't say never. I can't say never to you. I tried to make you my sexual companion and you've leapt to an exclusive, live-in girlfriend. If I had your track record with me, I'd relax."

I could only blink. My heart pounded in my chest. He pressed his lips to mine and moved to break our contact apart, but I deepened it. My tongue slipped inside his mouth and tangled with his, giving him my own brand of a claiming kiss.

When I broke away, we caught our breaths and he grinned at me. "You ready to relax and enjoy our vacation, Ms. Salomé?"

"Yes, Mr. Crane," I said. He pecked my lips and got up. "We have a short helicopter ride and then we get to enjoy our break."

I grimaced. "Helicopter ride?"

"It's fifteen minutes. I'll be right by your side," Jonas assured and gave me a quick kiss. He got up and took out a video camera. "We can take turns filming." I held the camera and he zipped up the case. We then made our way back to our seats for the landing in Seychelles.

We exited the plane and I squinted against the bright sunlight. A warm breeze billowed our shirts as we finished our arrival clearance. Once done, a male representative from the hotel greeted and directed us to a buggy. We rode a few yards away to a small helicopter. And without a moment to spare, we were strapped into the leather seats and given noise-canceling headphones.

My pulse sprinted as the pilot closed the doors. I stared out the curved plexiglass windows. "The weather is perfect today. You should have a clear view of the island," the pilot said.

The helicopter's lift was surprisingly smooth and it eased with an almost vertical glide to the ocean. Still, my hands shook as I took the camera from Jonas. Taking pictures was a welcome distraction, in conjunction with the pilot's discussion of island life. I panned around to film the islands. They appeared to pebble the vast breadth of azure water and were lush with greenery and large granite rocks. It was breathtaking.

I turned the video camera to capture Jonas's excited face. It was as alluring as the ocean view.

"We're approaching North Island," the pilot announced.

Jonas took the camera from me and the helicopter hovered close to where the blue ocean met a shallower turquoise water with reefs. It expanded up to a white sandy beach. A single palm frond-covered hut seemed to be the only pause in the scenery.

We stepped out on the stone helipad and quickly followed our representative down the beach. The closer we reached, the more there was to see of the hut. It stretched into a modern, spacious villa.

The representative unlocked and eased back a glass framed retractable door at the side of the villa for entry into an open, spacious bedroom. The décor included a reclaimed wooden desk and woven chests, brightly colored lamps, and lounge chairs situated around a silk and mesh curtained four-poster bed.

My face lit up and Jonas rubbed my back. He took my hand and we walked through a curtain of shells to follow our guide, passing natural, furnished lounges, wood-carved tables, and colorful daybeds.

"We will use every one of them," Jonas said and kissed my neck. He moved us outside to a plunge pool with a cascading waterfall. Farther out was a finished hut with silk netting and a large day bed out on the water.

"Would you like to discuss dinner?" the attendant said with a wide grin.

"One second." Jonas turned to me and said, "I'll handle it and lunch. Go explore and relax."

I wanted to sit out in the hut, but something else

tempted me more. I turned and walked through the kitchen and bathroom. The bathroom was dominated by glass windows and a large, sunk-in stone tub. Turning on the tap, I filled the basin, pouring in a selection of scented flowers and oils from a slate and bamboo tray next to the tub.

"Starting without me?" Jonas said, walking into the room.

"This is beautiful," I said, gaping at the panoramic ocean view. He came up behind me and circled my waist, his hands resting low on my stomach.

"Not as beautiful as you." The air seeped out of my parted lips. I shuddered as the jolt from his touch spread through me at his contact. I felt his chest expand against my back as he kissed the top of my head. He then turned me around and removed my clothes, like he was unwrapping a precious gift. He seemed to revere every piece of skin revealed. His gaze amorously lingered.

When he was done, I stood tall and naked with my hands at my sides, unashamed. I believed myself to be just as beautiful and special to him as he claimed. He stood back and the pleasure on his face warmed my heart. He hugged me and I hugged him back. "My Tiger Lily."

I helped him remove his clothes with all the care he had given to me.

A sensual light passed between us as we stepped down into the bath. We dipped our heads back, dampening our hair. He picked up the pomegranate shampoo and massaged it into my scalp.

"They are bringing dinner in a few hours. They brought a tray of fruits, cheeses, and fresh fish for us for lunch."

"Are we the only ones here?" I murmured as his hands massaged down my neck and back.

"In this villa and beach, yes. I thought we could use some privacy before we lose more of it with the book."

"Is the book mostly about your life, going up the ranks?" I asked.

"Partly. Along with some of the things I have learned that would hopefully benefit those who want to grow their business. Some of the passages are taken from some of my presentations I've given over the years, too," he answered. Filling a loofah with a lily scented scrub, he washed over my body without hesitation or question. I yielded, surrendering to his will. And once again, my insides warmed at the tender glide of his hands as they took loving possession of me. It was as if he wanted me to know just how much he honored having me as his own.

When he was done, I sought to do the same and we exchanged places. I put my feelings in my actions, and again, seeing the joy on his face made my heart constrict. I wanted to keep the happiness on his face forever. He turned his head, but I cupped his face, moving it back to me. His eyes shimmered and he shook his head. I pressed my lips to his and said, "I love you so much." Taking his hand, I climbed out. We didn't speak as we dried off, but we both knew where we wanted to go together next. So hand-in-hand, we stood and went into the bedroom.

Jonas moved ahead of me and pulled back the mesh curtain. I crawled on the bed and laid on my side, waiting for him to follow. Our eyes found each other and the world stood still, as if it was giving us a chance to capture the moment. I took it frame by frame in my head and heart.

"I love you," Jonas said and kissed me. My heart expanded so much I was overcome. He had shown me his love in many ways, but hearing his profession meant more. It was a balm that soothed the abrasions on my soul, the deep parts where I felt left behind, lost and alone. Unloved.

"You're mine," he said, adding on another layer of protection. I absorbed his words and his meaning. I was his to love. I was his to keep.

I wanted him now. I wanted him forever. I went into his arms. "My beautiful Tiger Lily. Whatever you want, it's yours," he said.

"You," I answered without hesitation.

"You have me," he said quietly and kissed me passionately on the lips.

Laying me back, Jonas went slow, kissing over my face and down to the hollow base at my neck. Filling his hands with my breasts. Light teases with his fingers, tender tugs on the taut peaks of each nipple. I moaned softly as my body heated and I arched into his caresses, my hands petting his dark silky hair. I followed the line of his beautiful sculpted cheekbones and placed my hands on the stubble on the sides of his face as he sweetly suckled and cherished me. His touches were like a message to my skin. *You are precious. You are loved.*

Jonas kissed over the curve of my hips. My eyelids fluttered, my chest rising and falling. He looked up the line of my body at me and I spread my legs right under his gaze. Once more, the pleasure of my response was evident on his face, but he went further and said, "I love that you have become comfortable with me."

I smiled down at him. I could see he was aroused by a glance in his eyes. The set of his jaw. His erect cock. But there was more. We had built this intimacy together. I was certain he wanted me.

He nuzzled the smooth skin at the top of my mound and a tingle went through me. He moaned as he slowly licked up and down my slit, then gently with his fingers he opened me wider and rolled his tongue around my clit. I shook as I tried to remain still, wanting nothing to stop the glorious sensation of his mouth on me. He paused and lifted my fingers and kissed their tips, then placed them on his head. *I love you*, I mouthed.

"I know," Jonas said and went back to pleasuring me. I gripped his head as he lapped through my slick folds and suctioned my clit. He was right where I wanted him and I broke apart, crying out as I came fast. But a taste wasn't enough for Jonas. He was there to consume. He added two fingers and struck the spot that had me coming again.

"I can't take more," I hissed, twisting away as my muscles contracted over and again. The dark look on his face let me know he was up for the challenge.

Jonas kissed my thigh. "Come back over here." His deep tone worked as its own aphrodisiac. I moved back and gapped my thighs the way I knew he wanted me to.

He kissed each thigh and started all over again, this time pushing me right over into madness. I came and wanted away. But the second he was gone, I wanted him back. Jonas met both with love. He pushed me over the edge just to catch me. He had the skill and confidence, but he still studied every quiver and tremor in my body. He loved and cared enough to try to find more ways of pleasuring me.

With that thought, I cried out his name, writhing as he fucked me with his tongue. When I came down, this time, he slid his body up mine and kissed my damp forehead.

"Seeing you come is addicting." Then, examining my face, he offered, "I can wait until later if you are too tired." His words ignited me once again. Truly, I couldn't get enough of him.

I gripped his firm ass. "I need you," I rasped.

He kissed me tenderly, stroking his tongue against mine. Giving me a taste of myself. I felt his need too. He rolled on his back and, while I wanted to take my time, I knew Jonas wasn't one to enjoy waiting. I laved over the head of his cock and sucked it in my mouth, tasting his pre-cum. He was throbbing in my hands, vibrating with need. And I sought to sate him, gliding him across my tongue to the back of my throat.

He gripped my head, stilling me, and let out a loud moan. From there, he set the rhythm and I aimed to please. My mouth moving up and down his cock. Stroking and squeezing his sacs until his breath was jagged and he asked me to stop. I still couldn't help but add a few licks and strokes with my hands.

Jonas kissed me and moved us to our sides and we faced each other. He lifted my thigh and I wrapped it around his back. He moved his leg between mine and with a long, deep thrust of his cock, we were pressed together. We looked at each other and an electric current surged through my body. Our bond.

This close, it was like we were molded to each other. Our hips grinding against each other. He gripped my ass and I held him tighter as we reached and took our bliss. We cried out as we erupted, clinging to each other. We gasped for air with our foreheads touching, our hearts hammering in our chests, neither one of us wanting to let go. Trying to stretch the moments of ecstasy into the infinite.

It was Jonas who finally broke us apart with a tender kiss on my lips. I turned over and he spooned me and we rested together.

I woke up on the bed tangled up in the sheets sometime later to find Jonas sketching. "What are you working on there?" I asked.

"My favorite muse." He said, lifting the paper for me

to see. It was of me sleeping on the lounge.

"Should I stay still?" I asked.

"No," he replied, placing his work down as he stood. "I can get back to it later. I thought this was a good time to get back to things that we enjoy, though. I haven't sketched since the hotel, but I'm hoping to do more when we return. There are things in the bag, too. Music, books."

I got up and padded over to the bag and found a bikini to put on. I started putting my clothes away in the dresser and a couple of dresses in the closet. When I got to the bottom, I discovered the paperback *Peter Pan* from the bedside table.

"You brought this?" I gave him a wistful smile and walked over and sat on the bed.

"Yes. I had hoped we could continue before…" Jonas paused.

"Before what happened at the prison," I finished for him. "I was devastated about the book, but some good happened there too. I'm happy it's over and thankful you were there with me."

He put his sketchpad down and crawled on the bed with me. "I agree. You were brave, strong, and gracious. I was grateful to witness your triumph."

"Hardly a triumph after what happened with Heather," I said. My voice caught.

"I'm sorry. I know how much the book meant to you," Jonas said, rubbing my hip.

"When he took it—it broke my heart. I thought it

was my fault. I was always talking about my parents and how much it meant to me," I said. My voice graveled.

"And there was nothing wrong with you doing that. You shared your feelings with someone that you cared for," he said, stroking the side of my face. "I know I was engrossed when you told me about it."

I ran my tongue over my lips. "On the first night I stayed with you at the hotel. You were nosing through my stuff." I let out a dry laugh.

"Yes, and you told me about your nickname and your parents. How the story inspired you to keep alive their legacy through the art program."

He moved on to his back and I shifted around to look at him. "When I realized we couldn't find it, I thought reading the story with me in the loft would help you."

I snuggled closer to him. "It did help. I thought a lot about you reading the book to me in the loft."

He traced my jawline with the tips of his fingers. "Your book inspired me to add it to the fundraiser gala last month."

"I thought you put my program in the gala to win me back," I mused.

He kissed my smile. "Giving you things doesn't win you over. You wanted me."

"I wanted you and your love," I admitted.

He tilted my face up and gazed into my eyes. "You have both." He kissed me passionately then got up from the bed.

"The book is more than a possession and I'm grateful that I have the good memories. I know they will never be taken away from me."

"This is the perfect time. I have something for you," he stood up and walked out of the room, winking at me as he said, "Be right back."

He came back moments later with a case, which he sat down facing away from me.

"You binding me again?" I joked.

He gave me a salacious look. "If you're good. You enjoyed that as much as I did."

I grinned and didn't deny it. I hadn't been up for it at first, but I wouldn't be opposed if he wanted to try it again.

"Not this time." He handed me a beautifully wrapped medium-sized box. I jokingly shook it. It didn't rattle. I tore it open, and my heart stopped. *Peter and Wendy by J.M. Barrie 1911.*

It wasn't the same as the one my father given me. This was a first edition. "Jonas. This is too much. I can't—"

"You will. I've inscribed this copy so you will have to keep it," Jonas said. My hands trembled as I opened the book and read Jonas's inscription.

To my Tiger Lily,

May you forever share your story and inspire generations to come.

I love you,
Jonas Crane

I gingerly placed it down and threw my arms around his neck. "Oh, Jonas. I love it. I love you. Thank you so much."

He hugged me back. "I love you, too."

"It's so…wow," I admired when we parted. I carefully lifted it and placed it delicately back in the box, to his amusement. "I'm going to have to put it in a locked display case."

"It's meant to be read," Jonas said, the side of his mouth turning up.

"It will be," I assured. He had given me a new book, but it was much more than that. He'd given me a new story that would be added to my others. Truly, I knew now the life I shared with my parents and the inspiration they gave to me was much more powerful than the physical book. While it was destroyed, it would remain in my heart and live on for those I shared it with. It may even inspire their lives or help others, like it did for Jonas and me.

"I'd like to read to you, if you don't mind," I said shyly.

"Are you sure you're ready?" he asked cautiously.

"Yes. I am," I said, and I believed I was. I wanted to move forward and go on. "How about at that little hut?" I said, pointing.

"I'll bring out our lunch," Jonas said and kissed me.

I met Jonas out by the small table near a silk-strung hut and ate the light lunch he produced. Afterwards, we crawled on the daybed inside of the tent and looked out over the sea. Then, with Jonas's arms wrapped around me, I took a deep breath and started reading the book from the beginning.

The sun was warm and we took a dip in the pool to cool off after an hour or so, only to rest again together inside. I was roused later by music. Beethoven's "Appassionata." It was evening and the room was casted in the soft light of candles. I sat up and looked out at the beach. The sky was filled with blues and whites.

I was about to get up and search for Jonas when I found a sketch of me sleeping propped up alongside a note. *Dinner in an hour. Beach formal.*

I rose and picked a pretty white cotton sleeveless dress from the closet and changed into it. I was brushing my hair back when Jonas appeared dressed in open-collared white linen shirt and tailored trousers. His full lips were turned up in a smile. "Ready?" I put the brush down and hugged him. "What's that for?" he asked.

"For everything." I said. "Thank you for this vacation."

"You look beautiful," Jonas said. He took my hand and led me out to the deck that was now lit by candle lights. A table set for two awaited us, with tiger lilies around a fluted ornate candle in the center. He held out my chair.

I melted. *It's like a dream.* "This is so beautiful," I prattled.

Jonas sat down and lifted his glass. "A toast from Voltaire. Love is a canvas furnished by nature and embroidered by imagination. I borrow this evening as an expression of the love I have for you, Tiger Lily." The sound of Beethoven's "Pathetique" played in the background as the wait staff came out with our grilled seafood and fresh salad platter. "I knew I was in trouble the second you walked into Sir Harry's."

"When I threw my handbag at you?" I teased and sipped my champagne.

"Good. You admit it now," he said and we laughed. "I knew you were special that night."

"I was nervous. You're intimidating," I said. "But you kissed me."

"You wanted that kiss," Jonas said confidently.

"Yes, I did," I admitted. "I knew I would fall in love with you, but you wanted a companion."

"I wasn't looking to get hurt again," Jonas said. "Then you left and that was hard because I missed you. I was alone." I took his hand and squeezed it. "I tried to move on like Dani did after our divorce. But I found you weren't replaceable. You were more than sex. You were kind, sincere, open, and loving. You were irreplaceable, unforgettable."

"I was scared and at my lowest. I didn't think I was worthy of you. I wasn't strong like the women you had in your life," I confessed.

"I'd say the contrary," Jonas said.

"I know now there are many different layers of strength. You picked me up at my lowest. You loved and cared for me. I found my way and got my life. For all that, I will never be able to thank you enough. It's not just what you do, it's who you are. You work tirelessly and still find time to be an amazing father and friend. I admire you and I'm so proud of you," I said.

He kissed the back of my hand. I smiled at him and went back to eating until we finished and the wait staff removed our plates. I looked out at the sea. "This was the perfect evening."

"It's not over. It's just beginning," Jonas said. He placed a small box before me and my heart leapt into my throat.

"I got this ring just before I picked you up from Arch. I told myself if you came back, I would never let you go again. And I won't. I want to wake up to you every morning and go to bed with you every night. I want to have our special conversations and listen to you ramble and watch you blush. I want to watch you reach for your dreams and be a part of them. This is where I want our relationship to go and grow, with you by my side as my wife. I love you. Will you marry me?"

Tears sprang to my eyes. I was trembling. "Yes," I answered without hesitation. I got up and threw my arms around his neck. "Yes! I love you."

He pulled me onto his lap, then reached over and collected the box. "You didn't look at the ring."

"You chose it for me. It's perfect," I said. He kissed me hard on the lips, then he took my hands in his and lifted the lid. It was a beautiful precision cut diamond and silver engagement ring. "I thought less flash, more feeling," he said. "Look at the inscription."

I peered down and read.

You're mine. Always.

"I am," I said.

He reached out and wiped the tears that were pouring down my face. I shook as he placed it on my hand.

The sound of a violinist playing "Unforgettable" filled the evening. Jonas stood us up, took me in his arms, and we swayed. We kissed through the night and forever.

EPILOGUE

A MONTH LATER

"LILY, JONAS AND Paul will be here soon."

I looked up from the computer to find Dani. She was wearing a white, embroidered churidaari, and I was still dressed in my T-shirt and jeans from the morning. I was running late for the Sunday dinner we were holding for our last weekend at the loft in Tribeca. Paul went with Jonas for the beginning of the promotional tours for his book, which was already a best seller. I had been working on the Love Legacy Art week that was starting in a few weeks and I hadn't left the office all day.

"I'm just making sure Betty has the additions to the instructors," I explained.

Dani smiled and shook her head as she walked over. "You have an assistant to do that for you now."

"I feel like she must be overwhelmed with the changes," I reasoned. "I can't believe all the volunteers we have pouring in. Penelope's networking has us creating a tristate program for next year," I said and hugged her.

"That just means you need to hire another assistant." She waved around at the boxes in the office. "And movers. You're moving to your new home in a couple of days. If Jonas finds you working on the art week instead of the wedding, you'll be in trouble."

"I'm working on the wedding. Jonas is in charge of the move," I said happily.

Truthfully, I would have married Jonas during our beach vacation even if it was, by conventional standards, fast. We were in love and loved each other and had no intentions of delaying it for too long. However, we wanted our friends and love ones there. "I can help with both," Dani volunteered.

"I'd love that," I said.

We walked together out of the office. The chatter in the living room had us turning to find Ian talking with Alan, Dani's husband. He was dressed in an embroidered Indian *sherwani* and jeans. Quite the contrast from Ian's designer pressed suit. He was a hugger, too, and gave me one.

"I'll take one too," Mary said and walked over and hugged me. When we parted, my brows rose at Mary, noting the change in appearance since her last visit. She was make-up free and wearing a high-collar, ankle-length dress. She shrugged.

"Why didn't you tell me you were here?" I asked.

"I just walked in and went to help Lin," she explained.

"I'll go help, too. You can go up and change," Dani

offered.

I hitched my thumb toward Alan and Ian. "What about them?"

Mary adjusted her glasses and walked away without a word as they all headed toward the dining room area.

Ian gave her back a pointed look and Alan laughed. I would have to ask later.

I went upstairs and took a quick shower and changed into a silver and black wrapped v-neck dress that hugged my curves. Thigh highs and heels finished off the look. I brushed my curls and put on a light bit of makeup, all the time anticipating a reunion with Jonas. I hated when he traveled, but I found he made up for it when he returned.

I heard the sound of laughter when I finally left the bedroom, as well as the beginning of Beethoven's "Pathetique" on the piano, and memories flooded my mind of my time with Jonas in the Waldorf. *Jonas must be back!* I took off my heels and rushed down the stairs and didn't stop until I reached the living room. My shoes slipped out of my hand and everything else faded away.

My Jonas. He had arrived and was standing next to the piano. He was looking incredibly handsome in a light grey shirt and dark slacks, the dark waves of his black hair slightly tousled. His sea blue eyes were all for me. The look he gave me was salacious, and my body responded. Without wasting another moment, he pulled me into a tight embrace and gave me a searing kiss that took my breath away. I answered with my own urgency and intensity. I would never get enough of him.

The piano keys banging got our attention.

"Dad, Lily, come on," Paul groaned.

"It's warm in here," Dani said, fanning herself.

"Maybe we should leave?" Alan said, grinning.

"Salomés always put on a great show," Mary said in her best impression of my father, and I giggled.

"No. I'm glad you're all here," Jonas said. He moved us a few steps away and cupped my face. "How's my beautiful Tiger Lily?"

"Happy you're back," I said softly.

He stroked the sides of my face. "Any time away from you is too long."

My heart swelled with love and I smiled up at him. "I feel the same way about you."

We kissed. "Let's have dinner so we can make up for the few days I missed," Jonas said before pecking my lips one last time. He released me and walked over to greet Dani and Alan.

Paul stared at Mary until she looked at him, but this time he boldly kept the eye contact until Mary turned her head. He even stood against the icy glare of Ian.

I laughed and he turned his head toward me and gave a wink. *He's going to be just like his father,* I thought proudly.

"Dinner is ready," Lin announced. Mary left for the kitchen while Ian joined in on the conversation Dani, Alan, and Jonas were having.

I walked over to Paul and beamed at him. "Thank

you for agreeing to instruct during the art week."

He put his arm around my shoulders. "I couldn't turn down the chance to walk around introducing you as my mom number two," he said.

"As you like. I'm not bothered," I said, giving him a hug. I knew better. He had already sent his classmates and instructors over to help with the New York Art Week for next year.

"So, do you think Mary would go out with me?" Paul asked.

I shook my head. "Not if she enjoys her freedom. You're only sixteen and that's illegal here."

"I was talking about in two years," Paul said.

I glanced over at Ian, who was clearly already missing Mary and walking toward the kitchen to join her. "I'm not so sure, but what about your girlfriend?"

He gave me a mischievous grin. "You're awfully nosy, Mom 2. Can't we keep a few secrets from you? You've changed Dad, now you're working on me. I've got to stop hanging around you." He pretended to run away from me, but I grasped his arms and we laughed.

"Come on you two," Jonas called out. We walked into the room and I took the seat next to Jonas, then stared up at him. I was going to be his wife and maybe the mother of his child? *Just get through the wedding planning*, I chided myself.

He leaned over and kissed my cheek, then whispered in my ear. "Baby day dreaming again?"

I bit into on my lip and nodded.

"Slow down, Salomé," he said in a low tone. He turned his head, but I caught the twinkle in his eye.

"I'd like to say the quote tonight," Alan said once we filled all the glasses. "By John Lennon. Count your age by friends, not years. Count your life by smiles, not tears. May we continue to be friends for many dinners and years to come."

Dani leaned over and kissed his cheek. "Absolutely perfect, Alan," she said. We all held up our glasses and I couldn't wipe my smile off as I stared around at the faces gathered at the table.

Mom and Dad, you can fly home and rest now. I have a family.

The End.

THANK YOU READERS!

If you enjoyed Tiger Lily Part Three, please review. For information about the story and my author's blog, please visit my website:

www.ameliesduncan.com

I'd love to hear from you.

You can reach me through my Facebook:

facebook.com/pages/Am%C3%A9lie-S-Duncan/572889196145981

or contact me through my website:

www.ameliesduncan.com

I'm also on Twitter:

twitter.com/AmelieSDuncan

SUBSCRIBE TO AMÉLIE S. DUNCAN'S MAILING LIST

To receive updates as well as a sneak peek at Chapter One, prizes, and updates on new releases, please sign up to be on her personal mailing list.

Subscribe now: http://eepurl.com/baQzb5

ACKNOWLEDGMENTS

This series means a great deal to me and I'm thankful to have the opportunity to share this story with you. There are a number of people I want to thank for making this trilogy possible.

First, I would like to thank my husband, Alan, for reading everything I have ever written. I want to thank you for your love, patience, and support. I love you so much.

Thank you so much to the incredible group of people that helped me with the Tiger Lily Trilogy. I truly appreciate it.
Silvia Curry from Silvia's Reading Corner.
Leah Campbell.
Julie Collins.
Hermione and Deanna for beta reading.
Thank you to Cassandra, Carol Eastman, and Paul Salvette.
Special Thanks to Jeannie, Tanya, Danielle, Belinda, Sam, and Kawehi

Thank you to all the bloggers for participating in the promotions.

Most of all, I would like to thank the readers for taking the time to read my story. I sincerely hope you enjoyed reading it as much as I enjoyed writing it for you.

ALSO BY AMÉLIE S. DUNCAN

Little Wolf

Tiger Lily Part One

Tiger Lily Part Two

Piper Dreams Part One

Piper Dreams Part Two

Made in the USA
Middletown, DE
29 August 2017